HOME ON FOLLY FARM

JANE LOVERING

Boldwood

First published in Great Britain in 2021 by Boldwood Books Ltd.

Copyright © Jane Lovering, 2021

Cover Design by Debbie Clement Design

Cover Photography: Shutterstock

A CIP catalogue record for this book is available from the British Library.

Paperback ISBN 978-1-80048-237-1

Large Print ISBN 978-1-80048-236-4

Hardback ISBN 978-1-80162-566-1

Ebook ISBN 978-1-80048-238-8

Kindle ISBN 978-1-80048-239-5

Audio CD ISBN 978-1-80048-231-9

MP3 CD ISBN 978-1-80048-232-6

Digital audio download ISBN 978-1-80048-234-0

Boldwood Books Ltd

23 Bowerdean Street
London SW6 3TN
www.boldwoodbooks.com

To my utterly wonderful sister-in-law, Debs, who manages to keep my brother, David, in line. I'm not sure how she does it... I think a cattle prod, but she says not.
Also to my assorted collection of nieces and nephews, Ed, Beth, Ben and Amy Lovering. They're a lovely bunch.
And this book is also dedicated to all the farmers of North Yorkshire, who work horrible hours in awful weather doing a largely thankless job, this one's for you, lads and lasses.

1

There are some people whose voices go straight through you, even if you are horizontal with your face in a bucket and your arm in a sheep. My sister's voice was one of them.

'What the hell are you doing?'

Yep. Like a steel toecap through slurry.

I hadn't heard her arrive. The jump it caused me made the ewe struggle against the pressure of my hand. 'I'm laying lino,' I said. 'Obviously.' I stretched my fingers to their furthest extent, felt the ewe strain with another contraction, and then pushed gently. The lamb's head popped down into the birth canal.

I would not show how surprised I was to see my sister; I would *not*.

'Yeah, but does it have to be *here*?'

I hadn't been expecting to see Cass for – ooh, another five years at least, if ever. I suspected there was probably a warning email sitting in my inbox from our mother who, although she could be a little bit distant, wasn't actively hostile, so she would have tried to prepare me. But I'd been so busy.

I had to work on not gritting my teeth too visibly as I gradually stood up away from the sheep, watched the lamb slither out onto the straw bed of the pen and sneeze, while I tried to think of something to say.

'Where would you suggest?' I asked. 'Benidorm?'

The ewe reached around and began to lick her lamb clean. Job done. I wiped my arm with the handful of straw that I realised I was clutching as though it were a stand-in for my sister's neck.

'Well, surely, the vet does that sort of thing?' Just on the edge of vision I could see Cassandra sitting down on a bale of hay, carefully folding her long legs up into a yoga pose, calculated to make me look even more graceless in my practical but unglamorous farming wellingtons and amniotic-stained jeans. 'I thought you were going out with the vet, anyway – would he not do you mates' rates? And your arm is disgusting. Don't you have hot water and a towel? Like in James Herriot?'

I sighed and climbed up and out over the metal hurdles that formed the lambing pen. 'No. And, yes, I was going out with Chris, but we split up six months ago. I did tell you I was having my heart broken, but you were probably, I dunno, getting a bikini wax or something.'

Cass tossed her hair, which she did more often than a dog groomer having a good clear out.

'A bikini wax is more painful than heartbreak,' my sister said firmly. 'And more frequent. Heartbreak you don't get every eight weeks from a perma-tanned sadist with acrylic nails.'

I thought about Elvie, who ran the local riding stables and who had, so I'd found out, been keeping Chris entertained, on and off, for much of the past couple of years. 'Oh, I don't know.'

'Not that you'd know, anyway,' Cass finished, looking me over as though she could see my pubic hair creeping its way up out through the waistband of my jeans and attempting to coat my torso.

'There's not much time for that sort of thing,' I replied tartly. 'What with the rare-sheep breeding and all, it's surprising I can find time to fit in my massage sessions and the weekly blow-dry.'

My hair was currently scraped into a ponytail and had hay tangled in it, so I didn't think the usual sarcasm alert was necessary, but I hadn't considered Cass.

'You should sue.' She looked me over again. 'I hope they aren't charging you for that updo.' Then she looked at her own hands. 'I get a discount,' she said smugly. 'They stamp this little card for you, and every ten visits you get a free gel polish.'

I took a deep breath. She was as out of place in the creaky old stone barn as I would be – well, getting a gel polish. 'Why are you here, Cass? I wasn't expecting you. Did you bring Hawthorn?'

'He's my *son*, of course I brought him – what did you think I'd do with him?'

I was tempted to say I would have expected her to have dumped him on Mum and Dad, much as she'd done on many occasions since he was born, but I didn't say it. There wasn't the time for an argument; I had eighty-five recently-lambed ewes to feed. 'So, where is he?' I looked around as though I expected my nephew to pop out from behind the feed sacks.

Cassie stood up. 'I sent him to explore.'

'*Explore!* Cass, farms are dangerous, you know that! You can't leave a child roaming around unattended!' I started towards the door, which was actually just a bit of tin propped against the crumbling cob wall. It didn't really stop much, except the worst of the wind. Three ewes and their lambs had belted through it yesterday and left it bulging and corrugated where it hadn't been before.

'He's twelve, Dora! That's, like, practically forty in child years!'

Cass came out of the barn after me, the familiar note of justification and complaint in her voice. God, had I really been listening to that since she learned to talk? How hadn't I brained her with the *Encyclopaedia Britannica*?

Twelve? Was he? When had that happened? Last time I'd seen my nephew he'd been a small, pale boy, the only one who could work the elaborate TV and programme the oven. 'I thought he was about seven.'

Cass did the hair toss again. The wind outside the barn came funnelled directly down the valley, and tossed it right back. Yorkshire in March doesn't give much quarter.

'Twelve,' she said again. 'As you'd know if you ever came to visit, which you don't because – actually, why *don't* you ever come home, Dor?'

We stood side by side for a moment, the sturdy walls of the old stone barn behind us, the unreeling endlessness of the dale in front of us. I waved a hand. 'Sheep,' was all I said.

'That's no excuse.' Cass pouted into the weather. The weather was not the least impressed and neither was I. 'And we're here because Mum and Dad are getting an extension.'

There must be some kind of consequential string of actions that led to Mum and Dad's potential extension sending my sister and her son from London to Yorkshire, but I wasn't sure what. 'Tell me,' I said, with the sternness of the older sister. 'But without references to your hairdresser, your yoga guru, Pilates or any one of your million friends. If you can,' I added, because Cass tended towards verbosity as I tended towards fruit cake.

We walked back across the yard to the house while Cass explained. To her credit, she managed to cut out most of what her friends said, why she went to twice-weekly yoga, how Jennet Reilly had had to leave town suddenly, the advisability of expensive shoes and the opening of a new Ted Baker shop on the high street. Not all of it, obviously, but she did her best.

'So, they're building a kind of granny-annexe for you and Hawthorn?' I tried to precis as I opened the kitchen door and we were greeted by a whirl of collie and the smell of ancient casserole.

'Yes. We were tired of sharing a bathroom and now he's getting older there's too many wet towels.' Cass pulled a chair from under the table and sat down wearily, as though she'd personally trudged the two hundred odd miles with her son on her back, rather than caught a train to York and taken a taxi the rest of the way. And Dad had probably driven her to the station in the first place.

'And you've come to stay with me?' I washed my hands at the big stone sink. Feeding the ewes could wait a few minutes, until I made sense of the situation, but I could hear the 'baaing' starting up. They'd heard my voice in the yard.

'Yeah,' Cass said. 'Hotels are too expensive, apparently.'

'What about school? And your job?' I looked in the fridge. I'd been sure there were some yoghurts in there and I was hungry. The ewe had been trying to lamb for a couple of hours and I'd had to carry her into the barn to sort her out, so I'd missed breakfast. And, actually, thinking about it, dinner last night.

'Job?' Cass looked blankly at me for a moment. 'Oh, the shop! Oh, God, no, I haven't done that for *ages*! It was just so restrictive, what with me being a single mother and everything. Oh, there's Thor now.'

The door opened again and stayed open, letting the wind circle the kitchen. It crept over my shoulder and whirled some milk bottle tops in the fridge, as though it too was disappointed by the lack of yoghurt.

'Thor?'

'Yeah, he decided Hawthorn is too babyish. Didn't you, sweet?'

Hawthorn, looking about as far from Chris Hemsworth as was possible whilst still being male and blond, slunk into the room. He was taller than his mother now, with a face that still held the soft traces of a child while his body had the height and long limbs of an adult. He needed to stop going up and start going sideways – there was a lot of filling out to do.

Hawthorn grunted and perched on the window seat, staring out across the yard as though waiting for a helicopter to rescue him. There was a suspiciously yoghurty smell about him and some smears down his jeans that told me where the four-pack of Müller Corners had gone.

'So, what did you do while I was catching up with Auntie Pandora?' Cass's voice had become high-pitched and cutesy and I knew this was just for effect by the way her son flinched.

'Updated my vlog,' he said. 'My followers want to know what's happening with me.'

'Thor runs a very popular YouTube channel,' Cass said, in a voice so bright that one of the dogs covered its eyes. 'He's got nearly a thousand followers, haven't you, sweetie?'

Grunt.

'He's going to be an influencer when he finishes his education.' She gave me a satisfied look, although I didn't really know what an influencer was, what they did, or why anyone would want to be one.

'Is that like hypnosis?' I put the kettle on, sweeping the crumbs of a long-forgotten meal off the range to do so.

'Actually, yeah,' Thor said. 'You're, like, paid to persuade people to buy stuff. Clothes and shi... stuff.'

'Thor is very Internet savvy.' Cass began wandering around the kitchen. I could see her comparing the small window, mismatched surfaces and bleak flagstone floor to our mother's – and, by literal extension, her – kitchen back in Streatham. This kitchen was typical of a Yorkshire farmhouse: small window set in thick walls, enormous Aga, dust, cobwebs and old feed sacks that the dogs slept on in the corner. There were almost no similarities between my kitchen and my mother's, except they both let daylight in and had a cooker. My mother's kitchen had a glass roof and bifold doors. Mine barely had a roof.

I had a moment of remembering my one brush with Internet technology, a blog I'd started as a way of publicising the flock, showing what could be done to bring rare breeds back from the brink of extinction. It had become clear that nobody read it; nobody was interested in the Upper Ryedale breed, and its extinction was a matter of concern to nobody except me. And possibly one other breeder, but he lived in New Zealand and was a touch obsessive about organic feed and pictures of feet, so I'd had to block him.

Cass and Thor continued to sit.

'Is it nearly lunchtime?' he asked eventually, not for one second relinquishing his gaze over the muddy yard, where two hens were lazily pecking up some dropped feed. 'I'm starving.'

'I'm sure Auntie Dora will find you something.' Cass poked one of the collies with her foot. 'Do you always allow animals in the food preparation areas, Dor? Or are they meant to be outside?'

I had no idea why she framed everything as a question. A habit learned from our mother, I supposed, who never liked to say anything directly but would instead rather skirt around a request or topic, closing in on it like a well-trained sheepdog bringing a flock down off the hill.

'They live here,' I said. 'And there's bread in the cupboard if you want to make a sandwich. How long are you staying?'

I hoped it was only a weekend. The lack of luggage, apart from Cass's overloaded Mulberry bag, gave me hope. But if it was going to be longer I'd need to get some food in. Apart from the bread and the lamented yoghurts, there really wasn't much in the kitchen.

'Not sure. Depends on the extension. Dad said he'll give me a ring when the house is habitable again. Maybe three months?'

'Three *months*?' I echoed in a tone that couldn't help but imply the end of the world was, not only nigh, but now. 'But – where's your luggage? And what about school?'

'Thor is home-schooled.'

I didn't miss the face that my nephew pulled at that. But then I shouldn't be surprised; Cass had been bringing up her son 'alternatively' since he was born. Anything that was mainstream, you could guarantee she'd turn her back on, at least until the alternative idea also became mainstream, when she'd turn her back on that too. She had largely rotated her way through motherhood.

'Mum hired a tutor for him. There's another taxi, all the luggage is in there too.' Cass looked distractedly towards the window. 'I wonder where they've got to. We've been here – well, it feels like forever now. And we haven't had any lunch,' she finished, pointedly.

The kettle began to boil.

'I think there might be biscuits in here somewhere.' I began a search of the counters and worktops, which ran around the kitchen walls at odd heights and angles, like a relief map of the county. They were mostly scattered with back copies of the local paper, brochures for feed and sprays, catalogues, show timetables and entry forms and DEFRA regulations, which I printed off the computer every time they were updated. So, practically every day.

It took a while to find the tin, and I suspected that it hadn't been opened since Christmas.

Thor and Cass both jumped up as I rattled the lid off. 'They probably aren't vegan,' I said. I didn't add *and they're probably six months past the 'best before' date*. They were biscuits. As far as I was concerned they just went soggy, not off.

'Oh, we won't worry about that.' Cass helped herself to a handful of chocolate digestives. 'That sounds like the other taxi. Dor, can you go out and give them a hand? Thor and I are eating.'

Thor, I thought as I slunk out of the kitchen, leaving the kettle and the biscuits. *What on earth possessed her?*

It was one of the local taxi firms and I was surprised they'd agreed to come all the way up to the farm; they usually refused to drive up the potholed, suspension-ruin of a lane and dropped passengers half a mile away down on the road. It really sorted out those who wanted to see me from those who had thought a fifty-acre farm in Yorkshire would be a great selling opportunity for double glazing or expensive feed supplements.

I stayed in the doorway, the bulk of the old house stopping the worst of the wind from reaching me. I'd spent most of the night checking on the sheep and trying to get them into shelter, and I was short on patience and energy for helping to hump suit-cases. If Cass wanted her tutor and luggage to be met and greeted, then she could damn well do it herself. I was limited to opening the door, with maybe a spot of 'ushering through', if I could muster the oomph.

'Sort your bloody lane out!' shouted the driver through his half-open window as he spun the taxi into a turn that sprayed mud and made the hens run for cover.

I just smiled. If it kept unwanted visitors at bay, an unmade track was fine by me.

The driver got out, still grumbling, opened the boot and

began pulling out a succession of suitcases, rucksacks, bags and carriers, dumping them into the murk that was the yard surface after a wet winter. The furthest rear door opened, there was a moment of mumbled consultation and a kerfuffle with a card machine and then the passenger climbed out, stretching a spine that probably felt six inches shorter after the pummelling of the trackway.

I took half a step forward, mustering a smile that, while it probably wasn't welcoming, might at least mitigate the worst of the wind and the mud, only to stop, horrified.

'Is this Folly Farm? Good, wasn't sure that taxi driver knew his way once we got out of York. Hello. I'm Thor's tutor.'

It was Leo. Fucking Leo fucking Drayfield was standing in my farmyard.

I wondered if it was too late to get a shotgun licence.

2

The sheep needed me a lot that afternoon. In fact, I managed to stay outside until well after dusk had flooded into the dale, driving the day into pinpricks of light from the windows and doors of distant buildings. There were ewes and lambs to feed and check over, some as yet unlambed ewes to bring down closer to the house to make the late-night walk round easier; the dogs needed work and it was *astonishing* how untidy the feed shed had got.

And while I worked, I talked to myself. It was a habit I'd got into lately. Mostly because it was nice to hear a human voice, above all the baaing and the barking and the occasional cluck of a broody or startled hen. It reassured me that I could still carry a conversation, even if it was rather one-sided; most of my vocalisations were shouted commands to the dogs or yelled imprecations at the sheep when the bastards had gone through another wall or managed to find themselves upside down in a bramble patch. So, a lot of what I did these days was to the monotone mutter that would have had me shut away a century ago.

'Why the hell is he here? At least he doesn't seem to recognise me, that's one thing to be grateful for, but how long can *that* go on? I suppose he never knew my family, so there's no reason to put it all together, but... and a *tutor*? I wonder if Cassandra knows about him – well, no, she'd never have let him teach her son if she did. Oh, who the hell am I trying to convince? Cass would let Jack the Ripper teach Thor if it meant she was free to go for a spray tan. No, that's mean, she loves her son, of course she does. But, let's face it, what kind of loving mother gives their child the name Hawthorn? And then abbreviates it to Thor? I suppose it's better than calling him Haw...'

The air had gone still, which meant there'd be a frost tonight. I checked the boundary fence of the little field where I put the ewes I thought likely to lamb overnight; I didn't want to be striding over the hills in search of an escaped ewe in trouble, or a lamb that had got separated from its mother. Not at four in the morning, anyway. And this far north we could still have snow even though it was March. Nobody had really got over 2013, when the snow had come suddenly, fierce and late, and people had been walking the high hills in drifts taller than they were, to try to find lost animals and bring them home.

One ewe, a little cockier than the rest, butted her head against my leg. It was Willow, a three-year-old whom I'd raised on the bottle when her mother died. She hadn't outgrown the attachment and tended to regress to lamb-hood whenever she saw me, which resulted in some interesting bruises down my legs and a reluctance to hand-rear orphaned lambs. Fortunately the Upper Ryedale was an excellent mother, tended towards single lambs or twins at worst, and lacked the usual ovine habit of dying given the slightest excuse.

'Bugger *off*,' I muttered at her, without much real conviction.

Willow baaed happily and trotted after me, her sides round with incipient lamb and a good fleece. I sold my fleeces to hand-spinners at a premium, and, in consequence, owned many of my ewes in the form of socks, hand warmers and, in one case, a fireside rug. They weren't pets, they were a commercial enterprise. They were my living and I had to remind myself of that sometimes, when I got particularly attached.

'Off! Go!' I shoved a booted foot out. Willow stopped, wrinkled her nose at me and then pretended that she'd seen a particularly juicy bit of grass over in the corner of the paddock. She was fooling no one – the place was mud, feeders and strewn hay, and if there was a blade of fresh grass in here, then I was her natural birth mother.

But at least she had stopped me thinking about the shitshow that my previously calm, if somewhat impecunious, life had just become. Three *months*? Of my sister, who made Lucrezia Borgia look like Mother Teresa, and her son, who appeared set to sharpen his teeth and eat his way through the flock, uncooked? And now Leo Drayfield? Maybe I could move into the old shepherd's hut up on the high moor and pretend that lambing lasted until July. I could let them have the run of the house and yard and only come down for supplies, like a particularly rigorous ascetic.

The idea had an appeal, and, in fact, wouldn't be too different from the life I lived at the moment, only it would mean peeing in a bucket instead of having a mostly functional bathroom. I doubted that online supermarkets would deliver to a hut in the hills, but, apart from that, yep, pretty much the life I was living now. And it would have the added bonus of keeping me well away from Chris, who had a bit of a tendency to pop over to check if I wanted what he called 'a bunk up' whenever Elvie was busy doing whatever it was she did with rugs and tack and fifteen horses and ponies. I never did want any kind of 'uppage' from Chris, been there and quite literally done that, but he kept trying. I supposed his determination not to accept a negative outcome was a good thing in a vet, but it was incredibly annoying in a bloke who'd disappointed me in just about every way.

At last I really couldn't stay out any longer. I was hungry, the dogs needed feeding, and the long columns of light laid across the yard showed that at least two bedrooms had been allocated. I ought to go in and warn them about floorboards and the random tendency of some of the doors to fall off. At least they'd had the decency to occupy rooms at the front of the house, overlooking the yard, which meant that I would still be sleeping in the wonderful isolation of the rear part of the farmhouse, which looked out over the moorland and where I'd mostly got to grips with the missing floorboards.

'Oh, *there* you are!' Cass was sitting at the table flicking her way through a women's magazine. There was no sign of the testosterone contingent. 'I've been online and ordered a delivery.'

'Oh, that was nice of—'

'I used your card. You left your details logged in on the shop's site,' Cass continued. 'It's coming in the morning, so one of us will have to be here to unload, but you don't really leave the place much, do you, so you'll be around?'

She turned over a page and made a face. 'Oh, now look, that's not really an outfit, is it? I mean, who can't co-ordinate shoes and bag? It's like Fashion 101, shoes, bag and, if you must, hat! Her people want shooting.'

'Where are Thor and Leo?'

'Who?'

I stared at her. I knew she didn't have a lot of short-term memory for anything that didn't come with a website address, but

I was fairly sure she'd remember those two. 'Your son. And the tutor.'

'Oh! His name is Nat. What did you call him?'

So. Leo had changed his name, had he? I wondered what else he'd changed about himself. 'Sorry, I must have misheard him. Where are they?'

'Thor's updating his vlog again, and Nat is prepping some work. We gave Thor a few days off for moving up here, but Nat's got a whole scheme of lessons for him based around the locality; history, geography, stuff like that, I think.' Cass sounded completely offhand. 'I leave that all up to him.'

'Did... did Nat say anything about me?' I asked cautiously. Maybe he had recognised me. Twelve years was a long time and I'd changed a fair bit since then, but *I* had recognised *him*, so maybe it wasn't that long. Unless – I thought hopefully – he'd had a severe blow to the head, or a bit of time in a coma or something and his memory had been wiped. Or maybe I had changed so much that he genuinely didn't recognise me.

I thought back to who I'd been then. Yes. I'd changed a lot. Just about everything, in fact.

Cass laughed. 'Conceited, much? Of *course* he didn't say anything about you! You only said about two words to one another in the yard and then you were off, shafting hefts or whatever it is you do out there. Nat barely even noticed your existence.' Cass folded the magazine closed on the table. 'I hope you're not going to start flirting with every man that comes around, Dora. I know you're nearly thirty-one and still single, but, honestly, it looks desperate. Try to relax a bit. I'm sure *someone* will want you before you're too old and wrinkly to have any looks left.' She squinted at me. 'Although it might be a wee bit late now, but, well, people find someone even when they're really old, don't they?'

I stared at her for a second. 'Did you originally come with a filter and it fell off in the wash or something?'

'Sorry.' She sounded completely unapologetic. 'But it's true.'

'Can I point out that you aren't in a couple either? And you're nearly twenty-nine, so it's not as though you're far behind me.' I began scooping feed from the sack of dog food under the sink, while the collies gyrated around my legs.

'But *I* have Hawthorn. I don't need anyone else.' Cass came to stand by the Aga, in the way. One of the dogs ran over her foot and she squeaked exaggeratedly and lifted her leg up. 'I don't think animals should be allowed in the house, Dora.'

'My animals,' I said, putting the two dog bowls down, pointedly, right in front of her. 'My house. My choice. If you don't like it, then maybe you should go back to Streatham. In fact, even if you *do* like it, why not go back to Streatham anyway? Just a suggestion.'

'We're not going to be in your way or anything. We'll live our own lives – even if that is practically impossible in this backwater of civilisation, but still – you'll hardly know we're even here.'

Two seconds later there was a thundering on the stairs and Thor hurtled into the kitchen, iPad held up in front of his face, shrieking, 'And *this* is where I'm having to eat! It's, like, medieval or something and there's, like, not a Nando's for *miles*!' Then he whirled around, presumably making sure that the video fully captured the awfulness, whilst his mother and I stood like a couple of film props. After a few seconds of spinning, he flashed us both a grin and slammed back out through the kitchen doorway and we heard his footsteps echoing off the main staircase as he headed back upstairs again.

'Vlog,' said Cass smugly. 'He's got nearly a thousand followers.'

'Yes, you said.' So a thousand adolescents had now seen the

inside of my kitchen. I didn't usually even let the *postman* in. 'What happened to privacy and consent and all that? This is my home, Cass.'

She stood up and stretched. At a guess, her jeans cost more than the monthly feed bill and her top was probably hand-knitted from unicorn wool by Atlantean refugees. 'Thor is just expressing himself. I don't want him to grow up all repressed and downtrodden like you, Dora. I want him to have a life! Excitement and risk and danger and adrenaline. Some thrills and spills. Not plodding on through life.'

From above our heads, where we could hear Thor thundering along the landing at the front of the house, there came a sudden crack and then his voice wailing down the staircase. 'Ow! Ow! Mum! My leg, Mum!'

'He's put his foot through the floorboards,' I said evenly. 'It's not a good idea to go running about up there.'

'Thor!' Cass started out for the kitchen door. 'Don't worry, sweetie, I'll get – I'll get some Germolene or something.' Then she turned to me, eyes narrowed. 'This place isn't fit for human habitation, Dora. Grandad would be turning in his grave if he could see what you've done to his farm!' She spat the words viciously over her shoulder and then slammed the hall door as she headed for the stairs, calling, 'How is it, sweetie? Does it hurt?'

I stood very still under the fluorescent tube that illuminated the kitchen. It hummed slightly, and the dogs were making growly gobbling noises over their dinners, but apart from that it was quiet now Cass had gone.

'"Excitement and risk and danger and adrenaline,"' I said, watching a small spider swing determinedly from a single thread up in the beams of the ceiling. 'Yeah, right.'

I would never, absolutely *never*, let Cass know how her words had hurt me. That she'd got right to the painful centre of everything I worried about. *What would Grandad think of how I ran the farm?*

Then I grabbed my torch and went out to check on the ewes again.

* * *

It was a relatively quiet night. Two ewes lambed, but easily and without me needing to intervene. They'd been standing, backed into the thick hedge that surrounded the paddock, wobbly lamb at foot and a slightly defiant look on their woolly faces, when I did the three o'clock check. They'd both had the sense to give birth tucked into the sheltered corner, where the frost wasn't too severe and the lambs looked sturdy and were suckling well.

Willow trotted over to make sure that I hadn't brought her a bottle – she still liked to check even though she'd been weaned for over two and a half years – and was severely butted away by one of the new mothers. It boded well for good, protective motherhood, so I climbed back over the gate and left them all to it; crunched my way over the frozen yard puddles and back into the house, where even the collies hadn't bothered to get up from in front of the Aga to accompany me. I hadn't put on the overhead light, just one of the small lamps over in the corner where I kept the computer, so the kitchen emitted a dull glow that shone through the window and the slightly open door, beckoning me back inside.

This was one of the times I loved. Everywhere was silent, even the milking machine down the valley wouldn't fire up for another hour or so yet. The only people walking the night were those who made no sound, even the house had stopped its creaking and settling and pretty much the only noise came from the occasional collie twitch against the feed-sack bed and the odd drifting baa as a worried lamb called for its mother in the far field.

Quiet. Dark. How I liked it.

So when I heard a voice from the far side of the kitchen, I nearly screamed in frustration and terror.

'I didn't think anyone else would be up.' It was Leo/Nat. Wearing a huge hoodie and sitting slumped over a mug at the table. 'Sorry. I didn't mean to startle you. I don't sleep well and I thought I'd make a cup of tea. Kettle's boiled, by the way.'

He was almost invisible, shrouded in the shadows that the kitchen kept even if all the main lights were on.

'I was – checking the sheep,' I said, as though I needed to excuse my presence in my own house. The kettle was still giving out a whisper of steam so I poured water into a mug to give my hands something to do. I could not think of anything else to say.

'It's good of you to put us all up,' he continued. 'Cass said it came as a bit of a shock to you. That you don't normally mix much.'

I gave a hollow laugh. 'I bet she didn't say it like that, though.'

'No.' His voice was measured but giving nothing away. 'No, she didn't.'

Did he recognise me? There was nothing in his tone that sounded as though he knew who he was talking to. Had he said anything to Cass? But then, she wouldn't know, would she? I was just her sister, just Pandora-the-boring. Pandora-the-normal. Pandora-the-no-trouble-to-anyone.

I had to make sure. 'How did you come to be recruited as Thor's tutor?' Vague enough. He could give me as much backstory as he wanted to that. I kept my back to him as I poured and stirred and checked the biscuit tin. It was empty.

'I grew up in London, got a master's degree in child development and psychology. Did a bit of private tutoring last summer and I enjoyed it, so when I saw the advert for a full-time tutor for Thor I reckoned I'd give it a go. Thor seems to like me, we get along well and he's a bright boy. I didn't mind coming all the way to Yorkshire to carry on, so, here I am.'

Grew up in London. So he didn't recognise me. If he did, he wouldn't have needed to say that.

My heart had stopped stomping its way up my throat, but my palms were still sweaty. 'Whereabouts in London did you grow up?' I hid the hoarseness of my voice by dipping my face into my mug. It was my 'Sheep Farmers Do It To Ewe' mug. Chris had bought it for me on my last birthday. It was the sort of thing he found hilarious. I used the mug around the house and yard in the hope it might shatter into a thousand tiny, unmendable bits, but it was proving surprisingly resistant.

'Streatham. I was surprised when I met your sister and your parents – it's not far from where I lived for a while. Still, London is a big place, no reason we would have all bumped into one another, is there? Funny that, you can live practically down the road from someone for a long time and never even meet them.'

I couldn't refute that. I'd lived here for seven years and only met the bloke from the next farm along twice, accidentally, up on the high moor looking for lost sheep.

'Yes. London's a big place,' I echoed.

He didn't know me. Well, he'd never known my name, my real name. Never met my family, and I'd never so much as mentioned him to them, and I looked – different now. No reason he would even think of me these days; he's clearly reinvented himself too.

'Well, I'd better...' I stepped out of my wellingtons, left them beside the Aga. 'Lots to do tomorrow.' I couldn't see his face, he was just a sketch of hoodie-and-mug; outlines drawn in shadow against the table, from the pool of light way across the kitchen.

'Of course. Goodnight.' He raised his mug in a toast to me.

'Goodnight, Nat.' With my socks making hushing sounds against the flagstoned floor, I shuffled my way hastily out of the room and up the stairs to my room, where I lay on the bed with my face hot and tight in a mixture of panic and half-satisfied relief.

3

I took the first lot of ewes and lambs, the ones that were big enough now not to need checking over quite so often, down to the far field in the trailer. It bounced about behind the tractor to the accompaniment of the odd, distracted baa, but nobody fell over as I inched the ancient Massey Ferguson down the little track. It wasn't quite the furthest field from the house, that was the ten-acre that bordered the road into the village, which I rented to Elvie for grazing, but it was still far enough to make getting the tractor out worthwhile, rather than trying to herd thirty ewes and their wayward lambs down. The dogs were good, but the hedges that lined the track weren't entirely stock-proof; I needed to get out with the electric fencing when the weather improved a bit.

Dax, the big collie, sat in the tractor with me. Bet stayed in the yard, eyeing the chickens and waiting for our return. When I drove back up, trailer empty and rattling like a bean can with rocks in, Nat and Thor were in the yard too. Nat was pointing up at the roof of the barn, while Thor was writing something down in a small exercise book. The sun had decided to make an appearance today and was illuminating the whole yard like a spotlight on a play.

I jounced over the final ruts and cut the engine, which died reluctantly and with many misfires and splutters. I really needed to get the thing serviced.

'Hello,' Nat said cheerily. 'The food delivery arrived while you were gone. Cass is sorting it out in the kitchen.'

Thor lowered his book and looked at me. 'Can I have a go on the tractor?'

'No.' I jumped down, preceded by Dax. The tractor was ancient; it had been on the farm so long that I feared its wheels might fall off if I tried to take it anywhere else. It had been Grandad's and he'd never got round to having a cab fitted, so it was just roll bars and seat, and he'd only added the roll bar when Grandma told him she'd divorce him if he didn't make it safe. They'd save you from the worst of the impact if the tractor turned over, but that was as good as it got. Grandad had been very robust in his attitude to health and safety. I definitely didn't want to risk Thor getting up on it – it would be like putting a baby on a racehorse.

'We've been studying the cruck roof of the barn,' Nat said. He carried on explaining something to Thor, probably trying to distract him from the tractor, at which he was looking much as Chris had used to look at models on Instagram. 'So, now you can go and sketch it, if you like,' he finished. 'Go inside, see how it has been constructed.'

Thor gave the tractor a last ogle and mooched off. He was wearing expensive-looking trainers, but they were getting scuffed in the mud and he hadn't even done up the laces.

'Sorry about that,' Nat said. 'He's easily distracted, unfortunately.'

I had to do it. I *had* to. It was like pressing a bruise.

'You're Nat Drayfield, yes?'

He inclined his head.

'Did you ever know someone called Leo Drayfield? He – went out with a friend of mine for a while. I just wondered...'

Nat had raised his head. There was an expression on his face that I wasn't familiar with. A kind of calm acceptance mingled with a little bit of – anger? 'Leo was my brother,' he said and his voice had the tiniest wobble to it. 'He died. Eight years ago.'

Leo. Dead. I felt my body flush with a feeling like grief, and my mouth was suddenly full of words I wanted to say, questions I wanted to ask, but daren't. And then came the feeling of relief, the slackening of muscle and the rise of laughter to the back of my head. Leo. Dead. It was all over.

'I'm sorry to hear that,' I said, trying to stop myself from smiling, whilst at the same time fighting the pressure behind my eyes that told me I might cry. 'You're very like him.'

A sharp look. Although, weren't Nat's eyes a little more hazel than Leo's had been? Wasn't his hair a darker shade of that undefined colour that went blonder in the sun? And he was taller, definitely.

'You knew him?' There was a tone of disbelief now, as though Leo had been kept in the cellar and denied to all but close family.

'I met him once or twice. Through my friend.'

We were standing quite close together now, as though what we were saying was secret. I didn't realise quite *how* close we were until Cass suddenly popped up behind Nat's shoulder with a look of horror on her face.

'What are you *doing*?'

Nat met my eye. Again, he had an expression I couldn't read. He gave his head the tiniest shake; I didn't know if it was aimed at me or whether he was just clearing his thoughts. Or it could have been the fact that Cass had practically shouted in his ear and he was checking that his eardrums weren't perforated.

'Your sister was asking about my family. Turns out she knew someone who knew my late brother.'

Cass looked slightly mollified. 'Well, OK, but you are being paid to teach Thor and I can't see you doing it right now. Where is he?'

'He's in the barn, drawing.' I felt obliged to say something in Nat's defence. Did Cass have to be *so* horrible? It wasn't even as though she were paying Nat – that would be our mother. Our mother had been paying for almost everything for Thor ever since the day he was born. According to Mum, Cass pleaded poverty, youth, lack of qualifications to get a good job, then when she got the job in the shop she pleaded lack of time. Now she was back to pleading poverty again, but I think our parents had stopped listening about a decade ago.

'It has a cruck roof,' Nat started to explain but Cass had glazed over.

'Well, all right. But don't distract them during lessons,' she said to me and then bobbed away again. Her strange gait was caused by her trying to avoid the mud and the puddles and the chickens in her cutesy little kitten-heeled shoes that were about as suitable for walking through a farmyard as my footwear was for hosting a society dinner.

'God, she's ghastly,' I said without thinking.

Nat laughed. 'She has her moments but she's my employer, so you never heard that from me.'

'Well, she's my *sister* and I still think she's awful.'

Nat turned to head towards the barn. 'I'm sure you love each other,' he said. 'Deep down.'

'If by "deep down" you mean "in hell", then that's probably what it will come to,' I said darkly.

He laughed and walked away, calling out for Thor as he went. Dax followed after them in case they might be doing something interesting in the barn; Bet trailed after me as I went into the house after Cass.

She was standing in the kitchen surrounded by shopping bags. There seemed to be an awful lot of them, and the food I could see spilling over the plastic rims wasn't anything I usually ordered.

'You'd better unpack.' Cass tittupped over the flags, her pretty little heels sounding like cats' claws. 'Before some of this defrosts.'

I went to the sink to wash my hands. I was absolutely NOT going to jump just because she said so. 'Why don't you unpack?' I said. 'You had no idea how long I was going to be down at the bottom field; it might all have defrosted while you were waiting for me to come and do it for you.'

I kept my back to her, soaping my hands more thoroughly than usual to drag the handwashing out for longer.

'The delivery man has just left; it will be fine. And I don't know where you keep all your food. If I put it away it would only be in the wrong places.'

Damn. This was logical thinking, which I was unused to from my sister.

'Anyway, I only had these nails put on three days ago. I don't want to snap one now, not with it being *miles* to the nearest salon.'

That was more like it!

I began unpacking, putting food for the pantry on the side, and food for the fridge, well, in the fridge. Even Cass could have managed to find that – it was huge and sulked in one whole corner of the kitchen, occasionally splitting the peace of the farm with its terrifying motor.

'So, what are you going to do with your time while you're

here?' I weighed a jar of peanut butter in my hand. *Peanut butter.* I hadn't eaten that since I was about seven, and, from the slenderness of Cass, she hadn't let a nut pass her lips since she discovered tight jeans. It must be for Thor. Did you keep it in the fridge or the cupboard?

'I thought I might do an online course.' Cass peered into another bag. 'People have always said I've got an eye for colour. I might do interior design.'

'Or you could, you know, help out around the farm. I could do with another pair of hands.'

She stirred the contents of the bag. 'Oh, no,' she said, distractedly. 'That wouldn't work for me at all.'

I contemplated throwing the jar of peanut butter at her head. 'But it's in your interests though, surely.' I tried to appeal to the fiscally motivated side of her character. Side? It was practically ninety per cent of her body. 'I mean, with the way Grandad left it. The more productive Folly Farm, the more money you make.'

Our grandfather had left the farm to me to work and live on, but fifty per cent of any net profit was paid to Cass. I guessed it was his way of being 'fair', since Cass had never had any interest in the place and he wanted it to stay in the family, but she seemed to think we should have sold the place. So she could buy more shoes, probably.

'Well,' she said, against all evidence, 'money isn't everything, is it, Dora?'

'Well, no. But it is a good proportion of these groceries, and I expect you'll be chipping in with expenses?' I opted for cupboarding the peanut butter. I don't know why I framed it as a question. Did Cass really think that she, her son and his tutor could live here free for the next three months? Seriously?

'I'll talk to Mum,' she said, pulling a pack of rice cakes from the bag. 'These are mine. I'm going to go and sit in the front room

– do you still use the front room, Dora? It's a bit difficult to tell which bits of the house are lived in and which you're letting go derelict.'

Derelict? 'Of course, I use the front room,' I snapped. 'But don't touch the freezer in there – it's full of colostrum. That's the stuff the lambs need as soon as they're born. We keep it for orphan—'

'Yes, I know what colostrum is,' Cass snapped back. 'I *have* had a baby, you know.'

'Twelve years ago!'

'Biology doesn't go out of date!' Cass picked up the slim leather case. 'I'm going to be on my iPad, if anyone needs me. It's important, so please don't interrupt unnecessarily.' She stalked out of the room, heels clicking, like a cat that's been confronted by a large dog trying to sniff its bum.

I threw the bread. It squished very satisfactorily as it hit the top of the dresser and was followed by a pack of hotdog buns, a madeira cake and, finally, a box of Bakewell tarts. I could feel tears of frustration threatening, so took it out on the baked goods instead of letting them fall.

My bloody sister and her sense of entitlement – I punched the bread back into shape and then punched it again for good measure. How *dare* they all pitch up without warning and take over... punch punch... my house? This was my *home*, not some *Country Living* centre spread – how *dare* Cass start insulting it? What did she expect from a working farm, Laura Ashley wallpaper and... and...? I couldn't think of any other manufacturers of furniture and fittings, so I settled for punching the bread again. DFS! That was one, the adverts were on all the time. Did she expect me to have DFS sofas?

I thought, with just a trace of guilt, about the sofa that actually was in the front room. I had no idea who it was made by; it had been in there since Grandma and Grandpa's time, so maybe

Noah had had a hand in its construction, while he was knocking up the ark. Plus, it was probably an ancestral home for many generations of mice. All right, maybe Cass had a point re the sofas.

'Are you taking an allergy to gluten a little bit personally?' a mild voice observed from the door to the yard. Nat and Thor were kicking off their shoes. Dax ran in to join Bet in front of the Aga and both dogs rolled their eyes at me in a 'how long are these people going to be here?' way.

'Where's Mum?' Thor ran through, his socks smearing the flags with mud that expensive trainers clearly didn't keep out.

'Front room,' I said, and carefully didn't add 'she doesn't want to be disturbed'.

'Cool.' Socks elongating by the metre, he took off out through the kitchen, sparing me and the half-unpacked shopping only the most passing of glances, which made me feel better about him disturbing Cass.

'Do you need a hand?' Nat was already pulling things from a bag and piling them on the table. Packets of things that I thought hadn't been manufactured since I was about nine were coming out like some kind of magic trick. Angel Delight, jam tarts, iced buns.

'What the hell is all this?' I waved a pack of butterscotch dessert. 'It's like I fell asleep and woke up in the eighties. There's more nutritional content in the curtains than in any of this.'

Actually, given the amount of splashed fat and smearing on the curtains, this was probably true.

'Well, I have noticed that Thor has somewhat traditional tastes in food.' Nat stacked all the packs tidily and then opened a cupboard. A pack of dog chews fell out and hit him on the head, which he ignored. 'He likes beige. Although he does sometimes liven up meals with tomato sauce.'

I shook my head and added several packs of fish fingers to the pile for the freezer. 'I thought Cass was raising him on organic quinoa and butternut squash.' There were two tins of spaghetti shapes under the fish fingers. I put them in the pantry.

'I think your mother had other ideas about children's food,' Nat said darkly. 'And Thor got a taste for the good stuff. He said that his grandma used to wait until Cass went out and then give him packets of Jelly Babies.'

I had a momentary image of Cass as she had been when Thor was small, cooking up batches of baby food in the sunny kitchen in Streatham. Pureeing carrots, if I remembered, with a sort of desperate housewifely look about her, while Thor – who had been Hawthorn then – sat on our mother's lap, all plump and big-eyed. That must have been not long before I left to come to the farm. When life had been different. When Leo...

The bread was carefully removed from my grasp. 'Have you got any ducks that want feeding?' Nat said carefully. 'Because I don't think this is going to be fit for human consumption now.'

'You shouldn't feed bread to ducks,' I said, automatically. 'It's not good for them.'

'This isn't good for anyone.'

I looked up. Nat was standing by the kitchen table and, for a second, he looked so much like Leo that it made my stomach ache. But then I realised it was just the outline, just the way he stood and the way his shape tapered from shoulders down to narrow hips, the way his face had cartoon-large eyes and a mouth that smiled more on one side than the other. *It's not Leo. You're safe.*

Nat put the bread down and carried on unpacking another bag. 'Did you know my brother well?' he asked, tone casual under the sound of tins of beans hitting the table.

His question so neatly fitted my thoughts that I dropped the six-pack of ready-made jelly. One of the plastic pots split and I managed to hide my expression under the cursing and search for a cloth, so by the time I needed to answer, I was composed, if somewhat covered in blobs of artificial strawberry.

'I didn't really know him at all. As I said, he went out with a friend of mine for a while, what, thirteen years ago? I think we may have met at a couple of parties or something. I remembered the name Drayfield and I wondered.' I was talking too much, too fast. I shut up and scraped. The dogs' attention on me was rapt and I could see Dax dribbling.

'Yes, you said. Which friend was it? I mean, Leo was a year or so younger than me so I didn't know many of his friends, but I might know the name?'

Nat sounded a bit breathless too, and his words came fast. It must be hard to lose a sibling.

'Sophie,' I said, pulling the first name of my fellow school attendees from my memory. 'Sophie Baxter.' Blameless Sophie, who'd been the daughter of a local solicitor. Skinny and dark and worried about her acne, that was pretty much all I remembered.

Nat frowned. 'Doesn't ring a bell.'

Well, it wouldn't. Sophie didn't do parties, she did showjumping and her dad wanted her to go to Oxford so she didn't hang out much. And then we lost touch...

I shrugged. 'Well, I didn't even know he had a brother, so maybe you didn't move in the same circles much.'

A sideways tilt of the head acknowledged my words. It made his hair flop over one cheek, just as Leo's had. I slammed down a few more tins of beans.

'It's a nice house you've got. Nice farm. Lovely location.' Nat was still trying to make conversation, bless him. He sounded as though he'd trained up on garden parties and kitchen suppers.

'Seventeenth century,' I said.

'Which bit? House, farm, location?' When I looked up from the seemingly endless supply of tinned carbohydrates, he was smiling. 'Sorry,' he said. 'I don't mean to sound nosey or anything, but I'm trying to ram some education into your nephew and I thought a bit of background history that's about his family might help. He might feel more engaged that way, because, God knows, it's pretty hard to get any other kind of engagement right now. You know about him wanting to be a vlogger?'

'Yes, Cass did mention something about it, but I don't know what a vlogger is. I thought it was some kind of lumberjack thing?'

'Video blogging. They get sponsors, they advertise stuff – all goes rather over my head, to be honest, but then, my teenage years are so far behind me that they're practically a history lesson. He's got—'

'Nearly a thousand followers, yes, so I've heard.'

I must have sounded sharp because Nat raised his eyebrows. 'I was going to say ambition, but yes, that too. But I thought that spending some time out here in the wilds might make him realise that there's more to life than the whole consumerist media nonsense.'

I thought about Thor, his expensive trainers, his general attitude. And then about Cass and her attitude to *his* attitude. 'The phrase "flogging a dead horse" comes to mind,' I said.

Another smile, somewhat rueful this time. 'Yeah. I'd pretty much come to the realisation that deceased equines were involved. But, hey, you've got to try. I wouldn't be much of a tutor if I let him sit on YouTube all day, would I?'

This was better. This was away from dangerous territory. Leo territory. And, although there was a gnawing inside me that was trying to make the words 'How did he die? What happened to him in the years after I knew him?' burst out of my chest, there was also a relief that the subject had been dropped.

The inside door banged open so hard that the handle hit the wall and made the dogs jump. Cass stood in the doorway, iPad in hand, looking furious, while Thor was trailing his way back up the hall, still dragging his socks.

'You,' she said, pointing at Nat, 'are being *paid* to teach my son. What you are not being paid for is to let him roam around during school hours, interfering with my life!'

'It's lunchtime,' Nat observed mildly. 'He's on his lunch break.'

Cass deflated. I noticed then that her hair had been expensively streaked to look as though blonde were her natural colour. It was not an effect that had been achieved with a box of do-it-yourself-at-home dye, and I tallied it up with the nails and the perfectly cut jeans. 'Cass,' I said, 'where do you get all your money from?'

Clearly taken aback whilst she was on a frontal assault, she widened her eyes. 'I do *work*, you know,' she said. 'I'm a remote PA. I do organising and – things.'

'Who for?'

Her eyes widened still more. If I wasn't seeing things, she was also wearing coloured contacts that made her eyes bluer than the steel-grey that was their real colour. I must admit to a tiny passing wonder if she was some kind of high-class online sex worker.

She shook her expensive highlights and sucked her cheeks in so her cheekbones stood out haughtily. 'Well, I work for Dad's company, of course,' she said, as though this should have been obvious to anyone with an IQ in double figures. 'I do his bookings, and make his hotel reservations when he has to travel, and sometimes I do receptions and things.'

As Dad was heading towards his seventies and had been semi-retired for nearly ten years, I hardly thought this was the kind of arduous employment she clearly believed it to be. 'So, you basically get an allowance off Dad.'

Behind Cass, Thor was obviously itching to get into the kitchen. The mounds of food all over the surfaces might have been influencing this desire.

'Well, yes, in a way. But you're living on family money too! This place!' Cass waved an arm. 'I mean, it's a grotty hellhole, but it's a roof over your head and the farm and everything!'

And again, that stab of guilt. No, not guilt. More like inadequacy.

Nat seized a random handful of foodstuffs. 'Come on, Thor,' he said. 'We'll go and eat in the barn and do some more sketching.'

'But—'

'Barn. Now.' I suddenly saw why Nat was probably a very successful tutor. There was a note of command in his voice that even a sullen pre-teen couldn't ignore. Thor shuffled his way back into his trainers and the two of them shot out of the back door and across the yard, their edible bounty clutched to chests and a definite air of 'scuttling' about them.

Cass and I confronted one another. We must have looked a very odd pair, like a before and after advert: her all glossy highlights and designer clothes, me with my scraped-back ponytail, torn jeans and a jumper with hay seeds bobbling the sleeves.

'I *work* on the farm, Cass. This is my *job*. It's not just where I live. And you get fifty per cent of the net profit without having to lift a finger!' I shoved my hands into the pockets of my jeans, mostly to keep myself from throwing the bread at her. The poor loaf had suffered enough.

'And how do I know that you aren't making up expenses? That fifty per cent doesn't look like much money by the time I see it. I mean, what are you spending money *on*, exactly? It's hardly home maintenance and good clothes. I mean, look at yourself, Dora. You look as though you haven't had a shower for weeks, you've got holes in your jeans and your hair – well. Least said about that, the better. And the house is barely fit for human habitation; the beds are uncomfortable, the sheets are the ones Grandma left and the place doesn't look like it's seen a coat of paint since Grandad died!'

'It's a working farm, not a Pinterest page!' I shouted back. 'And the money goes on paying the bills; there's feed and fuel and vet bills and semen.'

'I'm sorry? Did you say *semen*? I mean, Dora, there are some things that—'

'For the sheep. I don't have a ram. I use artificial insemination to keep the bloodlines going.' I almost laughed at her expression. 'One of the penalties of keeping an endangered breed, Cass.'

'Oh.' She looked momentarily chastened.

'And, yes, I realise I live like a hermit, and the place is looking a bit – well, threadbare, but farming is precarious. It's hand to mouth, and that's in a good year. A disease could wipe out the flock, a big hike in feed prices could wipe out my profit, if the tractor breaks down and a barn roof needs replacing, that money has to come from *somewhere*. You should be grateful that I haven't done up the farm because that would have meant that you didn't see any money at all for years!'

'Look, Dora.' Cass was making a visible effort to be the sensible, controlled one. 'Maybe it's time that we had a family meeting and agreed to sell Folly Farm. You could come back to London and get a proper job—'

'Like yours?'

She ignored the jibe. 'We could find you a nice little flat, you could do – well, I don't know, you must be good at *something*, temping in offices or cleaning work or something like that, and you wouldn't have to put up with all this.' She made a double-hand shrugging motion, which took in the kitchen, the hallway and the staircase. 'It's stupid, you rattling around in a six-bedroomed house that's falling apart, when you could have a lovely little studio. Maybe with a balcony!' she added, as though the prospect of two pots of wilting bamboo and a clothes airer would make up for fifty acres of Yorkshire moorland, a hundred sheep and all the bantams and dogs I wanted. 'And stop looking at me like that. You look like you've got a squint.'

Clearly my withering glances had lost some of their power in the last ten years; I used to be able to shut her up with a stern glare. I squinted a bit more and then turned and marched out of the kitchen, both dogs leaping up to join me. I would have slammed the kitchen door but one of the wooden panels was already loose and I didn't want to hear her confirming sigh if it fell out behind me.

There was no sign of Nat and Thor as I marched like a sergeant on parade across the yard and down to the lambing paddock, where my unexpected arrival caused a barrage of baaing and thirty heads of various sizes and colours turned to see if I'd brought a feed sack with me. Because there was no sign of imminent food, they all went back to suckling or grazing and I sat on the gate, dogs lolling at the base, and looked out across my domain.

The worst of it was that Cass had a point. And Cass hadn't had much of a point since the javelin incident at school. She'd got under my skin and released my worst fears. The farm *was* precarious. The house *was* under-maintained and in dubious condition. I'd had the roof replaced a couple of years ago and there was a low-level intent to do some internal work, but when I was out in the fields at all hours in all weathers, either trying to grow wool, lambs or grass, somehow DIY had fallen by the wayside a bit.

But, I told myself, watching a pair of twin lambs butting up to their mother for milk, I had all this. A farm that was perched in a small cleft in the heather-covered hills, where grass fields dropped down towards the village tucked out of sight below the curve of my, admittedly limited, horizon. Behind me, the moors rose, humped and heaved like a disturbed sleeper under blankets of bracken and whin. The air came in gusts, smelling of peat, lanolin, hay and cold. You didn't get this from a studio flat in Streatham.

If I turned round I could see the house, long and low as though it had been there first and grown the hills up around it. Two-storeyed, narrow-windowed, just a big stone streak against the hillside. Someone before Grandad had reformulated the rooms so they no longer led one into another and we had a proper hallway and landing, although the bathrooms were recent second-thought additions; the downstairs one had once been the cow byre and the upstairs one lay at the very end of the house and was too large, so the bath, shower and toilet took up about a tenth of the floor space and the bathroom looked like a sparsely attended party.

But I loved every mud-encrusted centimetre of the place. I could no more up and move back to London than... than I could be my sister. Besides, I was keeping an endangered breed going. This farm held ten per cent of the total world number of Upper Ryedales.

'You're important,' I told Willow, who had come to see whether my boots were bringing food.

She glared at me out of a long-pupilled eye, sighed, and headed back to give the mineral lick a good seeing to, giving me baleful glances now and again at the lack, once more, of bottle.

'Pandora...' It was Thor, squelching up behind me. The sheep raised startled heads for a moment. 'How far does the farm go?'

'What do you mean?'

'How many of these fields are yours?' He leaned his arms on the gate alongside me and I looked down at him. He had one of those hairstyles attempted by footballers, shaved at the sides and longer on the top. It made him look as if a shearing had gone badly wrong. There was an air of 'knowing' about Thor, almost a cynicism, which didn't sit well on a twelve-year-old.

'The farm stretches down to the village road, beyond that hill.' I pointed. 'And behind us, only as far as the end of the garden, where the moors start.'

'Oh. Okay.'

'Thor! You were supposed to look it up on the map.' Nat was following behind, exasperation clear in his walk.

'Using my initiative, innit.' Thor didn't even look up from his visual perusal of the acres. 'Why look something up if you can just ask?'

'You do have a point there.' Nat stopped at the gate too. Now there were three of us all leaning, sitting or standing in the gateway. No wonder the ewes were starting to get a bit restless; they probably thought we were plotting something. 'But, even so. This lesson is about how to use a map, so let's get back inside and have a look.'

Thor looked up suddenly. 'There's a car coming,' he said. 'Into the yard. Like, the fuzz or something.'

Nat and I looked too. There was, indeed, a police Land Rover bumping its way down the track. The road itself was a deeply incised line set below the level of the moorland, an old packhorse trail paved for traffic, and they hadn't turned on the lights or sirens, which explained why we hadn't seen it until it turned onto the property.

'It's Henry and James,' I said, although that will have meant nothing to Thor and Nat. 'Sometimes they drop in for a coffee if they're passing.'

The three of us headed back across the yard to where the two policemen were sitting in the Land Rover, window down and engine still running. 'Morning. Shall I put the kettle on?'

'Business call, Dora, sorry,' said Henry. He was copper-haired and lanky and kept asking me out for a drink. I'd gone once, but he'd been called out halfway through a pint, and that had been the end of our dating history. 'Some lads been reported in a lorry, cruising round. The rustlers are at it again, seems. You seen anything out of the ordinary?'

I shrugged and smiled into the vehicle at James, who was dark and brooding and more my type, but who had never so much as asked me for a biscuit. 'Nothing here,' I said.

'Sheep rustlers?' Thor asked, sounding more animated than I'd yet heard him. 'Like, pirates?'

We all frowned at one another.

'Like, they creep around at night and cut padlocks off gates and stuff, and it's all dead quiet and they have dogs and just put the sheep in a van and they're gone.'

Thor had clearly got a rather romantic view of something that was actually hugely unpleasant. 'Gangs of thieves, basically. And the sheep end up dead in a warehouse somewhere up north. Even my rare-breed sheep, who are frankly no use for meat. The rustlers aren't very choosy and it costs thousands to farmers,' I said.

'Concise as ever.' Henry gave me a grin. 'But yes. They're about again, so keep an eye open, Dora. I know you don't have any stock in the fields open to the road, but even so. They're cutting gates off and driving over arable to get to flocks.'

'Bastards.' I gritted my teeth. 'Oops. Sorry, Thor.'

'They are bastards though,' he said, reasonably.

'Well, yes.' Henry gave a generalised grin that included us all. James carried on brooding behind the wheel. 'That's kind of the point of us. We're like the anti-bastards.'

'My mate, Alexis, says you're bastards too,' Thor said, without any noticeable embarrassment.

'I expect we've had some good talks with your mate Alexis,' Henry said darkly. 'Over the years.'

'He's an Internet sensation,' Thor went on.

'Really.'

'We'll keep our eyes open for any unusual comings or goings, don't worry,' I said brightly, desperate to change the subject away from Thor's delinquent friends. 'I've got most of the stock close to home at the moment for lambing and the field that adjoins the road is let out to Elvie for the horses. She's got that locked up pretty tightly.'

James gave me a curt nod and Henry smiled broadly, then the Land Rover did a very neat three-point turn and sprayed its way back out of the yard, scattering chickens and mud in equal amounts.

'Wow,' said Thor, in a satisfied sort of tone. 'A run-in with the fuzz. I've got to put this up online.'

He dashed off, arms and legs flailing as though his extremities were still being grown into.

Nat and I looked at one another.

'He's due a break,' Nat said. 'Tutoring isn't twenty-four-hour babysitting, despite what Cass seems to think.'

'Can he really make money doing stuff on the Internet?'

Nat sighed and shuffled his shoulders inside his coat. 'No, not really.' He looked out over the dale, his eyes moving as though they were following the invisible road out towards civilisation. 'I mean, he could be the one in a million that actually *does* get somewhere but it's doubtful. I'm trying to convince him to think of other stuff he might like to do, but...'

'But having a mother like my sister, who still lives at home at twenty-eight and works for her dad – yes, I can see you've got a bit of a struggle on your hands.'

'This is why I think it's so good for him to be here,' Nat went on. He was looking at the sky now. I had to admit that the sky out here was particularly impressive; it went on forever, outlining the world and providing a huge, atmospheric background. You could see the earth curve and with the sky arching overhead it was like living between two elemental brackets. 'He can see that there's other ways to make a living. Working hard is a real thing.'

'I suppose it's natural though, isn't it? When you're young like him, to want to make a living only out of doing things you enjoy? When you don't really know what life involves and the big wide world is a scary place.'

I saw him jump. It was an odd movement, like a sort of double take. 'What did you just say?' There was a strange note to his voice.

'Um, only that it's hard when you're very young. You think that life is easy, everything seems so straightforward and it's only the adults that complicate it. Why?'

He was flicking me little glances. 'I suppose... I just never... thought of it like that.' His voice was distracted. 'I forget that, when you're young, you've got no idea what life is really like with bills and the great nine-to-five. You think being made to go to school contravenes your human rights to do whatever you like all the time and you don't realise it's training you up to accept more of the same for the next sixty years.'

Thor had reappeared, talking earnestly into an iPad held above his head.

'Nine-to-five sounds pretty good to me,' I said. 'Farming is more twenty-four hours on duty and you can never relax.' I watched Thor, who seemed set to document every inch of the farmyard in great detail, like David Attenborough in miniature. 'Like being a parent, I suppose.'

Nat was looking very distracted still. As though he'd seen something in the far, far distance that puzzled him and he was trying to make sense of it. 'Yes, I suppose,' he said vaguely, and I had the feeling that he hadn't really heard what I'd said.

'What's wrong? You're behaving as though you're watching French cinema without subtitles.' I watched Thor gesturing wildly at the field of sheep, presumably explaining 'rustling' to all his city 'crew', who probably thought it was the noise made when you shoplifted crisps.

'Me? Oh, no, nothing. It was what you said then about making a living out of what you enjoy and the world being a scary place. It just reminded me of something; something to do with Leo.'

I suddenly remembered. Sitting in a dark hallway, backs against crumbling plaster. Nearly thirteen years ago, when we'd first met. Noises in another room, a sense of anticipation, excitement and a conversation about the future. About the world being bigger than we knew and how we should enjoy every day, because you never knew what was coming. Leo, who always wore a donkey jacket and DM boots, had his hair long, and stubble, and who knew so much more than me.

I so desperately wanted to tell Nat. Wanted to share his brother, the way I'd known him. 'He—'

'Leo was a bit of a pillock,' he said. 'Stupid behaviour. Immature. Like he never wanted to grow up.'

Okay, I probably wouldn't, then. 'Well, he—'

'Risky behaviour, always pushing things that little bit too far and acting out. Probably something to do with family; parents who never paid him much attention and let him do his own thing too much. Too much freedom can be worse than too little, you know, Dora.'

'So, what about you? Presumably you never went off the rails? Good student, 100-per-cent attendance, straight off to university and studied hard?' I sounded bitter and tried not to. 'Maybe you were too much for Leo to live up to.' I didn't like the condemnation in his voice when he talked about his brother.

'Maybe,' Nat said, sounding vague again. 'Maybe.'

Then he flashed me a smile that was unreadable in its intent and walked off towards the house without another word.

'Weirdo,' I said to the sheep, and went off to fetch some straw bales to keep the wind off the lambs.

4

We all sat in silence around the kitchen table. The window was open, as the spring air was turning mild, and the breeze that blew in was lightly scented with the early-flowering daffodils that I'd planted along the borders.

'Well,' Cass pushed her plate away, 'that was – interesting.'

Nat and Thor were keeping their heads down.

'But then you never were much of a cook, were you, Dora?'

'Shall we go and finish those drawings in the front room, Thor?' Nat threw me the merest hint of a grin. 'It will get us out of the way.'

'Oh, yes.' Thor leaped to his feet. 'Can I take some biscuits?'

Without waiting for an answer, he seized the packet of custard creams from the worktop and the two of them lunged for the door with the eagerness of a couple of ferrets scenting a rabbit. I had no doubt at all that none of the biscuits would survive the evening.

'Cass, I was busy. I've been out sorting out lambs and ewes all afternoon, I don't have time to cook!'

'Then what on *earth* do you live on?' She pushed her chair away from the table and crossed her elegant legs.

'Well – this.' I pointed at my plate, which had, until recently, held tinned stew, tinned potatoes and a slice of bread. 'Whatever is in the pantry that I can heat up quickly.'

'But we can't be expected to eat that every night!' Cass almost wailed. 'We have takeaways from Zizzi's on "cheap nights".'

'This wasn't a cheap night. This is what I eat, Cass. I'm busy. I'm outside most of the time. I just want something that's hot, doesn't need much chewing and has the basic nutrients covered. A meal should also have the added benefit of being suitable for taking outside to the barn in a bowl if I'm having to keep an eye on a sick sheep. Oh, and Zizzi don't deliver out to here. In fact, I'm not even sure where the nearest one is.'

'How do you not have scurvy? And rickets, or whatever those diseases are that poor people get from eating everything out of tins.'

I didn't answer. The real question was, of course, why had Cass assumed I would be cooking for everyone, when I'd been out across the fields all day and she'd been in the front room with her iPad, pressing buttons and chuckling at amusing GIFS. I didn't feel that I needed to say anything about this, as I assumed my late entry to the kitchen, dripping mud and with my jumper unravelling, had been enough of a clue.

Cass stood up. 'This can't go on, Dora. I mean, it just can't. You're living like some kind of eighteenth-century peasant, only with less disfiguring diseases and more electricity. How Mum and Dad haven't called you home to stop this ridiculous charade of independence I have no idea! Let's sell the farm. If you really must, you could buy a little allotment somewhere, carry on with the chickens and the growing things. You could even keep one of the dogs, if you have to. If we did some work to the house it would be very appealing as a little holiday place; we could sell the land separately. I know lots of people in town who would love to have this as a bolthole for weekends.' She looked thoughtfully around the kitchen. 'Granite worktops, an island unit, a newer Aga,' she said, twisting her mouth as though the current state of the place was bitter. 'Yes. It could be lovely.'

'Grandad wanted the place to stay in the family,' I said sullenly, the guilt needling me under the ribs. 'Folly Farm has belonged to us for two hundred and fifty years.'

'And for two hundred and forty-eight of those nobody has done a thing to it.' Cass came over and put a hand on my shoulder, which was when I knew she was serious. 'Look, Dora, you clearly aren't managing. You're nearly thirty-one and on your own. You'll never find a man if you never come indoors – or, if you only come indoors for stuff like this.' She pointed a long-nailed finger at the bowl of brown gloop she'd toyed with. 'You need to look after yourself. Have some highlights.' She lifted a strand of my hair. 'Learn to put on make-up. Get some proper clothes. Stop all this nonsense about breeding sheep and come and live somewhere with heating and furniture and things.'

The worst thing was that, for the briefest nanosecond, I agreed with her. Maybe I did want to live somewhere where I could walk to shops. Buy an ice cream, walk in a park, go to museums and the cinema in my spare time. Actually *have* some spare time. Somewhere I wouldn't have to worry endlessly about tractor tyres and foot rot, dipping and shearing and feed deliveries. My life could stop being a constantly knotted ball of tension, forever poised on the edge of an overdraft and a credit card bill.

But then I glanced out through the window into the gathering twilight. I saw Willow, head shoved through the bars of the gate, trying to reach the edges of a bale of hay I'd put ready for the late-night feed round. Heard the high-pitched bleats of the newest lambs and the lower purring baa of their mothers answering them. The numbers of Upper Ryedales were starting to come back from the brink of endangerment. If I sold up the flock the breed would go back to being isolated twos and threes of sheep being kept for backyard spinners and pets, crossbred for convenience and marketability. Another couple of generations and the breed would be extinct. We'd lose that gene pool of easy breeding, eat anything, live on fresh air and dandelions that I'd struggled so hard to keep going. That Grandad had *wanted* me to keep going.

Selling up would be admitting that the last seven years had been nothing but a vanity project.

'No,' I said firmly. 'No. Grandad left the place to me. It's my home, Cass.'

She shrugged and turned to fiddle with the Aga, which was currently making disturbing bubbling noises as it heated the water.

'Oh, well. Have it your own way. It will come to Thor eventually, anyway, and he'll sell up in a heartbeat.'

She was wearing high heels again, I noticed, when she tapped her way over the flagstones to fill the kettle. Why on earth did she wear high heels in the house?

'What do you mean?' Grandad's will had left the place to me. Thor had been a small child when he died, and there was no mention of him inheriting after me.

'Well, Grandad obviously wanted the farm to go to a boy and you're clearly never going to reproduce, are you? So, who else would you leave the farm to, other than your nephew? And it's in my interests, as his mother, to make sure that the place is in a decent condition, so he can sell it when he inherits from you,' she said, smugly. 'We don't want some derelict barn of a place to have to bulldoze before we can get any money for the land.'

Every one of her words nailed my inadequacy more firmly into place and I couldn't believe her hard-heartedness. Although, no, the tragedy was that I could believe it all too easily. 'So you'd sell the place out of the family, after a quarter of a millennium? All that tradition, all those memories that Grandad built up? All those holidays when we used to come and stay here?'

'Dora, the *plague* was traditional! This place is a money pit that you don't have any money to pour into. What's your solution – you keep living here like Hannah Hauxwell, getting older and more decrepit as the place falls down around you? What then? Who's going to want fifty acres of mud and heather and a few fallen-down walls?'

I went to the door and flung it open and the sheep fell into an expectant silence. 'I am not talking about this now. Or ever. Folly Farm is *my* farm. I'm not selling and you can stop going on about it.'

The loose panel fell out of the door as I swung it shut behind me, but I didn't even stop to prop it back into place. I walked round the house to where a low stone wall stopped moorland and garden fusing into one entity. In the early days I'd dug a vegetable garden here, before I'd found out that there wasn't going to be the luxury of time for weeding and hoeing, and all the beans and peas had been subsumed under the growth of bindweed and bracken. A nasty outbreak of rabbits hadn't helped either, and when I'd realised that deer were coming from miles around to queue beyond the wall, waiting for me to plant nice juicy cabbages and lettuces for them to graze on, I'd given up. So instead I'd let most of the borders return to nature, except a few beds close to the house, where I'd put spring bulbs and some spiky bushes to give the illusion that someone actually gardened.

On this side of the house there were fewer windows, and the building stretched long and grey like a corpse along the hillside.

The grey slate roof wore its wig of occasional mosses jauntily though, and the beginnings of moonlight gave the whole place an agreeably literary sort of look, as though Ted Hughes were hovering about somewhere, trying to think of something to rhyme with 'mullion'.

Grandad knew I could do it. He'd left the farm to me because he knew I could do it. I just had to keep telling myself that.

A flash of brightness showed a door opening at the end of the house, where the nominal front door stood. Nobody used it and hadn't for over half a century, since Grandad had carried Grandma over the threshold as a new bride. Front doors round here were for ceremonies. Although both Grandma and Grandad had died in hospital, had they died at home their coffins would have been carried out of the front door, bidding the house a final, formal farewell. New babies were supposed to come through the front door too, but Mum had been born at home, in the bedroom I now occupied, so I couldn't imagine it had been in anyone's interests to take her outside simply to carry her back in again. The house would have known all about her arrival already, from memories of Grandma's tales of forty-eight hours in labour whilst feeding the sheep and mucking out the old pigsty. I understood there had been a significant amount of swearing involved; not so much whilst delivering her daughter, more at Grandad for letting her do farm work up to an hour before the baby was born.

Mum had been the only child. A girl. And then *she'd* only had two daughters. If what Cass had said about Grandad wanting the farm to go to a boy was true – we must all have come as small packets of disappointment.

And that little needle of guilt pricked deeper into my soul.

'Are you all right?'

It was Nat, a shadowy presence backlit by the bulb in the hallway.

'Yes. No. I don't know.'

The light was cut off as he closed the door and came over to where I was hovering by the wall, accompanied by a string of midges. 'Your sister again?'

'How did you guess?' I hitched myself up to sit on the wall and, after a moment's hesitation, he sat beside me.

'Well, one, because you only seem to be unhappy when you've been anywhere near her for a while, which isn't surprising when I look around at where you live and what you do. And secondly, because she just came slamming into the middle of Thor's homework session complaining about you.'

'Ah.'

We sat in the quiet for a while. At least, compared to urban living it was quiet; there was actually quite a racket going on if you listened. The last rooks were drifting off towards their nests, ack-acking to one another like gossips over a fence. The sheep in the far field were calling to their lambs, and the lambs mewed back with cries that sounded unnervingly human. An owl was clearing its throat in one of the trees near the beck and the birdsong was dying away in bushes and heather clumps. Somewhere along a distant road, a lorry was making hard work of the gradient.

'Cass thinks I should sell up and move back to town,' I said, eventually, when it became evident that he wasn't going to ask. 'I think her alternative is me living here until I die and am eaten by the dogs, when Thor will then inherit the place and promptly sell it.' I wiggled around on the wall to look out over the roof of the house. With the moorland at my back, the green dale stretched down in an illusion of agrarian tidiness. I could see the odd twinkle of light from the outlying houses of the invisible village tucked in the fold. The lorry ground its gears and continued to putter up the incline.

'Ah.'

Nat was taller than me and could rest both feet on the ground from the top of the wall, while my heels gripped into looser stones to stop my legs swinging as though I were five. I glanced at him sideways and had another sudden flashback to that hallway, when Leo was sitting very much like this beside me. 'Did you fall out with your brother much?'

'My...? Oh, Leo. No, actually, we got on very well when he wasn't being a tosser.' His tone was light, as though he could dissipate the force field of horrified annoyance that Cass seemed to cast around me. 'You and your sister have very different views though, don't you?'

'Different views? I'm not sure she's even looking out at the same planet as I am,' I said bitterly.

'Were you ever close? As children?' Nat adjusted his seat on the wall, and I didn't blame him. Grandad had been a demon drystone waller, but he'd gone for practicality rather than smooth finishes. This wall would stop a bullock, but it had a very uncomfortable coping layer.

'When we were very young, yes. There's only two years between us and we were thick as thieves when we were small. Up until Cass got to be a teenager, I suppose. Then she discovered boys in a big way, or, rather, they discovered her, and from then on she was all about the giggling and the Maybelline.' I shrugged. 'Mum used to bring us up here on holiday every summer and we helped Grandad out on the farm, but Cass couldn't be bothered then. She just wanted to sit on the phone to all her friends and laugh about how the freezer was kept in the outhouse and we had to light the range for hot water.'

'Everything worked out for you, though? You got the farm.'

'And she gets fifty per cent of the profits without lifting a finger.' I took a deep breath. 'Sorry. I know that's sort of fair really, but does she have to be such an utter *bitch* about it?'

'There's certainly a lot of resentment, by the sounds of it.' His voice was so even and bloody reasonable it made me angry again.

'Do you have to do that? Be all teacherly and "we can sort this out, shake hands, make up"?' I snapped.

There was a moment of wounded silence and then his voice, quiet in the dark, 'I wasn't aware that I was being "teacherly". I apologise.'

'Well,' I said, mollified somewhat. 'Some things can't be got over. Some things sit there, always in the back of your head. There are some things you can't shake off or run away from or just pretend never happened.'

The night carried on being agriculturally noisy around us. The lorry had chugged to the top of the hill and gone quiet, but the wildlife was still giving it the full pop-concert effect. One of Elvie's horses neighed in the bottom field to add to the cacophony.

'Yes,' Nat said, his voice almost inaudible. 'I know that.'

He was an outline now, a shadow with his feet braced into the turf and his body long and almost curled over his knees. He had his head in his hands and his hair fell forwards; there was another jolt of recognition in my stomach. Admittedly, in the twelve years since we'd last seen one another my memory of Leo had become blurred, overwritten with subsequent events and scribbled on by misery, but Nat really did look very much like the Leo who lived in my thoughts.

'How did Leo die?' I blurted out. Somehow it was easier to ask out here in the dark.

I heard Nat swallow. 'He... It was an overdose. In a squat in Balham.'

The vision I had of Leo, lanky and stubbled, with that tousled dark hair and those piercing eyes, was suddenly overlaid by a sick, emaciated figure, grubby and scarred.

'Oh.' Inevitable, maybe? That sparky intelligence, that offbeat humour; he'd never fitted in really. But then. Neither had I. 'I'm sorry. He must have only been, what, twenty-four?'

A sideways tilt of the head.

'Was he your only sibling?'

A moment's pause and then Nat stood up. 'I don't really want to talk about it, if you don't mind, Dora. Shall we go inside and see if Cass has stopped trying to bite the furniture yet?' His tone was so light that I didn't think I'd offended him by asking. It seemed that the story of Leo's death went so deep that he couldn't dredge it all up at once, here and now. As though he needed to formulate it in his head before it could be spoken.

'Of course. I need to go down and check the stock in the far field anyway in a minute.' I shuffled my bottom gingerly off the craggy stones.

'Come in and have a cup of tea or something first. Maybe Thor could go down and look at the sheep with you? He's actually starting to like – no, that's not true, he's actually stopped expressing his utter contempt for the countryside and I have hopes that he may pause in his influencing of his thousand followers for five minutes if the lambs can be persuaded to be amusing and or cute.' He gave me a flash of a grin. 'He may be a street rapper dancing to an urban beat, but underneath he's still a twelve-year-old boy.'

'He hides it well,' I said, and we headed off around the house to the kitchen door. I didn't think the front door could stand being opened twice in one decade.

* * *

'Dora,' Thor hooked a foot up on the gate and watched me heave another bale of hay across the field, trailing ewes all trying to eat as I went, 'why don't you have normal sheep?'

'What... do you mean... by normal?' I panted. 'They're woolly, four legs, go baa, in what other way could they be more normal?'

'You know. Like the ones in all the other fields. White ones.' He was eyeing my knife with interest as I cut the baler twine and spread the hay along the grass next to the feeder.

'Lots of reasons really. This is only a very small farm and I couldn't really make any money on just a few commercial sheep. Upper Ryedale wool has very long fibres, so it's in demand with people who spin and knit, so I can get more for their wool than I would for, say, Suffolks. They also don't need much extra feeding, even with the poor grazing round here, so they're cheap to keep. And they're an endangered breed, so lambs sell for breeding around the world.' Well, there was that weird bloke in New Zealand anyway. 'So, if you can only have a small number of stock, it makes sense to have something that is worth more, rather than try to keep a commercial breed and have to spend out on feed and vet bills.'

I wrangled a lamb that had got tangled in the string and it ran off to its mother, who eyeballed me as though I'd tried to disembowel it.

'But why not just build houses on the fields? You can get lots of money for houses.'

So, Cass had got to him already, had she?

'Do your laces up, Thor. You'll fall over.' I counted the lambs again, checked over the ewes to make sure none were coming down with mastitis or had mysteriously died. Even though the Ryedales made less of a hobby of dying than other breeds, that was like saying that my tractor was less likely to kill me than malnutrition. It was a very close thing.

'On point, innit,' Thor grunted and didn't so much as look at his feet.

'You would never get planning permission to build houses here. We're in the National Park.' And you can tell that to your mother, I added, silently.

'So where do they all live, then? I mean, like, if there's no new houses and people keep having babies and things, where do they all go?' He stared out into the darkness as though he expected to see the locals crawling out of holes in the ground. Like Hobbits. Or zombies. I shook my head to get rid of the image.

'Well, yes, it's difficult, obviously...' I didn't have the energy to get into local economics and politics with Thor now. I was still a little shaken from the realisation of how Leo had died. *In a squat. From an overdose.*

'I mean, what's the point of having, like, laws that say you can't build houses when there's people that need places to live?' Thor persisted with the subject. 'What are they going to do, stack up?'

'Let's go back to the house and see if they've left us any biscuits.' I figured that food would be the best distraction. My exposure to pre-teen boys was strictly limited and had been severely curtailed by my mother even when I'd been a pre-teen girl, so I wasn't quite sure what they did with all the food. Put it into growing upwards, if Thor's height was anything to go by; his trailing jeans hems and oversized sweatshirts seemed to be more of an attempt to put him in clothes he wouldn't grow out of before he got the chance to fasten them than a fashion statement.

'Yeah. Nat's got me doing this diary thing, and now I've *finally* got something, like, kinda interesting to put in it.' Thor bobbed along beside me as we headed back up the track. 'Can I drive the tractor tomorrow?'

'No.' And then, because I was actually quite enjoying this time with my nephew and wanted to erase his near-permanent frown, which gave him the look of a punitive accountant approaching end-of-year, I said, 'Maybe you can ride on it with me though. When I take the feed down in the morning.'

A sudden smile stretched his face, lit his brown eyes and wrinkled his nose until he looked more like the cute child that I remembered him as being. '*Wicked!* Can we do doughnuts in the field?'

'Er, no. No doughnuts. You'd be toast.'

Thor stared at me for a moment and then screamed a laugh. I didn't know if his follow-up hilarity was caused by my weak pun or the fact that he'd realised his distracted and somewhat disapproving aunt actually had a sense of humour under the furred-up jumpers and holey jeans. The giggles kept him going all the way back to the house, and made him far more endearing than any amount of street talk and followers had done so far.

Thor ran inside, barging through the kitchen door and past the bemused collies. I heard him clatter his way along the bare hallway down to the little study, where Grandad had always kept the farm paperwork and which Nat had taken over as the schoolroom for the duration.

I followed more steadily, the dogs getting up to greet me as I came in. I noticed that Dax, the older of the two, was getting a little less ready to jump up, a little stiffer in the hind quarters. I made a mental note to keep an ear out for collie pups to bring on and made the sudden decision that Dax would live out his days in the house and yard, keeping unwanted visitors at bay. I wondered if it was too late to train him to savage Cass.

'Oh, you came back.' Cass was swirling water into the sink. I didn't kid myself that she was about to wash up or anything.

'Yes.' I sank tiredly onto a chair. 'I thought about legging it for Patagonia but I had odd boots on.' I cupped my hands around the back of my neck. I was exhausted and only just realising it. Two more weeks should see all the ewes lambed and then life would quieten down a bit, except for the fact that Morgana le Fay would still be here.

'Do you remember,' she asked quietly, 'that summer when we came up and Grandad took you off to the sheep sales? I'd have been about ten.'

I thought back. The summers had, of course, all been long and hot and consisted of 'helping' on the farm, splashing about in the beck at the bottom of the long field, and eating endless picnics up on the high moors overlooking the house. As the only child, Mum had returned to see her parents a few times a year and we'd usually come too, except in winter. I used to think that was because Mum didn't want us to get snowed in at the farm, but I'd realised, after two winters here, it was because there was no heating and she didn't want us to go back with frostbite and missing fingers.

'I think so.' Yes, I did remember. In those days Grandad had kept a flock of Swaledale sheep alongside his few Upper Ryedales and we'd gone to the sales in York in his ancient Ford Transit van. 'Why?'

Cass shrugged. 'Nat told me to remind you of a time when we were young, that's all. That was pretty much the only thing I could remember. That and being bored as hell because Grandma wouldn't let me watch *Tracy Beaker*.'

I gave her a befuddled sort of smile. So Nat was trying psychology to stop us killing one another, was he? I gave him mental marks for the attempt, but he hadn't accounted for how shallow my sister could be.

'I remember falling asleep in the back of the van,' I said. 'And Grandad buying me an ice cream at the sales. It was hot.'

It had been hot in that old shed where the sale was taking

place. Hot and smelling of sheep and too many farmers who took personal hygiene as a suggestion rather than an actual practice. There had been dogs milling around, barking, and ewes baaing and the constant background rattle of the unfamiliar northern accent. The smell of pipe smoke and crushed grass took me right back to that baking auction floor even now.

'Mum used to say that was when Grandad realised he'd make a farmer of you.' Cass stirred the water in the bowl. 'Maybe I should have gone to the sale instead. *You* could have stayed here and listened to Mum and Grandma nattering on and made scones and learned to crochet. Things might have been different then.'

Yes, they might have been. It could have been *me* who'd got pregnant at fifteen and never left home and lived on pocket money and parental guilt.

'But you never had any interest in the sheep,' I said.

'Well, no, obviously I'd have sold them and turned this place into a boutique B&B, but that's not the point.'

She turned around. I wondered why she thought it was necessary to wear a full face of make-up every day, even out here when the only person we saw was Nat. And then I wondered if she was trying to attract him, and felt a little frisson.

'The sheep, well, the Ryedales, were important to Grandad. That's why I got the farm. They're important to me, too.' I had a tiny little moment of pride too, in knowing that Grandad had decided he'd make a farmer of me, but it was quickly subsumed under the knowing that there hadn't been anyone else to leave it to. While Grandad hadn't been overtly sexist, I still couldn't lose the feeling that crept over my shoulder in the early mornings when I struggled with the feed sacks, that he would rather I had been a boy.

Cass shrugged again. 'I've ordered some paint and fabric,' she said. 'That front room wants sorting out. I thought I might do the walls teal, it's very on-trend at the moment, and maybe re-cover the sofa.'

'Shit, Cass, there isn't the money for that!'

'I used my card.' Then, a sudden and rare flash of a smile that reminded me of my sister when she'd been younger and we'd been friends. A bright flick of amusement that lit her eyes. 'You've deleted your card details off the computer.'

'Well, dur, I'm not having you ordering caviar and Krug next time you do the supermarket delivery, not on the farm's account.'

We shared a moment so rare that it made the Upper Ryedale look positively common. A shared second of remembering who we'd been, how we'd been in a time before jealousy and resentment; when life had been no more complicated than who got to hold the bucket when we played down at the stream.

'The dishes need doing,' Cass broke the moment. 'I'm going to check Nat is making Thor do his homework.'

Without a backward glance, and with no sign that she'd felt any kind of sisterly communion, she strolled out of the kitchen, heels hard on the stone flags and her back straight in her designer sweater and carefully tailored jeans.

I wondered if she wore tight jeans to keep her forked tail from falling out.

5

Days passed. I managed, very efficiently, to keep out of everyone's way, which wasn't too hard to do. I was up and out before the house stirred, and there was plenty to keep me out of doors during the day. I made sandwiches or took food with me, so I only came into the kitchen from time to time, to feed the dogs or restock my pockets with biscuits or buns. It meant that any contact with my visitors was kept to a minimum of 'good morning's or smiles in the hallway. Cassandra I hardly saw at all. She was reduced to a thumping sound from the front room, some occasional raised-voice swearing from the top of the house. It was like living with a foul-mouthed poltergeist.

I did see Nat and Thor out on the farm sometimes. Once across a field, where I was checking a ewe's feet and they were walking the banks of the little stream, Nat pointing at plants and Thor mainly staring at the tractor, and once as they came back from the village when I was replacing some posts and connecting the electric fence to the battery. Nat raised a hand and called something I couldn't hear. I half raised my arm in reply, shading my eyes against the low-sloping sun that now carried enough heat to sweat me out of my jacket and make eating outdoors pleasant rather than a damp endurance test.

They walked on and disappeared into the house. I waited, half crouched over the wiring, in case someone was going to emerge and ask me if I wanted a cup of tea, or to chat, but nobody did. Willow, who was still waiting to lamb and, as such, was one of only a few ewes left in the paddock, butted my leg and distracted me and I went back to fencing.

So, it was a slight shock when I emerged from the barn late one morning, after a week or so of self-imposed isolation, to find Nat sitting on a straw bale and leaning his back against the sun-warmed cob wall.

'Hello,' he said cheerily. 'How're the sheep?'

'Er.' I looked up. Half the flock were now down in the big field with their lambs, the other half in the long field, where there was more shelter, with their younger offspring. 'Well, they're all upright, which is always a bonus.'

'Good.' Then he turned to look at me, screwing his face up against the brightness of the light. 'Hadn't seen you about much. I thought I should touch base with you, make sure you're still all right with having your house full.'

I shrugged. I couldn't see the point in saying, 'No, I'm not, bugger off now.' I'd only get the 'guilt calls' from my mother. 'It's fine,' I muttered, not very convincingly.

'Have you finished lambing now?' He hooked a foot up on the bale so his knee was under his chin. He was wearing dark jeans, which looked clean, boots and a thin sweater. I'd take bets that he was secretly freezing but too much of a 'bloke' to admit it and go and put a coat on. The thought made me smile.

'Nearly. Only two to go, Willow and an old ewe that's on her ninth season, so she'll go easily enough.'

'Do they all have names?'

I had to hand it to him, Nat had got this small talk mastered. He was probably in huge demand among the home-schooling fraternity in south London. 'No. Just Willow, because I had to hand-rear her and you can't keep calling them "the lamb" when they are the size of a Labrador and getting in the pantry every five minutes. You have to have *something* to shout so they know who you're cross with.'

'Right.' He stared off over the green hills again. 'You aren't much of a one for chatting, are you, Dora?'

'Nope.' And then, because I felt a bit sorry for him and because there was something very appealing about him sitting there, with the sun bouncing off the barn wall hard enough almost to be audible, and the bucolic scenery, 'I don't get much practice.'

'But you talk to the sheep. I've heard you.'

'Well, of course. It's a bit rude to go in unannounced and tip them up to feel their udders. I at least say "excuse me".'

The combination of his deep laugh with the sun, his crinkled eyes and his lean shape made disturbingly tingly things happen around my body. It was disconcerting. I'd last had tingly feelings about Chris, and he had the 'enough of me to go around' attitude that made any kind of tingly feelings, other than those occasioned by slapping his hand away from pinching my bum, a very bad idea.

'Well, I ought to get on with – stuff,' I said, not moving and hoping he would get up and go away and leave me to deal with my hormones with some energetic mud-sweeping. 'Shouldn't you be teaching Thor something nature-based?'

Nat eased his shoulders back. 'Your sister has taken him down to York for the day.'

'In *my car*?'

'She said you wouldn't have left the keys in full sight if you didn't want her to drive it.'

Damn. I knew I should have taken the keys from their place on the hook beside the sink. Although Cass would consider anything less than my burying them in the garden as 'in full sight'. 'What's she doing in town? If I'd known she was going I'd have given her a list. I might text her.'

'I think she found a salon that could do her a full body respray.' He grinned. 'Look on the bright side – she may come back looking like a satsuma.'

'I'd better not distract her with a shopping list, then. Spray tans are serious stuff. Although if the weather stays like this, all she'll have to do is stand outside and she can get a real one.' I looked at my hands. They were, indeed, brown, but most of that was marker spray. Some of it was mud. 'I'm Vitamin D'd to the max, at least.'

The knowledge that we were here, on the farm, on our own, made my skin prickle. There was almost a feeling of expectation in the air with the smell of grass and hay, but, from the way he was happily sitting on the bale, eyes scanning the roll and fall of field, it was all in my head.

'We should…' he started, but then the multicoloured stripes and rotating blue light of Henry and James's police vehicle slithered into the yard on a slick of mud. 'Hey, Dora!' Henry shouted out of the window.

I wandered over. The blue light strobed off the chickens giving them an interesting Avian Disco vibe. 'Hello. What's up?'

'Had a report of a suspicious lorry driving up out this way.' Henry opened the door and jumped down. 'Your neighbour down the dale there lost sixty sheep last night. Buggers took a gate off, backed a lorry in and were away before anyone knew a thing. I thought you'd have been out since early doors, so you might have seen or heard something.'

I thought back to last night and this morning. 'Sorry, no. It was quiet as usual up here.'

Nat came over too. Henry eyed him up and down but didn't say anything. I could hear conclusions being wrongly come to though, which really didn't bode well for a policeman.

'Keep your eyes peeled, Dora. They must have gone off down the dale, then, towards Pickering, if you didn't see them come up over the hill. But any sightings of big vehicles or trailers you don't recognise, give me a bell.' Another quick sideways look at Nat. 'You've got my number.'

And then they were gone, maybe to answer a call, because I heard the siren start up as they got to the main road. Or perhaps they just liked the noise.

'Does the other guy ever speak?' Nat asked. 'Cos he looks like he's pretending he's in an episode of *Starsky and Hutch*.'

'I think he's so used to being "bad cop" he finds it hard to get out of character.'

'Shall we have a coffee?' Nat began to wander towards the house. 'I feel we should make use of this time without Thor, to eat all the biscuits and lie on the sofas with our shoes on.'

'Coffee sounds good. I might make some soup too. It's been a while since I had hot food.'

It felt very domestic, pottering around the kitchen with Nat. The sun angled in through the window and gave the place a pleasing air of farmhouse chic, where the peeling paintwork and undulating work surfaces looked designer-shabby rather than impecunious-threadbare. The dogs stayed outside, curled in the sun, and we left the door open to let the fresh air in. It also let in a couple of bantams, who pecked at the crumbs on the flagstones and squawkily argued over some spilled spaghetti hoops.

'I should do some housework,' I said, scraping the table clear of what looked like Thor's breakfast remains.

'You're busy. I'll try to persuade Thor that cleaning is educational, if you like. I might get half a room out of him before he twigs he's been had.'

'We need to persuade Cass to help. What has everyone been eating?' I looked in the pantry. 'There doesn't seem to be much food gone.'

'Ah. Thor and I have been experimenting with food. We found some old cookery books in the dresser and we're working through the recipes alphabetically. He's up to cauliflower cheese and chicken rissoles. Early days yet, but he turned out a very acceptable baked potato. Still to master the art of not serving it rock hard, but we're getting there.'

'What the hell are chicken rissoles?'

'From experience, little balls of meat, raw in the middle and burned on the outside, but, like I said, early days.'

He poured boiling water onto the coffee and the smell made my mouth water. By the time he pushed the mug across the table to me, I was practically dribbling. I fell upon the plate of digestive biscuits like a starving person.

Nat was watching me. 'You should take better care of yourself,' he said, sipping at his mug. 'If you get ill, who will look after the sheep?'

'I'm fine,' I muttered round a mouthful of oaty deliciousness. 'Very sturdy. Robust, even.'

'I think your sister described it as "pig-headed and oblivious", but robust sounds better.' Nat sipped again. Two bantams squabbled over something in the doorway and Dax yawned pinkly in the sun.

'My sister isn't my biggest fan.'

There was a bit of a pause. I laid my hand on the sun-warmed pine of the table and wondered when the last of my nails had broken off.

'So, what happened?' Nat's voice was very gentle. 'What turned you from loving sisters into this whole "deadly mortal enemy" thing you've got going on? I half expect the music from *Psycho* to start up every time you two are in the same room.'

It was a question I had asked myself. I had also answered it myself, but I didn't know if the conclusions I had reached were accurate or fair. 'When Cass was fifteen she got pregnant.' I remembered the day as if it were last week. Mum and Dad both in tears in the living room, Cass banished to her bedroom. Me, ricocheting between all of them, not knowing quite what to expect from anyone. Mum was making plans, Dad kept saying, 'But what about school?' as though education had fundamentally failed us all. Cass was dry-eyed and determined; tight-lipped about the father and buying 'Your Body In Pregnancy' type books until WHSmith refused to let her through the doors again. 'Mum needed to look after Cass a lot and Dad went into protectiveness overdrive. Cass made having a baby her new hobby and, well, I had nothing in common with any of them any more.'

Mum was always telling me to be quiet, not to wake Cass, she was napping and needed her sleep. Dad was irritable and distracted, taking on some overseas projects to build his company profile and make more money. 'There's going to be an extra mouth to feed,' he would say, as though Cass were going to give birth to a killer whale.

'I went off the rails a bit, I suppose. I stayed out a lot. Went to parties, anywhere I could get in, and then I turned eighteen and I could hang out in pubs and nightclubs. Nobody seemed to care that I was never at home, and Mum actually told me not to come home if I was going to be late, because I might disturb my sister.' I shrugged. 'Cass was more important. And everything revolved around Thor. I sort of slid between the cracks.'

Nat nodded. 'You were a neglected teenager.'

I could never hear the word neglected without thinking *yes, yes, I was!* and then sense cutting in and denying it, loyalty overlaying the whole. 'No. I was a middle-class teenager whose parents had had a terrible shock and who were dealing with it as best they could. I had a home, a bedroom of my own, friends – I wasn't some Dr Barnardo's case. I just made some bad decisions, that's all.'

Nat put his mug down. 'There's lots of forms of neglect, Dora,' he said steadily. 'Practical. Emotional. Psychological. It's not all kids in alleyways being picked up by middle-aged blokes for sex or wet, hungry babies in a cot while mum goes out and gets drunk, you know. Teenagers need parenting as much as toddlers do.'

'Well,' I said robustly – this topic had gone on for long enough and I was feeling uncomfortable. 'Now I've got all this.' I held my arms wide to indicate the sunshine, the farmyard and the house. Behind me, the door panel fell off again. 'So, I think things turned out all right really.'

'Except for the fact that you and your sister are like two countries forced to be diplomatic, but underneath are itching to start a full-blown war?'

The sun had moved to shine in through the back door now. A wedge of light sliced across the end of the table and illuminated a small black hen, who'd brought her brood of tiny chicks in to feast on the unaccustomed bounty on the kitchen floor. I smiled at Nat. 'We're more like two adjacent parish councils, fighting over who mows the verge on the boundary line,' I said. 'It's fine. We don't need to have much to do with each other and we can generally manage to keep things at a stage of bitter well-mannered sniping. Nobody is going to die. Like I said, we're two very different people. Just because we're sisters doesn't mean we need to be sharing a bedroom and giggling all night over who fancies whom.'

He sighed. 'I guess not.'

From outside came the sound of a car coming down the lane far too fast for the suspension to accommodate the potholes. Nat and I were outside in time for Cass's arrival in the yard, my car squeaking and ever so slightly off centre.

'That was *wicked*!' Thor threw himself out of the passenger door. 'Like being on a Disney World ride!'

Cass slid her way out of the driver's seat. 'Your car needs a wash,' she said, walking past me and dropping the keys into my hand. 'And there's something wrong with the exhaust.'

'Well, there is now,' I muttered under my breath. 'It was fine before you took it.'

Cass was pulling bags out of the boot. 'Come and help, then,' she addressed Nat and I as though we were a pair of inept flunkies. Thor had run off into the house. No doubt his nearly a thousand followers were going to be treated to a blow-by-blow account of a day's shopping in York. I hoped they all had high boredom thresholds.

Nat and I exchanged a look. There was an element of complicity in it that caused the tingles to make a swift return and, when our hands brushed as we both reached for the same bag, the feeling shot to my fingertips like life coming back to frozen limbs.

'Had a good day?' The question was as neutral as I could manage, bearing in mind she'd probably ruined my car's springs by coming down the track too fast.

'We-e-e-el-ll...' Cass, holding one, very light, bag, tipped her head on one side. 'It was all right, I suppose. I mean, York is hardly Milan, is it?'

'It's not trying to be,' I pointed out.

'But the salon girls seem to know what they're doing. And there's the odd shop that's okay.' She stalked off into the kitchen, while we picked up armfuls of bags. A little scream came a moment later. 'Pandora! There are *birds* in the *kitchen*!' She emerged in the kitchen doorway making flapping motions, which I thought was a bit daft – I knew what birds were – but then I realised that she was trying to shoo the bantams out. The bantams were, as chickens do, dashing about in all directions like ladies with their knickers down, making high-pitched clucks of alarm.

I reached into the kitchen, took a handful of dog biscuits, and scattered them outside in the yard. The hens instantly waddled over to investigate the new bounty and started competing with the dogs to break the world speed-eating record. 'It's just the bantams,' I said to Cass, who was holding a hand to her chest and hyperventilating. 'Not a Hitchcock film.'

'But... they're *birds*!' She covered her eyes.

'They're pets.'

'And look! My tan hasn't set properly yet, I'm not supposed to touch my face! If I go streaky, Dora, you will be paying for another trip to the salon, and, let me tell you, that's not a cheap day out!'

I looked over at my poor little car, sitting slightly lopsided on its suspension. 'I can tell,' I said, dryly.

'Thor! Darling!' She ignored me and went to the hallway door. Nat was still bringing bags in, clumping them together on the table. 'Come and get your new outfits to show your followers!' She began dividing the bags into piles. Evidently Thor had benefited from the trip beyond appreciating the history and architecture of the city.

'I bought some paint.' Cass pointed to one of the heavier bags, which sat, sides roundly bulging like Willow, on the floor. Nat hadn't attempted to raise it as high as the table. 'I thought it would look nice in the front room.'

'Cass, you should have asked me first.' I moved aside to let Thor dash past, grab a handful of bags and then dash off, iPad still held up in front of his face.

'Oh, I've already started decorating.' Cass blithely shook the kettle. 'I would have mentioned it to you, but you've been so – *busy*.' She gave the word a pointed little spin, as though she suspected I hadn't spent the past week working with the sheep but had really been lying in the shed with six months' back issues of *Hello!* and a bottle of gin. 'I had to stop because I needed this paint and Farrow & Ball is much better if you see it in real life. It's so hard to colour match over the Internet.'

'You've already started? But where?' I looked around at the walls of the kitchen, which were not showing any signs of having been attacked by Farrow & Ball. In fact, I was sure I remembered Grandad slapping this primrose-yellow emulsion on during one half-term holiday when I'd been about nine.

Cass tossed her hair at me and stalked out, down the hallway, and then threw open the door to the front room, with a flourish. It would have blown her coolness to have declared 'ta-dah!' but there was something in her smug expression that held implicit 'ta-dah'ness.

'Wow.' I couldn't stop myself. 'It looks—' I had been about to say 'amazing', but Cass was already smug enough '—so different,' I finished.

The previously slightly bleak front room, which had held the huge sofa, a bookcase of dubious antiquity, a sideboard that had looked as if someone had nailed random planks together to form furniture, and the freezer of colostrum, had been transformed. The sofa, previously a sort of off-green draylon, was now covered in a grey and white striped fabric, which also swathed the windows. The bookcase had been cleared and now looked less like something from an M R James story and more like an actual piece of furniture. The freezer had gone. A slight trail showed that it had been moved across into the study, with some force, from the marks on the floorboards. The untransformed sideboard stood under the window where it looked as though it were sulking.

All the walls in the front room were newly painted a kind of off-white, the actual nature of the offness being somewhere between mushroom and beige, and the woodwork was a clean matt white. It was very effective.

'This—' Cass brandished the huge tin of Farrow & Ball paint '—is going on that wall.' She pointed to the big wall opposite the windows. 'I may do a feature on the fireplace wall. I haven't decided yet.' She popped the lid of the tin of paint. It was a bluey-grey, like the sea on a February afternoon. I bet it was probably called 'Winter Tide' or something. 'I'm going to restore the fireplace.'

'What to?' I asked, somewhat weakened by realising that my sister had an actual talent and could do more than waft. 'It's already a fireplace.'

'Some barbarian has decorated over the stonework.' She waved a hand. 'I mean, if you're going to have a seventeenth-century fireplace, you may as well make it *look* like a seventeenth-century fireplace, not something that the nineteen thirties spat out.'

The sun had climbed high enough in the sky to let a few beams in. They highlighted mouldings high on the cornices and the brightness of the new paintwork. It was as though the bones of the old house were showing through layers of more recent flesh. Cass was right though, the fireplace was hideous, with brown tiles and a marble-effect mantelpiece that might have looked acceptable in a suburban house, but looked ridiculously undersized in this big room with the high ceilings. Grandma and Grandad had never used this room, I remembered. It had usually been full of feed sacks. There was still the ghost of the smell of sheep cubes mingled with the smell of fresh paint and new fabric.

'Wow,' I said again.

Beside me, Nat made a 'yes, wow!' noise.

'So.' Cass looked at me. 'With your *agreement*, shall I carry on?'

'Don't be sarcastic,' I said. 'Of course. This looks brilliant, Cass.' I paused. 'Will you do the kitchen next?'

She shrugged. 'I follow my instincts with these things.' But I had the feeling that she was quietly pleased at my appreciation, and already planning a colour palette for the walls.

Nat and I left her to her paint-stirring and went back to the kitchen. 'I thought all her talk of interior design was just Cass trying to sound cultured,' I said. 'But she's actually quite good at it. Who'd have thought it?'

Nat was peering up at the ceiling. 'She's right too,' he said. 'You've got loads of seventeenth-century features in the place. It's a shame not to make something of them. Like – like I'm pretty sure that's a bread oven there above the Aga. The original would have been an open-fire range and that hole is where the bread would have gone to cook slowly.'

'I use it to keep the empty lambs' bottles in,' I said, pulling one out to demonstrate. 'Oh. And that's where I put the spare tractor key, I wondered where that was.'

There were voices in the hallway. 'Mum! Mum, will you come and do some stills of me in the new outfits, outside? I want to put a shoot up online for my followers, so they can see the stuff in daylight!'

'Coming, sweetie.'

Cass and Thor clomped into the kitchen and past us, without acknowledging us at all. Thor was still talking, holding his iPad out to his mother. 'I'm gonna sit on the fence. Not up here, it's all shitty with mud and stuff. I want to sit where there's, like, lambs and grass and stuff and it looks like we're in the real countryside. Gonna put my trainers on when we get out there, cos they've got to look box fresh. You take loads of pics and I'll put the good ones online, maybe try to get a modelling contract!'

'That modelling agency don't know who they turned down,' Cass said. 'They'll be sorry when they see these.'

I pulled a face at Nat. Thor was an average-looking twelve-year-old, and the 'my mother fell asleep with the clippers' hairstyle didn't help. He would probably turn into a good-looking man, but for now he was gawky and his features were too big for his face.

It struck me suddenly that Nat looked far more model-like than Thor, tall and slender but with shoulders that gave him a masculine shape and big eyes that made him look a bit elfin. The tingles pricked again. They were starting to annoy me now. Okay, so I hadn't had sex since Chris, and that hadn't so much been sex as naked wrestling, no falls, no submissions, although I had posited that either jelly or mud might have made it more fun. Chris was very much of the 'that was great for me therefore it must have been great for you' school of thought, but it had been nice to have a warm body there in the night to snuggle up to. Elvie clearly thought the same and she was, quite frankly, welcome to him, although having a vet instantly on hand had been useful at times.

So I reasoned the tingles were a side effect of having a man, any man, close enough to touch. The fact that the man reminded me so much of Leo was a drawback and advantage in equal measure, but it was a relief to know that my association with Chris didn't mean that I wanted all men pinned to a tree with a knife through their heart. I could still do it. I could still have that moment where my body felt as though it was growing towards a man a cell at a time; that if he turned towards me and held out his arms I'd fall against him, back arched and lips pursed like one of those women on the covers of the limp paperbacks Grandma had stacked in the attic. I might even have lifted one leg behind me and trailed a shoe, although that didn't look quite as alluring in wellingtons.

It was hard to know what Nat thought or felt. Maybe he got the tingles too and was wisely ignoring them. Or maybe he just thought I'd gone a bit quiet in the face of my sister's immediate obedience to her son's wishes, an attitude which wasn't going to do Thor any favours or help him grow up to be a mature and well-rounded individual. Nat was inscrutable, that was the only word for it. As though everything went on behind those wide, sparkling eyes but never got as far as the face in front of them. Which was probably a good thing in a teacher.

He moved so that his head briefly blocked the light, which meant that he was outlined by a pale halo. Yes, Nat really was too good to be true. He was good with children, well, with Thor at least, who I realised wasn't a representative sample, but he was tough to deal with, so it boded well. Thoughtful – he wanted my sister and I to get on better. Well mannered – he had to be, he hadn't thrown anything at Cass yet. And good-looking. So yup, definitely too good to be true.

Was it possible he was simply a nice, kind, uncomplicated man who'd lost a brother he'd clearly cared a lot about, in tragic circumstances?

Should I tell him about the Leo I'd known? Would that make his loss easier or harder to bear? Would it make him look at me differently? Would I become something other than the straightforward busy sheep farmer with the annoying sister and the slight air of resentment at my upbringing?

But on reflection, it was best I didn't. Nat was just Thor's tutor. And once the three-month endurance test that was Cass and Thor staying here was over, they'd all be back off to the newly built extension in Streatham, no doubt with underfloor heating and all the storage space Cass could need. Me and my tingles were my own problem and the best way to deal with those was hard work and isolation.

'Dora!' Thor came dashing into the kitchen, clearly midway through an outfit change. He was only wearing a T-shirt and a pair of boxer shorts; trainers flopped untied on his feet. 'Come quick, there's something wrong with one of the sheep!'

I sighed wearily. In summer there was always the odd person up from town making the trek down my trackway to tell me that a sheep was dead in the field, only to point out a ewe lying blamelessly and innocently on her side in the sun. She'd usually get up as we watched, like an old lady embarrassed at being caught resting, and I'd smile and thank the visitor for taking the trouble, and silently swear all the way back down the driveway.

'What sort of something wrong?' I asked, wondering if I should make more coffee and whether Cass had bought any of her preferred expensive biscuits in town.

'She's lying down!'

Well, of course she is. I opened a cupboard. 'Yes, and?'

'She doesn't look well, Dora, please come and look. It's that little one up in the paddock. She keeps kind of baaing and wriggling.'

Willow? 'Okay. I'm coming.' I grabbed my jacket from the back of the door. Willow was due to lamb any day now and she'd been scanned with twins. She'd had a large single last year without any problems, maybe something had got caught up?

Willow was jammed in the corner, by the barn. She'd been fine when I'd done my last check, although maybe she had been a little quieter than usual, and I cursed my self-involved musings that had kept me from properly addressing this. I could have isolated her in the barn, but there was no reason to suspect she'd have a problem lambing.

I grabbed the lubricant from the shelf inside the barn and dragged off my jacket and jumper. With my arm nicely slippery, I began feeling inside Willow, who was contracting strongly, but with no sign of any lambs imminent.

'That's disgusting,' Cass said from outside the field. 'Don't look, Thor, darling.'

'Is she all right?' Thor was standing on the top of the fence, half leaning into the paddock. 'Dora?'

Willow was in full labour, trying to expel her lambs, but her cervix hadn't dilated. I could only fit one fingertip inside.

'Nat, please can you phone the vet? The number is stored in my phone, which is in the pocket of my jeans here.' I sort of indicated with my head.

There were no tingles when he touched me this time. He got down beside me and slid the phone out of my pocket. 'It's locked.'

I told him the number to unlock it. It was Leo's birthday. A stupid, sentimental gesture that I'd liked at the time because no one would ever guess it. My birthday, Cass's birthday, even Thor's were all a matter of record and anyone could have looked them up. Leo's? Well, nobody even knew I'd known him. So, safe enough.

Nat didn't appear to have registered the significance of the numbers. He tapped the phone, scrolled through the list, while under my hand Willow baaed and struggled.

'Tell them we've got a ewe down with ringwomb and trying to deliver now.' I held Willow's head as there was nothing more I could do at the other end. 'They'll need to do a section.'

'Will she be all right, Mum?' Thor sounded less like a street-gang member and more like a little boy now. 'Mum?'

'I think we should go inside now.' Cass sounded a bit strained. 'The vet will be here in a minute and we want to leave room. Let's go and unpack all your clothes and get them hung up before they crease.'

'Is there anything I can do?' Nat's voice was soft in my ear, trying not to alarm Willow. She was panting now, eyes rolling as she tried to look at her belly.

'No. We just have to wait. She may suddenly dilate and deliver them and the vet will have had a wasted trip,' I said hopefully. But I didn't like this. Ryedales didn't usually suffer ringwomb, they were easy lambers, so I didn't have much experience with it. I did know, however, that it didn't often put itself right.

We stayed there for what felt like hours. Willow continued to strain. I checked once or twice but there was no further progress. Nat stood with me, still holding my phone, until we heard the disturbance on the track that was the arrival of the vet.

It wasn't Chris, thankfully. I didn't think his brand of jolly bonhomie was quite what I needed now. It was Jen, the down-to-earth and serious partner in the veterinary practice down in the village; she must have come immediately.

'Ringwomb,' I said shortly.

'Okay. I'll operate on her here, no point in stressing her out more than we need to. All right, old girl, let's get you sorted.' Jen began changing her clothes.

'I'll go and get the hot water,' I said. 'Anything else you need from the house?'

'Just the water, thanks. I've got everything I need in the wagon. Oh, and a cup of tea wouldn't go amiss either. I've been out calving at Peter's all morning.'

Her practicality and treatment of the situation as an everyday occurrence was very calming compared to Chris's habit of behaving as though he were in an episode of a James Herriot drama. Not that Chris exactly made the situation worse, but he did have a degree in flirting with every woman within ten miles by over-dramatising, which could be wearing when you were in a life-or-death situation. 'We'll let you get on with it, then.'

I nodded to Nat, who was finding it hard to tear his eyes away from the sheep down on the ground as Jen went to fetch her bag from the car. 'She's...'

'Let's leave it to Jen. We'll bring her some hot water and a cup of tea for – after.'

'You don't sound hopeful.'

I gave Willow one last look. 'Caesareans are not always successful in sheep. I don't want to lose Willow or the lambs, but – Jen will do her best.'

I walked briskly back across the yard to the house, where the kitchen door stood ajar. I couldn't afford tears. Keeping animals involved loss; that was how it was. I couldn't get emotionally involved otherwise every time I sold a ewe or something went wrong with a lamb I'd cry. I would have dissolved by now. The animals were a business and I should no more cry over them than I would cry over a desk falling to pieces or a non-delivery of stationery.

Grandad had taught me well. I remembered him standing,

unspeaking, with his pipe between his teeth, when the vet had come to his old sheepdog. Zip had worked with him every day for ten years, been his companion when Grandma died, hadn't left Grandad's side except to sleep. And Grandad had just nodded at the vet, said, 'It's time,' and stroked Zip's head before turning to go out to the yard and feed the sheep.

There had been no tears. Except mine.

The water ran into the bucket and steamed. I stared at it until it overflowed and the sink began to make the slightly urgent noise that meant it was beginning to block up again.

'I'll take this out.' Nat grabbed the bucket handle, tipped a quantity back down the sink, which made regurgitation noises again. 'You put the kettle on.'

The house was silent with expectation. There wasn't even the slightest thump from elsewhere to tell me where Cass and Thor had gone. I couldn't hear anything from the paddock and the edge of the barn blocked my view. I stood by the window, staring out over the yard where the sun shone innocently and the birds sang.

Nat didn't come back. I put the kettle on. Jen might have needed him to hold something for her or he might have wanted to watch an ovine caesarean section, I didn't know. Maybe he was just giving me space. When I saw him and Jen coming towards the house, I could tell from the set of his shoulders and her brisk manner what the news was going to be. I had time to prepare myself.

'Sorry, Dora.' Jen was still wiping her hands on a roll of blue paper. 'Couldn't save the ewe, I'm afraid. But you've got two healthy lambs there that are going to need hand-rearing.'

The kitchen was instantly overlaid with memories of Willow as a lamb, dashing all over the floor with her ridiculous legs splaying, butting my legs constantly in search of a bottle. The high-pitched little bleats as she hurtled down the hallway following me wherever I went. Her tiny black-and-white face popping up around corners and following me to the toilet.

'Oh,' I said. 'The kettle's boiled. I'd better get some colostrum defrosted, then.'

I left Nat to make Jen her tea and went off to the freezer in the study, where I stood and let myself have the luxury of crying. Not for long, just as long as it took a couple of sobs to emerge and the freshest of the memories to disperse. I had my head bent over the freezer lid, both hands flat on its surface, when I felt someone come up behind me.

'You're allowed to be upset,' Nat said softly. 'You don't have to pretend.'

I half turned and he put his arms around me. There was a friendly familiarity about the smell of him, and I burrowed my face into his sweater and let the tears fall as my body absorbed the impact of a world that no longer had Willow in it.

* * *

'Can I have a go?' Thor asked, hanging over my shoulder as I tried to bottle-feed both lambs simultaneously. They were lying in the dogs' spot in front of the Aga on a bed of old duvets, still looking slightly dazed. We'd rubbed them down with straw and got the first colostrum into them before Nat and I had carried them through from the barn and put them in the warmest place in the kitchen. The dogs had moved to lie in their corner – they knew the drill, but from their expressions they were disgruntled at best. There was lots of heads-on-paws and deep sighing going on.

'Here. Hold it up so that they get a constant flow of milk.' I showed him how to tip the bottle, and then carried on feeding my lamb whilst Thor sat back against the Aga and patiently persuaded the other lamb to suck.

'Do you really have to do this all the time?'

'I don't often lose a mother. Willow's mum was the last.' I'd never have to push Willow away from under my feet again. I turned my face away. 'So, it's not that bad.'

'I mean, do you have to bottle-feed them like this all day?' He stretched his legs out. The designer jeans were covered in fluff and feathers from the duvets, which usually lived in the cupboard in the hallway for such occasions, and his shirt had a yellow stain from the lambs' amniotic fluid. He looked as though he'd lost half a decade.

'Oh, yes. Until they're a bit older, they need regular feeding.'

'Can I do it? Can I, Dora? I could have them in my bedroom and feed them and everything!' Thor looked down at the happy little face suckling from the bottle, ears flopping and tail waggling furiously. The lambs were strong, a pair of ewes, which was great for the bloodline, and didn't seem to have suffered too badly from their struggle into the world. 'I'm gonna call them Flick—'

'That's a cute name for a lamb.'

'—and Knife.'

'Hmmmm. Maybe something a *wee* bit fluffier?' I suggested. 'When they're older they may get separated, and you'll be left with a sheep that's called Knife on its own and everyone will wonder why. Unless you're going to give the whole flock weaponry-inspired names.'

Why was I talking as though Thor had already inherited the farm?

'Yeah! Like – Sword and Katana and stuff.'

'Bit tactless,' Nat observed. He'd come back in from wherever he'd been and was watching our lamb-feeding with an air of amusement. 'When you consider what happens to a lot of sheep. In the end.'

Our eyes met. His were checking that his joke hadn't upset me. Mine – mine were probably still full of the embarrassment that I'd felt when I'd finally disentangled myself from his hold and left him standing in the study with my tears still on his jumper.

'Not Upper Ryedales. There's not really enough meat on them to go for commercial slaughter, and we're still building up the breeding numbers.' I averted my gaze and concentrated *really hard* on my lamb. It still had the vacuum-packed look of the newly born, but each breath and each mouthful gave it a little more substance.

'So, what do you do with the ones that aren't suitable for breeding?' He wasn't going to refer to my little breakdown, which was good.

'Oh, most of them go to places like the National Trust. They'll graze land that you can't keep much else on and stop undergrowth taking over, and they sell the wool in the shops. Some become pets, of course, to people who spin and knit their own wool.'

'Is that what you'll do with Flick and Knife?' Thor's lamb had finished its bottle and the effort had tired it out. It sat down on the duvet with its head on his leg.

'No. These girls will stay here and go into the breeding flock.' And now I'd be doomed to a lifetime of beating them off my wellingtons whenever I went out into the field, but that didn't matter. The only thing that mattered right now was the two tiny shapes spread out in the kitchen, gradually coming to a sort of life.

'It's amazing,' Thor said, stroking the head of his lamb. Nat and I met eyes again and this time we shared a little smile. Thor's world-weary rapper air had gone, replaced by a wide-eyed wonder at new life. He was a proper twelve-year-old for these few precious moments. 'My followers are gonna *love* them! God, I am gonna get so many new hits with these guys.'

And just like that the awestruck child was gone and the number-hungry wannabe Internet star was back in the room. But those moments had given me hope that there really was a normal pre-teen inside the over-indulged premature adult that he seemed to be most of the time.

'Better get the iPad. Should be filming all this.' Thor disentangled himself from the now-sleeping lamb and flew to his feet with the ease and flexibility of his youth. 'Cool.'

The kitchen door slammed and his feet thundered up the stairs. I heard the little skip as he avoided the broken floorboard and my heart ached. Thor was feeling at home here now. It had only been a matter of ten days, or was it a fortnight, I'd lost track, and he was treating the farm as a home, rather than his own personal hotel. I wondered if Cass had told him that Aunt Dora was doomed to a life of spinsterhood and lone working and the farm was practically his already. His ownership of the contents of the fridge seemed to indicate this was the case. I hadn't seen a yoghurt since they'd arrived and the biscuit tin was permanently empty. I'd had two angry calls from the local supermarket delivery team about the state of the driveway, so I gathered food was arriving at regular intervals, but had no idea where it was all going.

Thor's exit had left Nat and I staring at one another. I absolutely wasn't going to mention my earlier tears and held a nervous hope that he wouldn't either.

'Thank you for helping with the lambs.' I stood up and took the bottles to the sink to wash up. 'They've made a bit of a mess of your shirt.' He had lamb meconium in a dark smear down his front.

'It'll wash out.' He looked down at himself. 'Eventually. Do they really live in the house? The lambs?'

'Only until they're big enough and the weather is reliable enough for them to go outside. We'll let them out once they're on proper food and not likely to get the crap kicked out of them by the big sheep.'

'I think Thor is hoping they'll be pets.' There was a careful tone to his voice, as though he was trying to give me the opportunity to talk about crying over Willow.

I didn't want to. 'Well, I'd better go out and feed the others,' I said, rinsing the bottles. 'Life – life goes on. Maybe you can use this opportunity to work up some lessons for Thor on sheep breeding?' I didn't add 'because clearly this is going to be his future'. I couldn't quite see how a career as a YouTube star was going to be compatible with living in the wilds of North Yorkshire and working outdoors for twenty-eight hours a day in mostly atrocious weather. There's not much influencing to do in a field in the dark.

'Good idea.'

Nat stayed in the kitchen. When I looked back over my shoulder as I crossed the yard, I could see him, tinged a pale pink by the sunset light. It was a colour that Cass would probably have put all over a bedroom, but reminded me of Elastoplasts. I could only see his top half; he looked as though he was watching the lambs sleep, with his arms folded across his stained chest and his hair falling forwards over his cheek. I thought of Leo again, but it was too close to thoughts of Willow so I distracted myself by heaving hay onto the trailer and heading down to the far field. A flock of hungry sheep is enough to distract anyone, from almost anything.

6

The lambs grew incredibly quickly under Thor's tender care. Cass wasn't happy about them living in his bedroom but, since she didn't seem to have said no to him since he was six, the state of affairs continued. Nat now had to teach to the accompaniment of shrill, happy baaing, constant butting for bottles and eight extra legs trundling about the house and yard. Everywhere Thor went, the lambs went too. In the afternoon, when things were quieter, Nat would take Thor into the study for book work and the lambs – who were now, incontrovertibly, Flick and Knife – would lie on their duvet beds at his feet. They were going to be the only sheep in the world with a working knowledge of the dissolution of the monasteries and algebra.

The last old ewe lambed, alone and safely, and all the sheep were now out together in the far field. I could see them from the bathroom window, dotted along the ridge of the hill that dipped down towards the village like little black-and-white nails in a green board. Sometimes a couple of Elvie's horses would potter up to the dividing fence and sniff at the lambs, and there would be much joyful pretence of fear, and cavorting about in the sunshine as a result. It never failed to make me smile, watching the lambs play like children in a schoolyard, jumping and prodding and generally larking about. They had all the exuberance and energy of the very young and that, combined with the longer, warmer days, made my heart lift.

My heart was also doing disturbing amounts of aerobics whenever I saw Nat. The tingles had migrated north, had stopped bothering my extremities so much, but now were giving me a weighty feeling in my stomach instead. It was ridiculous. It was as though Thor and I were passing one another on the adolescent ladder – he was heading upwards towards thirty as fast as he could and I was regressing towards being fourteen again and giggling behind my hands whenever a boy looked at me.

I managed the worst of it by staying busy again. The older ewes were going to need shearing very soon so I spent as much time as I decently could on the phone to the local shearing unit, arranging times and locations. I phoned them so often, on spurious excuses, that I was sure the guy in charge of the team thought I fancied him. But it kept me out of Nat's way, mostly. The odd occasions we were in the same room I managed to negotiate by having Thor or Cass around. Cass was throwing herself into redesigning the inside of the farmhouse along the lines of a French chateau, with elements of beach hut thrown in for good measure. She painted the front room and hired a sander. I didn't know what else she was doing in there, but she emerged every now and then on a tide of paint splatters and ferocity, like a mixture of Kirstie Allsopp and Genghis Khan, to terrorise us all into agreeing that teal was the new black.

So I suppose it was inevitable, with the new awkwardness, that I'd next meet Nat alone, in the dark of the kitchen again. It was late night, rather than early morning this time. I'd been out with the dogs for a last walk round before bed, tidying up the yard and checking that all the beasts were up on their legs and not upside down, and that none of them had fallen in the beck.

The single lamp was on in the corner of the kitchen when I went in, illuminating movement. I hesitated for a moment, but the dogs barged on ahead of me, losing me the element of surprise or the chance to creep out around the yard again and sit in the barn until everything had gone quiet, so I went in.

Nat was fiddling about in a cupboard while the kettle piped its cheerful boiling into the silence. 'Hello,' he said without looking up. 'Where are the biscuits?'

'I have no idea. I can only assume that Thor is building a model of the Taj Mahal out of Hobnobs,' I said. 'There were some fruit shortcakes in a packet in the pantry, if that's any use, but they're barely biscuits by anyone's description.'

'They'll do. I'm desperate.'

He didn't look desperate. He looked chilled and relaxed in loose sweatpants and the enormous hoodie that he wore in the evenings. His feet were bare, which was brave on the flags of the kitchen floor, and he looked as though he'd just got out of bed.

The tingles were back.

'Why are you desperate?' I put a teabag in another mug. He was clearly halfway through making his own, and tea and biscuits sounded reassuring and the sort of British thing to do when you meet up with the guy that you... umm... well, when you encounter a man in the middle of the night. In your kitchen. In loose sweatpants and bare feet.

'I let Thor cook dinner tonight.' His voice came from deep in the pantry. 'Ah. Here they are. Yes. Thor cooked. And if you ever tell him this I will have to kill you, but he produced the most inedible series of substances outside of a meth lab. I'm not *quite* sure what they were, but he had the main food groups covered: crunchy, rock hard, sloppy and burned.'

I sat down at the table with my mug. 'Did you eat it?'

'Oh, yes. Well, some of it. The rest, I'm afraid, is outside in the garden. Well, I wasn't going to hurt his feelings, was I? I waited until he'd gone to fetch the lambs and tipped it out of the window.'

'Did Cass eat it?'

'I'm not sure your sister *does* eat. I think she lives off fury and human blood. Sorry, no. She emerged from her *Changing Rooms* lair, made herself a sandwich, and went back in.' He tore open the packet and endeared himself to me by stuffing three biscuits into his mouth at once. 'I think I may take over cooking duties tomorrow.'

'I'm sure it was very educational.' I tried not to laugh. I didn't want him to think I found him amusing – hell, I didn't want him to think I thought of him at *all*. I just had to stay calm until the shearing team arrived to distract us all. Their behaviour and language would be the perfect anti-dote to any romantic notions I might be brewing; four sweaty men in filthy vests making sexist jokes and leering was usually enough to put me off men again for another year.

'It was certainly educational for me. I've been looking up all the major causes of food poisoning.' He washed the biscuits down with a gulp of tea. 'I think we might need to go back to chicken rissoles and build up more slowly.'

I reached over to take a biscuit from the packet and our hands touched. There was a romcom moment where we both hesitated, fingers in contact, and then he handed the packet over with a sort-of smile.

'How are things?' we both said simultaneously, still in keeping with that romcom.

The smile became a definite grin. 'Sorry. How are the sheep?'

'Still doing their little sheepy things. All continues normal in the World of Wool.' I dunked a biscuit. Hell, he either liked me or he didn't; if he was going to be put off by me dunking, then he wasn't a man I wanted to have anything to do with. And, besides, when it came to fruit shortcakes, dunking was all they were really any good for. 'How's Thor getting on?'

Nat leaned back and raised his eyebrows at me. 'He's really getting into history. Thor is a very bright young man,' he said. 'I have no doubt that he will achieve everything he sets out to do.'

'Including being an Internet sensation?'

'Well, maybe not that.'

There was a pause. One of the dogs drank noisily from their bowl. Nat and I sipped tea across the table from one another.

'And how are you?' His voice was very soft.

'Me? I'm fine, of course. No problems.' But my heart wasn't fine, was it? It was on the edge of some kind of event, lurching up and down in my chest in defiance of all biological reasonability.

'Are you sure? It's a tough life out here. I've seen it. Working all hours for not much reward. Is this the life you always thought you'd have, Dora? Or did you want something else for yourself?'

Oh, no, this was getting too serious. I didn't like this. But I did like *him*, and in that get-up he was hotter than hell.

'Are you always this intrusive in the lives of your students' families?' The words were soft but pointed.

'Yeah.' He went back to sipping his tea. 'We're in a bit of a reverse Jane Eyre situation here, aren't we?'

It had been *years* since I'd read Jane Eyre. Was that the one with the woman going mad skipping about on the moors and falling in love with the abusive idiot?

'Er,' I said and then something caught my eye out of the window over his shoulder. 'What the hell is that?'

'Sorry, it's these trousers.' And then he looked too and we both stood up. 'What is it?'

I was already grabbing my coat again, and pulling the door open. The dogs, sensing the urgency, were up and out before me. 'I think it's a lorry,' I said. 'Parking at the end of the track.'

Nat stepped into a pair of wellingtons at the door. 'Sheep rustlers, do you think?'

I was heading across the yard. 'Well, I don't think it's a Tesco delivery.' And then I was belting off down the drive, the collies running ahead of me, Nat behind with the wellingtons making a 'clop clop' noise against his legs as he ran too, and we legged it over the potholed surface out towards the main road.

'Your sheep... aren't... there?' Nat panted.

'No, but the next farm over has some out on the moor just up there.'

I could hear barking and see the light from a couple of torches bobbing about. I groped into my pocket for my phone. Took a couple of pictures as I ran and tried to dial Henry's number but it was hard to go through even quite a short contact list whilst charging along in a waxed jacket and work boots so I had to stop.

Nat leaned forward with his hands on his knees and puffed. 'We... shouldn't... confront them,' he gasped. 'Could be... dangerous.'

'I'm not going to confront them.' I found Henry's number. 'I'm going to stop them stealing my neighbour's sheep.'

Henry answered, bleary and obviously off duty, but was awake and alert when I told him what was happening and where I was.

'Police are coming,' I said. 'At least, Henry is. He may not have the Land Rover. I expect James is posing with it in Pickering. Come on.'

We moved on, more cautiously now. There was a lot of banging and a bit of muffled shouting. There were three men, by the sound of it, and a couple of dogs. They'd dropped the ramp of the lorry and were trying to use the dogs to get as many sheep inside as they could.

'Dax!'

He came bounding up to me, tongue lolling and the mad gleam of the collie about to get to work in his eye.

'Go back around!' I whispered the command that would send him out around the edge of the flock, bringing them together. His ears went down and he shot out into the night, running to the left to circle the entire collection of men, sheep and other dogs.

I heard the shout. 'There's another fucking dog here!'

'Get 'em in! Get on!'

'Someone's seen us!'

A confusion of voices, the stamping of hooves on a wooden ramp, the snarl and snap of a dog confronting another dog and then the revving of the lorry engine, slamming of doors and a lorry the size of a large minibus squealed past us, lights off and the ramp only half secured at one side.

Dax had rounded up the remaining sheep, which milled about looking confused, and he and Bet held them there. I sweated inside my coat.

'What if they'd been armed?' Nat sounded shaken.

'It's dark. They can't see us, we're too far away, they would have just fired to scare us off.'

'That doesn't make me feel any better. We still could have been killed. It being an accident wouldn't make us any less dead, Dora.'

The adrenaline of the moment was trickling away now,

leaving me cold and shaken, and the sweat of running nearly half a mile in a heavy jacket was pricking at my skin. 'Well, they got some of the sheep but not this lot.' I called the dogs back. 'Hopefully not too many were lost.' Dax pressed against my leg and I fussed his ears.

'What if they come back?'

'Unlikely now they know they've been seen. Come on, we'll go back. Henry will be along in a minute and we might as well tell him what happened indoors where there's food and warmth.'

We began the walk back down the driveway. I hadn't walked along here in a while and I noticed how big the potholes were getting. Maybe all those people shouting at me about fixing the track had a point?

'That was pretty quick thinking on your part.' Nat had got his breath back now and was walking alongside me, Bet close to his leg. 'You probably saved a few dozen sheep there.'

I shrugged, feeling the damp clamminess of my coat over my shoulders. 'We tend to look out for one another's stock all the way out here. You save someone's sheep one night, another night they could be saving yours. It's the way it works.' I got my phone out again. 'I took some pictures, I was trying to get the number plate of the lorry, but I think it was too dark.'

I saw Nat give my phone a quick look. Was he remembering my passcode? But it was four numbers. It could have been my bank PIN or four random digits. No reason for him to associate me with Leo just because they were his birthdate. After all, I'd hardly known him, had I?

Henry passed us as we got to the yard and was in the kitchen before we were. The kettle was still warm.

'How many do you reckon they got?' He was writing things down, and he was keeping proceedings very formal, which felt rather out of character for Henry – usually it was James who did all the dour, broody stuff.

'They weren't there for long, so maybe they got away with a half a dozen? You'll have to get him—' I jerked my head to indicate my neighbour further up on the moor '—to check. The pictures are no good, but there were three men and two dogs, maybe more, but I only heard two.'

We told him everything we could remember. Nat was better on the type of lorry, the colour and size, and I knew which way they'd headed out. Henry ate the remaining fruit shortcakes, drank two mugs of coffee and headed off to do something official with the information. I didn't comment on the fact that he had his pyjamas on under his police jacket, and odd shoes. I was just grateful that he'd got here so fast.

When he'd left, I was suddenly exhausted. Shattered and, Nat's hotness notwithstanding, not keen to restart the conversation we'd been having before the arrival of the lorry. I was itchy with cold sweat and awash with tea and I wanted to go to bed and not lie there analysing what was going on with me and Nat. I also wanted to read a quick precis of Jane Eyre, to make sure I was thinking of the right book.

But Nat seemed reluctant to end the evening. He wandered around the kitchen like a dog that's had its blanket washed, leaning against things and then getting up again, pacing, pacing. I finished the washing up, tidied the table and checked the Aga.

'You were brave out there,' Nat said at last. 'I really thought you were going to go head to head with those guys stealing the sheep.'

'I'm not stupid.' I emptied the bowl into the sink. 'And I don't have a death wish. But I *do* object to people taking what isn't theirs because they think it's there for the taking, when it's someone's livelihood.'

'It's...' He started to speak and then, as though correcting himself, stopped, swallowed and started again. 'Do you think it's changed you? Living out here, where everything is so precarious and based on the weather and the land?'

'Changed me from what? You make it sound like I wasn't a human before.' There was a note in his voice that made me – feel something. I wasn't sure what. Scared?

'I'm just thinking about Cass and Thor.' Nat spoke quickly. Almost as if he'd sensed me recoiling and wanted to hurry to reassure me. 'Do you think it's going to change *them*? Having all of nature spread out in front of them and the big sky and everything depending on the sheep to pay the bills and... all that...' He trailed off.

I'd turned the main lights on when Henry had come into the kitchen. But even with the big fluorescent tube overhead humming and flickering, there were still shadows in corners. Shadows that would never be properly lit, even when the sun came in. The whole room felt like a reflection of my soul if I dared to think about it.

'It's late, Nat. I'm going to bed,' I said on a sigh. 'Can we keep the metaphysicals for the morning, please, when this has all receded into being a bad memory?' I left him standing there, barefoot again and loose-clothed with his hair all awry after our mad dash, and his eyes thoughtful, and I went to fall into a sleep of half-remembered and slightly erotic dreams.

* * *

'Did you really scare off the sheep stealers?' Thor's eyes were wide over a breakfast that seemed to consist of a bowl of milk flavoured with two Rice Krispies and four spoons of sugar. 'Nat said you sent Dax in to bite them!' He showed his teeth as though

I were unfamiliar with the verb and made snarling noises that made both dogs glance up from their bed.

'It wasn't as dramatic as that.' I turned away from the toaster. 'Nat and I frightened them off, that's all.'

'And then the fuzz came and interviewed you! Did you have to go to the police station and, like, wear handcuffs and get cautioned and all that stuff?'

'Have you been letting him watch repeats of *Heartbeat* or something?' I asked Cass, who was nibbling the edges of a crispbread as though the centre were arsenic and only the rim were edible.

'Nah, I was watching reruns of *Luther* the other night.' Thor scraped his bowl noisily and suddenly found himself the centre of collie attention. With a half-ashamed, half-defiant look at me and his mother, he put the bowl on the floor and the dogs almost cracked heads in their eager desire to lick the last remnants of sugary milk.

'I've told you, that is disgusting.' Cass put her half-eaten crispbread down on her plate with a sated sigh. 'Humans have to eat out of that bowl later.'

'Yeah, but it's gonna be washed first,' he said with the tone of one who hopes this is the case but has never seen it actually happen. 'So it doesn't matter.'

'Well, at least put it in some water or something.' Cass threw me a sidelong glance. I think she suspected that I picked the bowls up and reused them straight away.

'Can't. Meeting Nat outside in ten.' Thor stood up, Flick and Knife tracking his every move. 'And I gotta feed the girls first.'

'Their bottles are on top of the Aga.'

'Thanks, Dora. Come on, girls!' and he picked up both bottles and headed away, followed by two happily bleating lambs, who'd filled out nicely and now looked far too rounded and woolly legged to really still be in the house. Thor was too attached to hear of them moving into the field yet, and I'd agreed that the weather was still unreliable and they'd be better staying with him until they were bigger.

I hadn't told Cass that they'd normally have been out in the day now. I think she thought that they had to live indoors until they had lambs of their own, and neither I nor Thor felt like disabusing her of that notion. Besides, it was cute to see Thor actually behaving like a child: laughing at the ridiculousness of the two spotted-faced and gangly-legged lambs as they played and skipped about. It was far better than hearing him talk like a gangster.

My phone buzzed a text. I looked at it, puzzled, and then shook my head. 'The feed bill has bounced this month,' I said to myself. 'That's odd.'

'Hmmm?' Cass had a magazine spread out on the table. 'What do you think of this as a colour scheme, Dor? I mean, those WAGs have very little taste, but they do buy in the best designers, so maybe this is on trend for next year?' She held the page open, but I was checking the farm's account. 'All right, don't bother to look, just don't complain when I do the next room in stripes and leopard print and tell me I never warned you.' She put the magazine back down again. 'I rather like it. It's a bit busy, but anything to distract the eye from the fact that the walls haven't been actually upright since eighteen hundred.'

'Cass...' I said slowly. 'Have you been taking money from the farm account for all this decorating?'

She looked up. 'Well, of course. I'm not doing this out of the goodness of my heart, Dora. And you really should think about all the sites that you leave your card details logged in, you know. It's ridiculous. I'm amazed you haven't had your account stripped bare by now.'

'I have,' I said, teeth gritted. 'By you. Cass, I can't afford it!'

She looked down again, flipping the pages with an immaculate nail. 'Don't be silly,' she said. 'Of course you can. You don't pay rent, you get – grants and things. And what do you spend it all on, mmm? I mean, look at you, you haven't bought new clothes in a decade by the look of those jeans.'

'I spend it,' I said, with my voice so tight it almost cracked, 'on bills. Electricity. Council tax, tractor fuel, hay, feed, fertiliser. Keeping my car on the road. Vets' bills. All the things you don't have to worry about because you live with Mum and Dad and haven't ever had to think about. And if I make *any money at all* after those are paid, then you get half of it.'

'I am aware.' Flick flick went the pages.

I snatched the magazine from her hand and thrust my phone under her nose. 'Look at it, Cass! Look at the farm bank balance! You're forever prancing about with paint and swatches and colour-matching fabrics – but that's my feed bill for the month you've spent!'

Cass glanced at the phone and gave an exaggerated sigh. 'Oh, all right! If you're going to be petty about it, I'll transfer the money over to you. Will that be satisfactory?'

'You mean you've got the money?'

Cass looked smug. 'I,' she announced, 'have *savings*, Dora. Investments. I've got an ISA. But be aware that you are taking money away from me that would normally have been put into Thor's account to help him save to buy his own place one day.'

I stared at her. She was living here rent-free, spending the farm's money as if it were tokens in an online game, and she had *savings*? I hadn't got a penny put away anywhere, unless you counted the jar of fifty-pence pieces on my dressing table.

'Please transfer me the money before the bank charges me, Cass.' I tried to keep my voice steady. It wasn't her fault. She didn't live out here on the edge. Someone who's never lived without money can't understand what it's like to have to check, check and triple check before you spend, and she'd been bankrolled by our parents all her life.

I had the tiny, treacherous moment of wondering if they would have done all that for *me*. If I'd come home and announced I was pregnant, would I have been cosseted through the rest of my adult life? Or would I have been thrown to the wolves? Would I even have *wanted* to be cosseted?

Then I looked at the peeling paint in the kitchen, the serpentine effect of the unlevel work surfaces and the cupboard door hanging from its hinges, and thought that a certain amount of cosset might be nice.

Cass sighed again, heavily, like a fourteen-year-old who's been told to take off her make-up. 'All *right*,' she said. 'But it's not fair.' She picked up the magazine from where I'd flung it onto the table, ostentatiously scraped off a blob of butter and stalked from the room, closing the door with a nascent slam behind her.

She was really keeping her inner teenager alive and well. But I did have to admit that, money or not, she'd done a fabulous job of the front room. It was now all grey stripes and cool colours; there was even a carpet down in there. I'd not really had much chance to look, but the absence of footsteps against boards when she or anyone else went in told me that the floor was now covered in something classier than old newspapers and empty feed sacks. I would not have admitted it to her, but it was a great improvement.

I stepped into my boots and the dogs dashed over. Behind me the back door opened, and there was Nat. He seemed surprised to see me, which was a bit rich since this was my kitchen.

'Hello,' he said. 'I'm looking for Thor. He's supposed to be out here learning to calculate the height of a tree.'

'Any tree in particular?' I looked over his shoulder, assessing the weather. It had been unseasonably warm, but there were some clouds building on the horizon that usually boded some kind of weather event and I'd missed the long range forecast this week. I wanted to know if I'd need my coat.

'There's a formula.' Nat looked behind him as though he thought I'd seen something.

'Don't you point your phone at it? And that tells you how tall the tree is?'

'Well, yes, but don't tell Thor that. He's already told me he doesn't need to learn most things because he can just look it up on Google. Honestly, textbooks would be the thickness of pamphlets if the answer to every question was "Just look it up on Google". Are you off to do something noteworthy or just anything to get away from us?'

He looked much more 'tutorly' today. No sweatpants, no baggy hoodie. He was wearing a proper shirt under a thick jumper and a pair of chinos that had probably started the day clean, but clean clothes in a farmyard lasted about ten minutes. The mud had dried to dust that stuck to everything and mysterious stains appeared out of nowhere. They did on my clothes anyway, and the chinos had a patch below one knee that looked as though he'd leaned too close to an exploratory lamb.

'I'm going to worm some of the lambs. Everything over six weeks old, in fact.' I decided on the coat. I'd rather be too hot, and it gave me more pockets. 'So, I'm bringing them all up to the small field. Takes too long running round after them down at the big field, and I want to check all the ewes over properly.'

The doorway was too narrow for me to pass him, so I waited for him to step back and let me out. The dogs shot past his legs and they ran out to circle in the sun. Nat didn't move; instead he looked as though he was lost in thought for a moment.

'Sorry, can I come through?' I didn't want to shoulder-charge him.

'Oh! Yes, I'm – I was just thinking. Sorry. Would you like a hand? Moving sheep sounds like hard work.'

I stared at him. 'I have done it by myself before, you know. I've been here seven years.'

'I understand that, but wouldn't you like some extra people to help?'

It was a simple question. One that had a long, long answer that contained a lot of 'I would desperately like help but I can't afford to employ anyone and there's nobody close enough to pop over to help with little jobs like this and Chris always said he'd come and be an extra pair of boots on the ground but when it came to it he was always somewhere else when I needed him and I've never dared to rely on any help because I have to be *able* to do it all myself to prove to Grandad that I can handle the farm and he was right to leave it to me.'

'Aren't you supposed to be estimating the height of a tree?' was what I did say.

Nat grinned. 'He can look it up on Google,' he said. 'You can't learn how to move sheep from Google.'

Thor came bursting out of the house, trendy jacket half done up, trainers still trailing laces. The lambs scooted along behind him.

'Go and shut the girls in and put some boots on,' Nat called across to him. 'We're moving sheep today.'

Thor's expression changed from a semi-resigned-but-enjoy-ing-being-outside to a big-eyed open-mouthed one. 'Really? *Wicked!*' And he turned around, the lambs wheeling behind him, and hurtled back into the house. Two seconds later he was back out. 'They can stay in the kitchen, can't they, Dora?'

'Yes. But boots.'

'Aw.' Then another thought. 'Can I vlog this? It'll be *amazing*. 'Specially if Nat falls in the shit – I mean, in the poo,' he corrected himself, and I didn't know if this was Nat or Cass's doing. Nat's probably. Cass didn't even seem to listen to Thor particularly, other than to things that required an 'oh, *darling*' response. It struck me that she wasn't a particularly applied mother, which was strange. When she'd been pregnant she'd been all about the parenting. Maybe it got harder as they got older? Or maybe she'd lost interest, as she had done with so many of her hobbies over the years. But then, a child is for life, not just for showing off to your friends.

'All right, but it will be entirely your own fault if you drop the iPad and forty sheep run over it.'

'That would be a hundred and sixty hooves,' Thor said smugly. 'And I did that in my head.'

Nat and I exchanged a glance. We were both trying not to laugh. 'This tutoring thing is really working out for you, isn't it?' I said to him.

'Looks like it.'

Thor looked at both of us. 'Are you laughing at me?' he asked warily.

'No, we're not. We're laughing at – oh, it would take a long time to explain.' Nat pushed his hands into the pockets of the chinos. It made them go very tight across his groin, not that I was looking or anything, but my eyes had to be pointing *somewhere* and that was where they'd come to rest at this particular moment.

Had he seen me looking? I flicked my eyes away quickly to investigate a blameless patch of rutted dirt near his feet just in case. Out of the corner of my eye I saw him raise his eyebrows but that might have been something to do with Thor, who was wearing a pair of the farm wellingtons four sizes too large and on the wrong feet.

'Okay, Brains,' Nat said. 'Sort your boots out and then we are in the capable hands of your Aunt Dora for today. She will be guiding the activities, so be prepared to be educated.'

I talked myself down. I didn't get out very much, that was all. He was a man and I was noticing him. That was normal. The tingles I felt when I looked at him – well, they were normal too. But they needed to stop.

'Right. We're going to drive the sheep up the lane, pop them in this paddock, sort out the lambs that are old enough to worm. I'm going to dose them and mark them so we don't do the same ones twice. We'll check their mothers too while we're at it. Then we can leave them up here overnight, to make sure none of the lambs have any horrible reactions to the wormer, and take them back down to the field tomorrow. All right?'

We brought the flock up and set to work. Thor did enjoy a bit of lamb-wrangling but mostly he was busy vlogging or recording or whatever it was he was doing, sitting up on the fence with his iPad and shouting instructions to us, which was only a little bit annoying.

The sun heated up. The air smelled of warm wool and hot sheep, of pounded grass and a bit of bracken and peat from the moorland beyond, and the birds sang competitively from the hedges. Nat and I got red-faced and sweaty, fingers greasy with the lanolin from fleeces as we grabbed lambs and pulled ewes; some of the marker spray went adrift now and again and Nat ended up with stripes of it up his trousers. Thor had a moment of finding it funny to try to spray it at us until I had firm words, whereupon he knuckled down and marked lambs while I held them.

I discarded my jacket, then my jumper. It didn't really matter that I was wearing a T-shirt so baggy that all three of us could have hidden out in it; there is a reason that fashion magazines don't tend to do their shoots on sheep farms. Nat kept his sweater on though. Probably because he didn't want to risk me ogling his chest in the same way as I might possibly have ogled his groin a little bit. Nobody needs a sex-starved sheep farmer throwing themselves at you when you're up to your knees in shit and you've just had a discussion about castration with an over-interested twelve-year-old.

At last all the lambs of the right age group had been dosed. The ewes with lambs had had their udders checked for mastitis or damage ('Ew, gross!' – Thor) and the gimmers, which were the younger ewes who had been too young for putting in lamb this year, had had their feet looked at. We were all panting and laughing, probably at different things, and Thor had filmed enough to give his nearly a thousand followers a glimpse at a life they would probably only ever see from the grill and mint sauce end of things.

'That was *brill*, Dora.' Thor leaned on the fence. 'Can we do it again tomorrow?'

I had to restrain myself from ruffling his hair. Besides which, he was nearly as tall as I was, and it would bring my armpit closer to his face than anyone needed. 'Don't be daft. We've only got a few lambs left to do and they aren't old enough yet. It'll be another fortnight before we need to go through this again. But the shearers will be coming soon, you can give them a hand if you like.' Although Thor would probably pick up some turns of phrase that he had better *never* use in front of his mother, I didn't add.

'Aww, *cool!*' Thor broke away and dashed off to the house, presumably to upload content or whatever it was he did with his vlog. It must be like eternally watching someone's holiday videos, I thought, and wondered about the followers. Maybe they were all confined to their homes by ankle tags or something? It was very hard to see what could possibly be so entertaining about watching sheep.

'That was excellent, thank you.' Nat pushed a filthy hand through sweaty hair.

'I don't know how educational it was though.' I carried on leaning on the fence. He was standing right next to me, his shoulder brushing mine, but I wasn't giving the tingles house-room right now. I was too shattered and grubby.

'Oh, I don't know. He's got a whole new vocabulary. Gimmers and hoggs and you buggering bastards will probably feature in his essays from now on.'

'Ah. Yes, sorry about that. I do tend to get a bit annoyed with the sheep sometimes.' I wiped my forehead with my arm, which just transferred sweat and muck about a bit.

'To be fair, they were behaving like buggering bastards.' Nat propped himself up on his elbows. 'Do they always have to run away from you? It's like watching a flock of grounded and woolly starlings all swooping about.'

'Yes. It's in their contract. Run away at all times. In quite big letters.' I yawned. 'I need a bath and a big cup of tea.'

Nat gave me a sideways look. 'What about wine?'

'What about it?'

'Well, I was wondering if you'd like to go down and have a drink? In the pub which I understand the village boasts, along-side a very small shop that's only open if there's a Q in the month, and a telephone box?'

'Oh.' I was so taken aback that I practically reared up in his face.

'I mean, you don't have to, obviously, it's only a thought. You never seem to get away from this place and I'm not sure I can take another evening of sitting alone in my room reading improving literature. I'm going to come away from here so improved I'll be six foot seven and look like Jason Momoa. It's read or watch *Strictly*, and I'm not a big fan of that either.'

'Oh,' I said again. 'No. I mean – yes, that would be nice. A drink. But only one, because sheep with a hangover is the worst thing you can imagine. Or not. I should think getting up for early milking with a hangover might be worse. Or pigs.' I finally got my mouth under control.

'Great.' He pushed himself away from the fence. 'Shall we meet out here at seven, then? That gives us plenty of time for a shower, and I have to teach Thor how to make himself eggs on toast. I'm assuming your sister will cook for herself, or drain a passer-by of blood, whichever she does.'

'That would be – lovely,' I said weakly. Well, it would be an experience, not necessarily a lovely one, as our local pub wasn't what you might call tourist friendly. It made The Slaughtered Lamb look like Spearmint Rhino. But it was Out, and I rarely went Out. In fact, when had I last left the farm? I couldn't remember.

'Right. Here, seven o'clock.' And he walked off. I told the tingles to ignore his back view in those chinos, but they didn't listen.

* * *

'This is – interesting.' Nat looked around at the inside of the pub. 'Brutal, but interesting. It's rather like what you'd get if you asked the Kray twins to do your interiors, I'd imagine.'

The local pub was one up from spit and sawdust, but only by a couple of centimetres. The walls were still stained by nicotine from when you could smoke indoors, and hung with such choice items as a man-trap, two old shotguns, which I devoutly hoped had been put beyond use, and some kind of huge scythe-knife thing. It was probably an agricultural implement, but I wouldn't have put it past the landlord to use it on people.

'I did warn you,' I said.

'I know. But I thought all the pubs in North Yorkshire had Michelin stars and chefs and a tourist trade these days.' Nat sipped at his pint. It was cider of an unspecified type, as Brig, the barman, had sneered openly when he'd asked for lager. 'This is so unreconstructed that it's barely built at all.'

'It serves beer to people who spend most of their lives working on their own.' I had a glass of what was probably gin and tonic. Brig had had to blow dust off the bottle. 'It's a serviceable pub, not a tourist trap.'

'I worked that out from the easy-to-hose-down floor.' He sipped again. 'Are there many fights?'

'No one's got the energy. When you get up at four and don't stop until dark, you've barely got the energy to raise a glass, never mind a fist.'

There were two other people in the pub apart from us. One was a very old man sitting at the bar reading a newspaper with a terrier at his feet and the other was a young lad in milking overalls playing on the fruit machine in a very desultory way.

'It says in here,' announced the man with the newspaper to the pub at large, 'that them sheep rustlers been back about.'

'Aye. They got a dozen of George's from up the high moor last night,' Brig said, helping himself to something green and fluorescent. I suspected that he drank cocktails when no one was looking. 'You chased 'em off, eh, lass?'

This was directed at me. I was unsurprised. In a dale this small the news travelled faster than the light. 'They'd stopped at the top of my lane,' I said. 'We just went up to move them on.'

'Bastards,' said newspaper-man, with no particular heat.

The men all nodded and agreed that, yes, sheep rustlers were bastards.

'They reckon they're putting them somewhere local,' said the lad on the fruit machine. 'Collecting them up, like. Then they takes them up to Teeside to slaughter, all in one go. Police been poking around in our old barns, but Terry had a go at 'em for trespassing. He's growing weed in them barns.'

Brig snorted. 'They'll not be bothered about a bit of weed. It's them buggers taking the stock they're after. I heard they've had near three hundred head this year alone.'

Nat rolled his eyes at me but fortunately the men started talking about football shortly afterwards so we could concentrate on our drinks again.

'Three hundred head?' Nat whispered. '*Just* the heads? Isn't that a bit – weird?'

I tried not to laugh. 'It's how we count stock. It means three hundred.'

'Then why not just say three hundred? Why bring the heads into it? I've got horrible mental images now.' He took a large mouthful of cider. 'And this stuff isn't helping. Do they still put laudanum in drinks and then bop you on the head when you go outside?'

I knew he was trying to make me laugh. 'Not for a couple of years or so, no. Body snatching got unfashionable. It's all a hundred illegal things to do with a ferret now.'

'So, tell me about your past.' Nat put his glass down onto the table. 'You said you went off the rails a bit when your sister was pregnant? I'm only asking so that I can make sure Thor doesn't do anything similar. I want to know what signs to watch out for.'

I pulled a face, only partly occasioned by the gin. 'Oh, it was nothing really. Staying out all night at house parties given by people I didn't really know. Drinking too much and not paying attention to my A levels – nothing terrible. When I left school I spent eighteen months working up here with Grandad, then went to agricultural college and did a qualification in sheep management; halfway through my last year Grandad died so I came up here as soon as I finished and took over the farm.'

'Wow, you've really got "life story" down to an art form. It's like those study notes.' He drank another mouthful. 'Did you date much?'

'Well, I was at agricultural college, so there was a fair bit of choice. Even with equality we girls were still outnumbered three to one. But it was all a bit cheerfully chop and change around for me, being asked out by four different lads a week. Very good-natured and all that, but I was there to work. So, I dated a bit, but nothing serious. How about you? What about your life growing up? It must have been hard for you and your family, losing Leo like you did.'

The alcohol gave me the courage to ask. He was asking questions about my past, so I felt I was entitled to prod around in his a bit. And, I'll admit, I was curious. Curious about him, how he'd managed to turn out seemingly well-rounded and educated when his brother had hung around in squats and – well, things had not ended well for Leo.

'There's nothing much to tell. I pratted about a bit when I was young, then went to university and on to do a bit of teaching. And now, here I am.' He raised his glass to me.

'So, were you away when Leo – died?' It was still hard to say those two words in conjunction. And it was still almost impossible to imagine that lively, soul-searching boy no longer in the world. Maybe, if I didn't say the words, then I could imagine he was alive somewhere, living in a suburb with a wife and two children. But no, that wasn't Leo – he'd be backpacking round

Mongolia, living in a yurt and trailing hand-reared goats, learning a thousand languages.

'I was – away, yes.' Nat looked down into his pint. It was yellow and cloudy, with what looked like small bits floating around in it. It looked like an unhealthy urine sample. 'It was a difficult time. It made a big impression on us all.'

'And how did your mum and dad cope?'

He closed his eyes briefly as though he was trying to remember something. 'They were already divorced. There was a lot of shuttling between houses, I remember, but no real animosity. Reading between the lines, I think they had both spent too much time at work and grew apart.'

I thought of my parents. Mum hadn't worked since I was born. She'd wanted to be there for us while we were growing up, and then, just as she must have been preparing to return to the workplace, Thor had arrived and she'd started all over again. Dad worked away a lot when we were small but since he'd semi-retired he'd been around more for Thor's growing up than he had for ours. I remembered him playing football for hours in the garden, Thor as an energetic three-year-old kicking endless balls ineptly while my father pretended to try to save them from rolling between the goalposts. ''Nother one, Grandad! 'Nother one!'

It hit me, as suddenly as if one of those balls had missed the target more spectacularly than usual and caught me in the chest, that Thor might be the son that my father had always wanted.

'Are you all right?' Nat put a hand on my arm. 'Is it the gin? It does rather look as though it was brought in under the noses of the Excise Men and never opened.'

'I'm having a little moment of realisation,' I said softly.

'It still might be the gin. What are you realising?'

'Family stuff.' I didn't want to go into it. It was too raw, too new a thought to look at closely yet. 'Shall we go?'

He'd finished his pint. I drank the second-to-last mouthful of my drink, left a little bit in the glass to indicate that it could, maybe, do with a little more tonic that wasn't flat, and we put on our coats. With a nod to Brig and the elderly man, a rumple of the head of the terrier and a grin at the youth fresh from milking, we went outside.

'Meanwhile, back in the twenty-first century,' Nat said, breathing deeply. 'I feel if I turn round the pub isn't going to be there any more. There will just be ruins and the money we used to pay for the drinks sitting on a stone in the middle of a grassy knoll.'

'Nope. That pub will be here forever. It shrugged off the Black Death like it was a nasty cough.' I looked over my shoulder. 'And it will still be here after The Bomb. I've no idea how it keeps going, but it does.'

We started walking. There were no street lights, so the village was illuminated only by the lights from the incredibly clear sky. I sniffed. 'Wind's changed. It's going to get colder.'

'Can you tell by the feel of the air? Or the clarity of the cry of the owl?' Nat sounded amused.

'No, I can tell from the weather forecast that I listened to before we came out. I might keep the sheep up in the paddock for another night, then. Just in case it turns really bad.'

We turned up the road. A single row of houses stuttered along, broken by yard entrances and driveways; the light from the still-operative phone box was the only noteworthy thing for miles. At the end of the village the road branched; left would take us out of the dale, up over the hill and down towards the nearest town of Pickering. Right took us deeper into the moors and home to the farm.

'So, you had a realisation.' Nat was trudging along beside me, hands in the pockets of his coat. 'Anything you want to share?'

'Did you ever want children?' I asked. There was something about the dark and the rhythm of our walking that made thoughts like this easier to voice. 'Only, the way you treat Thor, it's sometimes more like a father than a tutor.' I turned to him suddenly, my mouth falling open. 'Oh, God, you *aren't* his father, are you? Pretending to be a tutor so you can watch him grow up and then he turns twenty-one and you pull some kind of "Hawthorn, I *am* your father!" stunt?'

Nat looked at me, resignedly. 'You've watched too much *Mrs Doubtfire*,' he said. 'Of course I'm not Thor's father. Besides, that would imply that I'd slept with your sister, and I think she might bite the heads off her men after mating.'

'Oh, yes, that's true.' I felt relieved. *Why* did I feel relieved?

'And to answer your question, to be honest, I've not really thought about it. I mean, there's plenty of time and all that. I need to meet the right woman first.'

'Don't try to make me feel sorry for you,' I said briskly. 'You look like you've had your fair share.'

'Right, so I look like a player, do I? Shouldn't I have interesting facial hair and a sports car for that? Only I feel I'm missing out if I don't. Can you even *be* a player if you spend most of your time with adolescent boys? And, no, don't answer that, I realise it did *not* come out the way I meant it to.'

Beside us the beck trickled, accompanying the road downhill. An owl called, loud in the clear air, and some rooks argued sleepily over their nests in the big ash tree. He hadn't answered my question.

'So, women?' I tried again.

'Yes, please, I'll take two.' A quick, cheeky sideways grin. 'Some. A few. Nothing really serious. Are you checking me out?'

His voice was amused, but I didn't dare look properly at his face. I was too afraid that he'd see that I was blushing a horrible sweaty scarlet.

'Of course not. Just wanting to make sure you haven't got anything that might make your knob fall off into the silage,' I said, brisk again.

Nat laughed out loud, then put a hand on my arm and pulled me to a stop. 'Pandora,' he said. 'I'm trying to chat you up. You bringing my knob into things is not helping me keep this on an even keel.'

'Not even if it's by hinting that you might have some horrible disease?' I turned to face him. The blush had died but only because all the blood had gone elsewhere. In this starlit world he suddenly looked a lot more like Leo, and I wasn't sure I was ready for all the implications of that.

'I must admit that it has put a bit of a damper on things.' He was standing very, very close. His coat, which was undone, flapped in the breeze and was trying to wrap itself around to include me in his space.

All right, it was probably hormones and it had been a *long* time since Chris and I had had any more than what he would call 'a bunk up'. The tingles ran down my spine and spread out until I could hardly stand. 'Is this what you want?' I moved in, pressed myself the length of his body, feeling the roughness of his sweater, the hardness of him, the catch and snatch of the zip of his coat as it blew around, and then, finally, the firm warmth of his mouth.

There was no doubt that it had been what he wanted. His arms came around behind me, pressing me in tighter, his lips pushed back against mine until the pressure of the kiss nearly made me stumble.

We stayed like that for a while, mouths exploring, until a car coming down the dale illuminated us in its headlights and a window wound down to a passing shout of 'get a room' and some raucous laughter, when we stepped apart amid much clearing of throats and adjusting of clothes.

'Well,' I said. 'That's awkward.'

'Is it?' His voice sounded a bit rough and slightly higher pitched than normal. 'I mean, yes, it is, a bit. But, you know, we don't have to – well, it doesn't have to go any further. We can just say that we fancy each other.'

'We could if we were sixteen,' I said. 'But we're not. And, for all I know, you do this with all the families whose children you tutor.'

By unspoken agreement we started walking again. It was either that or I was going to throw him backwards in the heather and tear his clothes off with my teeth.

'Well, I don't.'

The cold air was helping. Deep breathing, occasioned by the slope up towards the moor, helped even more. 'Okay.'

'Could we, perhaps, have a fling? Do people have flings still? Is that a thing?' He was puffing a bit too, but it was fine, I could see both his hands, so I knew it was only the gradient.

'No. I don't do "flings". Anyway, I think it's "friends with benefits" now, isn't it? And I don't do that either, despite Chris's insistence that it's the best thing since antibiotics. And that's probably not an unconnected thought.'

'You've got a real thing about sexual diseases, haven't you?' He was trying for light-hearted now, bless him.

'As has any right-thinking human.' I stopped walking again so suddenly that he'd gone a few steps before he realised I wasn't beside him. 'Look. All right, yes, I – I *like* you. But you're Thor's tutor. It's not really ever going to work out, is it? And I'm not looking for anything complicated right now.'

'And you've got a mad person in the attic.'

I was ready for it now and secretly slightly smug that I'd checked. 'Well, I'm no Edward Rochester and you most *certainly* aren't a plain little governess,' I snapped back.

There was a bit of a pause. 'Did you have to look it up?' he asked.

'Yes, but you started it.'

'Fair enough. Shall we just admit that there's an attraction and leave it at that?' He started walking again. 'But I warn you now that I'm not above a bit of flirting.'

'That's fine. I've – well, there hasn't been anyone for a while and sometimes it gets the better of me. Just now was a blip.'

'Yes, I had a bit of a blip too.'

'I could tell,' I said waspishly. 'Those trousers are too tight for that sort of thing.'

'So, we can laugh about it?'

'Of course. Laughing might be the best thing.'

We hauled up the slope and turned down into the lane to the farm. A few lights were on: the kitchen lamp, which we'd left on when we went out, and two bedroom lights gleamed out from upstairs. Cass and Thor were in their rooms. A blue flicker from Cass's showed she was watching TV, and the utter silence from the other said that Thor was probably listening through his headphones to music with lyrics that went 'gnnaarrrrrr!!!'

'I'm going to go round and check the sheep,' I said as we came into the yard. 'They'll be needing some hay.'

'Do you want a hand?'

I gave him a stern look. 'I don't want any part of your anatomy right now, thank you.'

'Ooh, that "right now" gives me hope.' He grinned, his smile wide and very appealing in the light from the window. 'No, you're right. Stupid idea. Sorry. We're too close for comfort, and, like you said, there's Thor and your terrifying sister, who ought never to know about this.' He held up his hands in an attitude of surrender. 'And the madman in the attic.'

I laughed. 'Go away. Thank you for the drink. And the kiss.'

'Did you kiss Aunt Dora, Nat?' Thor's voice came out of the darkness in the corner of the yard.

'Oh, shit,' said Nat, succinctly.

7

'Do you think Dad wanted a son?' I asked Cass a few days later when I found the chance to talk to her alone. 'Instead of daughters?'

'What on *earth* makes you think that *now*?' Cass had her hair tied up and a pair of my old overalls on. She was stroking a rag-covered roller along a wall, making a marbled effect in the pale blue paint she was currently using to decorate the bathroom.

'I just wondered. He's very attached to Thor.' I was sitting on the edge of the bath, swinging my legs. Nat and Thor had borrowed my newly fixed car to drive into town and do – something. They had told me what, but I'd been writing stuff on the farming calendar and not really listened at the time.

'So attached that they've sent us up here for months with no end in sight, in some kind of horrible agricultural purdah.' Cass stood back to admire the paint effect. 'We've been here for six weeks and they still can't tell me when the extension will be finished!' She pulled the scarf off her head and shook her hair out. 'I'm sure it contravenes the Geneva Convention.'

I didn't know whether I was glad or not about there being no hint of when she'd return to London. Nat and I had managed to steer round one another; a few flirty remarks here and there and the odd hand touch had been all that remained after our talk. But the weather had been mostly good, so he and Thor had been out and about, studying various things, and I'd been busy making sure that the grass was growing in all the fields, fertilising and topping off weeds and pulling ragwort. I still didn't know whether or not I'd miss him when they left.

'He's their grandson, and looks likely to be the only one, so of *course* Mum and Dad are going to dote on him.' Cass looked at her watch. 'I need a cup of tea.' Then she looked expectantly at me. 'Well, go on. I'm working here.'

It took all my forbearance not to point out that I'd been out in the fields since six and this was the first time I'd sat down today. But I managed to keep quiet and went down to the kitchen to put the kettle on. Flick and Knife were under the table, lying on an old rug, waiting for Thor to come back and feed them. They looked hopefully at me, but I ignored them.

When I took the tea upstairs, Cass was standing in the doorway to Thor's bedroom, looking in with an odd expression on her face. She looked almost wistful, if I could ever imagine my sister having an ounce of wist in the first place.

'It's nearly Thor's birthday, isn't it?' I asked, handing her a mug, which she received as though I were handing her her tea in a gravy boat.

'Yes, next week. He'll be *thirteen*, Dora.' There was a note of sadness in her voice. I almost remarked on it, but stopped myself when she said, 'Don't you have *any* bone china in this house?' She shook her mug at me. 'It doesn't taste the same out of these builders' mugs, you know.'

'Nothing wrong with being thirteen.' I ignored her tea jibes. 'Everyone has to grow up, Cass.'

'But he's my *baby*!' Then she collected herself. 'They grow up so fast though.'

They do if you let them watch *Luther* and rap videos, I thought. But I sipped at my tea, which didn't taste any different whatever I served it in, and said nothing.

'But his YouTube channel is doing well,' Cass said brightly, as though trying to distract herself. 'He went over the fifteen hundred followers mark last week, you know! Loads of people are messaging him wanting him to update about being here on the farm. He's so popular!' She grimaced at her mug. 'Not that you'd understand, of course. YouTube is a video-streaming thing on the computer – it's all the thing with young people now. I have some make-up tutorials up on there,' she finished smugly.

'You're not that young,' I said. 'Is that the problem? You don't want to be seen as old enough to have a thirteen-year-old son? You'll have to start lying about *his* age now, until you meet him coming up as you're coming down. When you're both thirty-two people are going to catch on, you know.'

'Don't be silly, Dora.' But the way she dropped her glance down to her tea again told me I probably wasn't far off the mark. As a mother to a cute young child she could get away with it, once he was a teenager she was either going to have to pretend she'd had him when she was seven, or stop shaving off those pesky odd years.

'But *do* you? Think Dad would have liked boys?' I'd found an unattended packet of digestives in the pantry and brought them upstairs. Thor ate biscuits as though he was afraid they were going to be rationed, and I was lucky he hadn't seen these yet.

'Mum wanted a boy,' Cass said, unexpectedly. I'd dunked my biscuit, and I was so taken aback by this information that the end went soggy and fell into my tea. 'But she had three miscarriages after me and the doctors told them to stop trying.'

'How on earth do you know that?' The idea of my sister having information that I'd never even suspected was incongruous. '*Seriously?*'

'She and Grandma used to chat. While I was here and you and Grandad were out on the farm. They'd set me up with some baking or crochet or a jigsaw or something and then it was as though they thought I went deaf because I was busy. Mum and Grandma both thought it would have been good to have a boy on the farm, because of the heavy work. They were disappointed that there was only us.'

Something inside me felt as though it had been punched. 'Grandad never said...'

'Of course, he didn't! Who's going to say to a child, "You can't have the farm because you're a girl and we're all very frustrated about that"? And I don't know how he really felt about it because I only ever listened in on Mum and Grandma. Do you know that Grandma lost five babies? Mum was the only one who got past two and a half. She had three boys and two other girls. Mum was the last so she didn't know any of them. Their pictures are all up in the attic in one of the chests; I saw them once. I went looking,' she finished, slightly proudly.

'Oh my God.'

Cass shrugged.

'You knew all that and you never thought to tell me?' The mug was so hot it was burning my knuckles but I couldn't really feel it.

'Why would I?'

I tried to think of a context in which it might have come up, but failed. 'When you were pregnant? When you had your scan and knew he was going to be a boy?'

'Oh, come on, Dora! You weren't around then to talk to! You

were off out with all your fancy friends, dancing and partying and who knows what. You hardly said a word to me once you knew I was having a baby, like I was some weird anomaly.'

I stared at her. 'Do you actually know what anomaly means?'

'Isn't it like an animal, like a unicorn or something?' She tossed her hair back and put her mug down. 'Anyway. I'm going to carry on in here. I can't do much about the bathroom suite, unless you're going to pay for a new one?'

I shook my head.

'So we'll have to put up with it. Lucky it's white, so I can work round it colour-wise. I'm going to go for a sort of nautical theme, with maybe a touch of industrial. A chrome towel rail and some metalwork basket things...' She tailed off, lost in her own world of *Perfect Homes* magazines and artfully trailing plants.

I was too stunned to try to bring her back. She'd clearly said all she felt she needed to for now and it was a lot for me to absorb. She had confirmed so many of my secret fears. Mum had wanted a boy. Grandma had lost all those children. It was as though two people I knew really well had been replaced by others; people who looked like them but had had different lives. And then I remembered Grandma, as she'd been when I'd known her, comfortable and competent, working on the farm and in the kitchen with equal zeal and, apparently, contentment. No hint that there was a whole other life that she could have been living, with a house full of raucous children rather than just Mum, who'd grown up happy and loved but always, I'd felt, slightly lonely. How had she felt, knowing that she should have been the youngest of six, three strapping older brothers out helping with the sheep and two sisters to gossip and bake and travel to school with? It was as though she'd been cheated out of a life.

I went back downstairs, my tea cooling rapidly and slopping unnoticed over the rim of my mug. The kitchen looked the same.

It was the kitchen Grandma had presided over through my childhood: tea and scones on the table, home-baked bread in the Aga, often along with a couple of orphan lambs in the warming oven, if they were born during bad weather and needed keeping snug. She'd been plump in home-knitted jumpers and pleated skirts from M&S, all varicose veins and lost glasses and observations on the weather and how fast we were growing. She'd died, suddenly, of a heart attack when I was fourteen and Grandad had run the place alone for nine years. And how had *he* really felt, under his Yorkshire-farmer exterior of the flat cap and tweed, dogs in constant attendance and a pipe clamped between his teeth? Lost sons, lost opportunities – and only girls to inherit.

So much loss. So much hidden. Well, not hidden, not really; Mum and Grandma had talked about it between themselves, half kidding themselves that Cass wouldn't be listening or wouldn't understand or wouldn't care.

But nobody had thought to mention any of it to me.

I slumped down at the table over my tea. Dax came over and put his head in my lap and Bet sidled over to eyeball the lambs, who were sniffing my feet and sucking the leg of my jeans in an experimental way. A swift and wintery shower scattered past the window on a rising northerly breeze, but the forecast wasn't for covering level snow, so the sheep would be fine.

Sheep. After all that I'd found out, I was still thinking of the sheep. It was new information about my family and information that only built further on that feeling that I buried so deeply that it only jutted occasionally through to the surface. I gritted my teeth and forced it down again. The farm was important. There was nothing I could do, right now, with the knowledge that Cass had handed me, but I could care for the farm.

So I washed the dishes that had been sitting by the sink waiting for someone to give in. Then I wiped the table and swept the floor – except for the bit the lambs were lying on – with the dogs following me around and doing the canine equivalent of 'are you sure you're feeling all right?' with worried tail wags every time I caught their eye. I shook out the rag rug, tidied up the paperwork, put the curtains and tea towels in the washing machine and scraped something unidentified off the Aga, where it had burned on in a black excrescence that made it look as though hell were trying to come through the hotplate.

The activity helped. Not only did it occupy my mind, it grounded me. It gave me the renewed feeling that this was *my* kitchen. All right, I might not be in possession of a penis, but the farm was mine nonetheless. It might not have been Mum's or Grandma's, or even, for all I knew, Grandad's, first choice to leave it to me instead of any unborn brothers, but in their absence – well, here I was. And doing a bloody good job, if I said so myself. This year's clutch of lambs was doing well, growing in the sunshine. The shearers were booked and the wool would be on sale soon. I'd got a few possible buyers for two of the gimmers that would be ready to lamb next year and English Heritage were interested in taking the ram lambs that had been castrated to go and graze some of their coastal sites in conjunction with Exmoor ponies, to keep undergrowth down. Life was, actually, pretty good. This morning I'd been gazing out over my acres and the only sense of dissatisfaction had been down to the fact that Cass had been moaning about how long it took Internet deliveries to arrive.

Now – now I felt inadequate again.

'Wow, it's clean in here!'

In my self-absorbed state I hadn't heard the car come into the yard, so Thor tearing into the kitchen and stopping, wide-eyed, in the doorway, was a bit of a jolt.

'Don't say it like that. It's always fairly clean.' I'd even waxed the pine table. I must have been desperate.

'Well, yeah, like, not *botulism* bad, but now it's all—' he waved an arm as the lambs hit him somewhere around thigh level '—like, decent. Gotta feed the girls.' He snatched up the bottles that I'd pre-made and tore off further into the house, with Flick and Knife following giving happy little bleats. They were eating solid food now quite happily and their time for heading out into the field and being proper sheep was coming rapidly. But for now they were the only things that made Thor behave like a young boy, so I was keeping them close to home.

'Gosh, it looks—'

'Don't you start.' I rounded on Nat, who was struggling into the kitchen with bags of shopping. 'Thor's already told me that the place is normally one step away from giving hovels a bad name. I had some spare time, that's all, okay?'

'I was going to say, nice and sunny in here, but now you come to mention it—' Nat put the bags down on the table, widening his eyes at its new, shiny appearance '—it does look a bit rejuvenated. Where are the curtains, rag bin?'

'They are in the washing machine,' I said, with dignity, then looked more closely. 'Where the soap has proved too much for them and they have disintegrated into sludge, apparently. I don't know what's the matter – surely most people don't wash their curtains more than once every twenty years, do they?'

He didn't reply, probably wisely. Instead, he began unpacking shopping bags onto the table, pulling out Scotch eggs, cold meats, bottles of wine and more biscuits. 'While we were down in town, being all cultured, I bought some food.'

I clutched a clean tea towel defensively. 'That's not food. That's picky stuff. The sort of thing that looks tasty on a shelf. The sort of thing they have in fridges in TV programmes.'

He ignored me. 'I thought a picnic might be nice.'

'*Really?* Have you ever had a picnic in real life? Ants and rain and inquisitive cows and really hard rocks under your bum and all that? Plus it's only April.'

He opened the fridge and jammed loads of the tiny packs inside. 'You. Me. Tomorrow. Picnic. Yes or no?'

'Um.' I weighed up the list of things I ought to be doing, realised that if any of them had been *that* important or enthralling I would have been doing them right now, rather than cleaning the kitchen, and put them against sitting in the brief sun with Nat, eating what looked like delicious little morsels of things. Plus, wine. 'Yes.'

'Good.' Nat picked up another bag. 'Now I have to go and try to beat some local history into Thor – where is he?'

'Feeding the lambs. Hopefully in the study or the back room. If he's taken the incontinent twosome into the front room he will currently be a small pile of bones outside the back door, courtesy of his mother.'

Nat gave me a big grin and went out after his charge. I double-folded the tea towel and hung it carefully over the Aga rail. Then I went outside to walk around my flock, slowly.

* * *

I had to admit that my idea of picnics had been formed in my youth, when our mother had taken Cass and I out to various local sites of interest in the car. Bottles of warm squash, sandwiches with unidentifiable pink stuff in and biscuits from the custard-cream end of the spectrum had featured heavily. There had also usually been arguments and a lot of exasperation from our mother, who had seemed to think that two prepubescent girls would be enthralled by old houses or ruined abbeys and would spend their time filling in educational worksheets or nodding wisely along with tour guides. Instead, we'd mainly giggled at boys, tried to force inedible food down one another's collars, rolled on the grass or squabbled about who got to sit on the less-sicky side of the back seat of the car.

Nat had clearly had a classier upbringing. We sat at the end of the big field, where the beck left my land to flow down into the village, giving rise to picturesque footbridges and long sandy stretches of riverbank. We hadn't wanted to go too far afield, so walking to the edge of my land had seemed a good compromise. It was Sunday, and even Cass couldn't insist on Thor being actively taught seven days a week, so Nat had the day off and Thor and Cass were productively smearing decorative finish around my upstairs bathroom, in a mother and son bonding exercise.

'I had a word with Thor about his vlog.' Nat leaned lazily back against a sapling that grew out of the narrow bank of the beck. 'Just to make sure he wasn't giving away any information. He's pretty okay with Internet security, but he's picking up more local followers and I didn't want him blurting anything that might give those sheep stealers inside info on your flock.'

It hadn't even occurred to me that Thor's now over a thousand followers might have evil intent.

'Oh,' I said, feeling a bit dim. 'Right.'

One of the big cobs that Elvie was currently providing grazing for wandered over and stared at us.

'Are you sure we're all right to be here?' Nat looked at it anxiously. 'They won't worry us to death or anything?'

'It's my field.' I picked up another tiny little thing. It looked like deep-fried pastry of some kind, with a filling of mushrooms and garlic. 'I rent it to Elvie, but I'm still allowed in it. I have to check the fences and things.'

'Oh. Good.' Nat relaxed as the skewbald wandered back off. He'd even thought to bring cushions to sit on, and I was currently reclining like a Roman emperor on a bed of downy softness, eating one-handed while propped on an elbow. The sun was a little too piecemeal for warmth but it gave an illusion of heat and the buds of the trees were bursting into soft green around us. Blackthorn blossom gave the hedges a decorative dusting of colour, enhanced by the jigsaw of birds fluttering around in them. The odd car curled its way down the road past the gate, but we were mostly hidden from view by the sloping bank of the beck.

'This is nice.' I helped myself to some olives.

'I thought it was a good way to get you on your own.'

'That sounds ominous. I should warn you that the water here isn't deep enough to dispose of a body. I'd get snagged on the rocks and someone would find me within a day.' I looked into the black peaty water that gurgled along beneath us.

'Oh, right. Anyway, I was just going to chop you into pieces and feed you to the pigs.' Nat stretched lazily.

'What pigs? There aren't any pigs for miles here. Maybe down near Pickering.'

'Okay, scratch the pig idea. Wine?' He lifted the bottle.

'Please.' Nat had even thought to bring plastic wine glasses. This man had had exposure to some very classy picnics. I thought back to the thrown grass and woodlice down the necks of our growing up. 'So, if you don't want to kill me and haven't properly planned on the disposal of my remains, why do you want me on my own?'

'I'm still trying to chat you up. And that's remarkably difficult with a nearly thirteen-year-old boy standing right beside you all the time, you know.'

'Well, I have to say...' I lifted the wine glass; there were little bubbles in the wine, that rose and fizzed and looked like I felt right now '... that this is a remarkably pleasant way to be chatted up. Much nicer than...' I stopped. Covered my sudden lack of words by drinking a large mouthful of the wine. 'So, you get extra points for that.'

'Oh, is there a scoreboard?' Nat drank some wine too. 'How am I doing?'

I made a so-so face. 'I hear the south of France is very nice.'

'Sorry, I only get one day off. I'll have to settle for being somewhere around the middle of the rankings, then. What's the top of the scoreboard as the best date you ever had?'

Date? I hadn't really had many dates, had I? Then I remembered another hallway. Sitting next to Leo on the bare boards and talking; listening to everything going on around us as we sat in our own little bubble of quiet. He'd touched my hand. Just that, just a casual brush of fingers. And stupid, eighteen-year-old me had thought it meant something. I'd held that brush of fingers close to me throughout everything else that went on. It had been the last time I'd ever seen Leo.

'There was someone, once,' I said. The wine was going to my head, aided by the bubbles. 'A – boy, man, I suppose, he was a couple of years older than me.' How could I say to Nat that it had been his brother? That he'd led me into things that I'd have been better staying out of, both of us too young to know better. 'It was nothing, really. But I felt...'

That had been it, really. I'd *felt*.

'What was his name?' Nat asked softly.

I put the wine glass down. 'I forget.' I started to collect up wrappings and empty packets. 'It was a long time ago. Doesn't matter. Come on, let's get all this packed up.'

'There's no hurry.'

There was absolutely no way to broach the subject. How could I ever do it anyway? After Cass's revelations I knew how it felt to know that you were a second-best choice. That you were only chosen because all other similar avenues were gone. And I knew how it felt to have that fear of not quite living up to what had been expected of you. So if I told Nat that I'd fallen for his brother, why would he ever believe that I liked him for who *he* was, rather than because he reminded me so much of that slender, dark boy who'd shown me excitement and another life away from my uninterested parents and baby-obsessed sister?

Even if that other life had been bad for me.

And didn't I like the me I was now rather better? The me that Nat saw? Careful, reliable, the dedicated farmer who put all her energy into rearing good stock and looking after the land? If he found out about me and Leo, he'd find out about the old me. The one I'd left behind, the one I couldn't admit to.

'The shearers are coming next week,' I said.

'Now, there's a non sequitur to illustrate the phrase "non sequitur".' He lazily refilled his glass. 'I must use that one on Thor.'

'I meant that I need to get back to put all the non-shearlings together so we only have to bring the ewes down for the shearers.' I half stood, half crouched. Nat wasn't making any move to stand up and I didn't want to sit down again and restart the conversation we'd been having. Equally, I couldn't just walk away, so I continued in my awkward, bent stance.

'Do you know what Thor told me he wants for his birthday?' Nat didn't react to my peculiar posture.

'If it was a baby cousin, it's not going to happen.'

'He told me he wants you to teach him to drive the tractor,' he went on.

'Oh, bugger, does he?' I thought of my poor old Massey being gunned around the yard by a Lewis Hamilton wannabe. 'He's a bit young.' But then, weren't the local farmers' sons helping out on the combines by the time they were Thor's age? When it was harvest time it was all hands on deck, and however young you might be, you had a job to do and sometimes that job was driving machines that were worth more than my house. 'But if it's what he really wants, then maybe it's time. If he's taught properly he's less likely to do something daft one day if he finds the tractor standing in the yard with the keys in.'

'It's his birthday on Wednesday.'

'That's the day the shearers are coming,' I said.

'Is there some kind of contraindication that means shearers and tractors can't exist in the same universe?' Nat was still relaxed, eating a biscuit from a pile.

'Of course not. It's that I'm going to be busy. Watching.'

He tipped his head on one side. It made his hair flop and again I had that flashback to Leo, which punched me in the heart. 'Do they need full-time ogling? Because I volunteer to stand in and stare at men in vests wrangling sheep for an hour or so if you need to get away.'

'That's noble of you. I should warn you that they take their vests off sometimes. There's a lot of naked chests and tattoos.'

'That must be awful for you.'

'It's tough, yes.' I smiled at him. He was working so hard to lighten the atmosphere after the questions about my dating past. I hadn't realised that my discomfort at answering them had been so obvious. 'So, if you still want to take my leering shift, just be aware. I will happily go off and give Thor a lesson in tractor driving and leave you to the burly blokes with the ripe language and the T-shirt tans.'

He'd drained his glass now and I waited to see what he'd do next. Maybe he'd copy me and stand up, start tidying cushions and picnic accoutrements back into the bag.

But he didn't. He sat up and hunched his legs up to his chest.

It was that pose, the one that brought Leo so powerfully back into my head that I felt myself entitled to bounce back some of the questions he'd been using to upset my psyche. 'What was your best date?'

'Oh, now that's a question.' He stared over the beck at the far bank, where a tangle of undergrowth and brambles was providing cover for a whirl of small brown birds.

I waited. My heart was beating really fast and I wasn't quite sure why.

'My best date.' His voice was a bit dreamy. 'If we're doing rankings, this one comes quite high, to be honest. There was one that ended with me losing my trousers and having to jump some garden walls, although that wasn't so much "best" as sexually adventurous; I like to think I've refined my dating technique since that.' He gave me a quick look, half over his shoulder. 'I think good dating comes with age, doesn't it? When you're young it's more about imposing your world view on other people to see if they disagree or whether there's some kind of match. Oh, and sex. I like to think that it becomes more about the discussion and less about the blow jobs as you get older.'

I gave him a stern look. 'Sex complicates things.'

He sighed. 'I know. And some of the best relationships I've had haven't involved sex. For me, it's got to be a mutual compatibility, if you see what I mean?'

'Like a meeting of minds?' Leo had once said something like that to me. That what went on in the head was more interesting to him than what went on in the bed.

'Yeah. I'm done with lust. I mean, not completely, obviously, it has its place, but it's not a great basis for an entire relationship.' Nat sighed and stretched his legs out again.

'Great, that means I don't have to worry about you and the shearing gang, then.' I wanted to get him back to the farm, away from this isolated spot with occasional horses stomping past and the difficult questions. Once I was back on my home turf it was easier to distract him, easier to distract *myself*, and thoughts didn't become tangled and heated by the flame of the past.

'Oh, I don't know. Tattoos, didn't you say?'

I threw a cushion at him. It was the only sensible response.

8

Wednesday dawned fair and bright. The shearers arrived at ten, raucous and fun, a gang of four, two New Zealanders and two local lads, who travelled to all the farms in a fifty-mile radius, shearing and hoof trimming. They presumably had other jobs that they did during the rest of the year, but I couldn't see any of them being accountants or traffic wardens, and our conversations usually revolved around Upper Ryedale fleeces, so I wasn't sure what they could be.

I took Thor, who was practically rotating with excitement, down onto the flatter part of the far field and began to teach him how to drive the old Massey. I linked up the brakes, showed him how the hand throttle worked, gave him some basic clutch instruction and let him get on with working out how not to stall and the niceties of steering.

Thor behaved like a boy who's being allowed to drive his father's Ferrari for the first time and the smile on his face when he finally got the ancient tractor up and down the field was my reward for missing out on the shearing action. I could hear the sheep yelling their annoyance at being upended and rapidly relieved of their coats in the paddock, but they were in safe hands. Nat was, true to his word, hanging over the fence and watching. He had strict instructions to call or text me if anything arose that the boys couldn't deal with, but the phone in my pocket stayed quiet.

I travelled the first few circuits of the field up on the tractor with Thor. There were a few nerve-jangling moments, when he tried to turn too sharply on the slope and I feared we'd roll over, and a couple of failures to brake and steer, so the old vehicle lurched into rabbit holes. After a while, though, he seemed to have got the hang of it and I jumped down and let him circle the ten acres alone, with varying degrees of acceleration. The Massey wouldn't do much more than twelve miles an hour these days, even on a downhill slope, and as long as he kept focused and didn't let it head into any fencing or bramble patches, and didn't go into the far corner where the slope was a little bit precipitous, he would be fine.

The sun on my back made me drowsy. Once I was sure nothing dreadful was going to happen, I didn't have to do much more than observe, and walking round and round the middle of the field, keeping him in view as he circled the perimeter, as though I were lunging a horse on a very, very long line, was boring.

My mind wandered under the weight of the sun. Once it had done its duty, assessing the grass in the field, visually checking the fencing, wondering about the quality of the fleeces being stripped off up in the paddock, it began to dwell on Nat. Nat, who wanted to 'chat me up'. Who clearly derived some sort of entertainment from my company, who didn't seem to want instant gratification, and who'd taken my sensible 'this can't go anywhere' talk with good humour and a degree of resolution. So, we couldn't have an actual relationship. I didn't *want* an actual relationship, not with a man whose brother had been – well, whatever the hell it was that Leo had been, that kept bringing him back into my memory. Anyway, no man wants to feel that he's having to measure up to a brother who's been dead for nearly a decade, does he? Plus, they'd all be going back to Streatham soon, please God, because otherwise I might just carry out Nat's plan and feed Cass to some pigs, even if I had to travel to Norfolk to find some.

So, no. On so many levels, no. But, on the other hand, he was hot. Probably literally, since he never seemed to take his jumper off, and clearly regarded Yorkshire as being only a couple of inches away from the North Pole. But when he wore his 'evening' clothes, those loose sweatpants and the oversized hoodie, and padded around the kitchen in bare feet, it took all my willpower not to fling him backwards over the table and discover whether the actuality measured up to the promise.

Eventually Thor pulled the tractor up alongside me. 'That was *amazing*,' he said. He was red-faced and sweaty but, to be honest, given the way my thoughts had been going, so was I. 'This tractor is *brill*! I'm gonna vlog all this later. Can I drive it again and show my followers?'

'All right.'

'*Cool!*' In his excitement he abandoned the tractor in the field and headed off towards the house. Cass had promised him that she'd make him a birthday cake, which might have influenced his speedy rush. Although with Cass there were two ways it could go: either a perfectly baked cake in the shape of an F1 racing car with a scale model of Jensen Button rendered in icing alongside, or a lopsided chocolate lump with incidental buttercream and some decoration taken from the ageing Christmas cake that was still lurking in a tin at the back of the pantry. It depended on how involved she'd got in the upstairs bathroom.

I left the tractor where it was. I wanted to haul some feed later, so I'd be moving it to put the link box on anyway. I'd walked up the lane towards the yard when I heard the wolf whistles break out, and the shearing handsets stop.

'I brought you all some tea,' Cass said, tottering on her heels as she came out across the yard with a tray of mugs. I instantly felt guilty that I'd not been there, supplying tea and beer for the lads shearing, as I normally would. Then I saw their reaction to Cass and stopped feeling guilty. She'd clearly made their day with her delivery, although that was mostly because she was wearing skin-tight jeans and a low-cut top, as though she were visiting from a *Carry On* film. I could tell the admiration was mutual. Cass leaned over the fence, giving her breasts – which I was almost sure were fifty per cent plastic – a good exposure, and gazed upon the acres of tanned chests appraisingly.

The lads were, despite their loud and overt sexuality among themselves, respectful when women were present. I didn't count as a woman, so I usually got the other end of the conversations, but Cass was faced with four bashful blokes all being deferential over the tea mugs and complimentary over the biscuits, which she'd brought out to accompany the tea. By the time I turned up on the fence, it was like a vicar's tea party, if the vicar had been six feet of tanned ruggedness and his housekeeper had done Victoria Beckham impersonations.

Nat and Thor were in conversation over the iPad at the far side of the yard. Nat was, presumably, getting a blow-by-blow account of tractor driving and I didn't want to intrude on Thor's glowing happiness, so I stayed leaning on the fence, unnoticed because I was overshadowed by Cass's boobs.

The fleeces were piled on a clean tarpaulin in a corner of the shearing area, and the newly shorn ewes, looking thin and a bit shell shocked, now roamed around the paddock. Only a half-dozen or so remained to be done, plump and matronly and trying to look dignified in the little holding pen, calling for their lambs, who we'd penned together at the far side of the small field.

At last the mutual admiration society brought its Annual General Meeting to a close and Cass tittupped back across towards the house with her tray of empty mugs. I lifted a hand to the lead shearer, who nodded back, and then I went after Cass. I needed tea. And a biscuit. Teaching Thor to drive had exhausted my attention span, and my state of overheated boredom needed builders' tea and a Hobnob.

'Thank you for taking them tea.' I sat down at the table. She was filling the sink, but I didn't hold out any hope for her carrying the nineteen-fifties-housewife thing through as far as actually washing up. 'That was nice of you.'

She looked a bit taken aback. 'Well, it's warm and they're working hard.'

'Plus, it's always nice to help four burly blokes with their shirts off.'

She gave me an un-Cass-like grin. 'That hardly occurred to me at all.' Then she turned back to the worktop and started doing something with a cake tin and a bowl. 'Nat seems to like spending time with you,' she said, with a voice that lacked any inflection at all. I couldn't tell if she was going to turn around with a smile or a carving knife. 'Thor says he took you on a picnic at the weekend.'

'We like hanging out, that's all.' I got up and checked the kettle. 'He's quite fun.'

'I don't want any element of hanging out, thank you.' Cass took the cake out of the tin and put it on a plate. 'He's here to tutor Thor, not seduce anyone.'

There was a bit of a 'tone' to her voice now. 'Did you have a crack at him?' I poured water onto my teabag. Because I knew about her hatred of the mugs, I was making tea in the biggest one I could find. 'I wouldn't have thought he'd be your type.'

I only said it to annoy her. I had no idea what Cass's 'type' was. She'd never said a word about Thor's father, which I took to mean that she either had no idea who he was, or he was someone local that we knew and would have mocked her for ever sleeping with. I had money on it being Kenny Oliver, who was thick as privet but who'd been a very pretty teenager. He'd lost all his hair now and worked with his dad laying driveways.

'He's Thor's tutor,' Cass said again, although this did nothing to deny my allegation. 'He's an employee, Dora. One doesn't sleep with the hired help.'

'You got that from a *Downton Abbey* episode, didn't you?' I took a biscuit. 'Nat's hardly the boot boy.' I watched her carefully stroking icing onto the sponge cake, stepping back now and again to assess the evenness of the finish. 'And *did* you have a crack at him?'

Nat had never said anything about Cass flirting with him, and he did seem to regard her in the same way as I did, as the result of a random mating of Stalin and Elizabeth Bathory.

Cass put the icing spatula down and took a packet of chocolate buttons out of the cupboard. 'He *can't* fancy you,' she said, and her voice was the quiet, even-toned voice of someone who is either trying not to be heard, or is about to go apeshit with a chainsaw. '*I'm* the pretty one. It's all I've got.'

Then she stood away, bringing the cake plate down with a flourish onto the table in front of me. 'There. What do you think?' As though the previous words hadn't been spoken. Maybe she didn't realise that she'd said them aloud. She'd got her usual expression of slightly dissatisfied complacency, and the cake was beautifully decorated – this had clearly just been the finishing touches, but there was a tautness about her that made me wonder.

I was about to ask her what she meant and why she thought she only had her looks, but there was a clatter in the doorway and Thor and Nat were there, lambs following and the dogs preceding.

'Is that my cake? Wicked! I said I wanted all the chocolate, didn't I, Mum?'

'Did you thank your Aunt Dora for letting you have a go on the tractor?' Cass's voice was still even. Very controlled. I wondered, for the first time in a very long time, what was going on in her head. I normally thought of my sister as a kind of cardboard figure, one who went about her day-to-day business reacting to things. I never wondered about the life she led inside. Her hopes and her fears – she only ever spoke about these as they related to her son. As if she'd stopped living the day he was born and now only existed in relation to him.

'Yeah, thanks, Dora! It was *amazing!*' Thor began to rattle through everything he'd learned about tractor driving, as though that hour in the field had equipped him to operate every type of farm machinery from now on. 'And I vlogged, and some of my followers who live down the dale said I should go to the local Young Farmers' club and they do all things like go to shows and have competitions and stuff and they do tractors and learning how to build an engine and shi... err... things like that.'

'We're not going to be here long enough for that,' Cass said, and I felt a momentary leap of hope, followed by the sinking sensation of loss.

'Have Mum and Dad said anything about the extension, then? Is it nearly done?'

If they all went back to London soon, all my problems would

be over. Well, all my prevarications regarding Nat, anyway. Plus I wouldn't have to live with the Spirit of Kirstie Allsopp any more.

'You sound like you want to get rid of us,' Nat observed.

'Yeah, you don't want us to go, do you, Dora?' Thor looked at me, wide-eyed, from over the top of his birthday cake. The sun this morning had brought out freckles over his nose, and he looked wholesome and young.

'Besides, I'm only halfway through doing that dreadful bathroom,' Cass put in. 'If we leave now it will never get any further than two marbled walls and a stripped pine lavatory seat. And no, they haven't said anything about the extension. I meant that if Thor joined the Young Farmers, he wouldn't get chance to do all those things because we won't be here for long enough.'

'Oh,' I said, hope subsiding.

'You don't have to sound so cheerful about it,' Nat said.

I don't think he saw the sharp look that Cass gave him, but at that point the head shearer came to the door to report that they'd finished and were heading off. There was a confusion of big boots and stomping as they got into their truck and went on to their next job, while I checked over the wool and pulled it into the shed on its tarpaulin.

'What happens to it now?' Nat was standing in the doorway, blocking the light.

'It goes off to be processed and sold.' I picked up a handful. 'Hand spinners and knitters like it. Some of it is even sold raw, like this.'

'What do they knit with it, more sheep?' Nat touched the bundle with a fingertip.

'It's full of lanolin. That's what makes it smell like that, but it also makes it very waterproof.'

'You could knit a tent. A very smelly tent that attracts other sheep.' He was looking at the huge pile of wool. 'And this is how you make money, is it?'

'Well, you can't knit money, no.'

'You know what I mean. This is your income?' He shook his head. 'I don't know how you do it, Dora.'

'Usually when people say that, what they really mean is "I don't know *why* you do it",' I said.

'There is a bit of that, yes. I mean today, all sunshine and lambs and birds singing – it's lovely. But, like before, when a sheep dies and it's raining and cold and the bills keep coming...' He wasn't looking at me. He kept his eyes on that multicoloured heap of fleece.

'The bills keep coming for everyone, Nat.' I took a deep breath. 'Did my sister ever make a pass at you?'

Now he looked at me. Clear hazel eyes, pupils wide in the shadow of the little barn. 'I turned her down,' he said. 'If that's what's worrying you.'

'It isn't. You're free to sleep with whoever you like.'

'Great! I've just got time to go after the shearers.' His tone was light but there was something else in his words. 'Was that an issue? That I might have slept with Cass? Because my taste in women tends more away from those who look as though they may have a cupboard full of corpses in the attic.'

I shook my head. 'I just was wondering, that's all. It was something she said.'

Then Thor was there again, wanting to look at the wool, wanting to touch it and throw it around, but I stopped him, and Nat and I were having a long, unspoken conversation through glances and eye rolls. It hadn't actually occurred to me that he might have slept with my sister first, and of course how hypocritical would it have been of me to not want him for that reason? But knowing she'd tried...

'—and I've got two new games for the Xbox!' Thor was running through his present list as we went back out of the shed into the sunshine. 'There's this one where you've got to find and kill all these people...'

'Teletubbies aren't what they used to be,' Nat said and caught my eye again.

'What's that?'

'A programme from before you were born,' I said hastily, before Thor started to think we were laughing at him. 'Thor, Nat said he had a word with you about your vlogging.'

'Yeah, yeah.' Thor pulled a face. 'I'm not, like, *stupid*, Dora.'

'No, I know you're not. It's just that these people, the ones who steal sheep, they pay people to follow farmers' blogs and... vlogs.' The word sounded ugly and awkward, as though I'd acquired a speech impediment. 'They go through them all to see if people mention when sheep are being moved, which fields they're being put in. They wait until they know the sheep are a long way from the farm, or until they know that the farmer isn't going to be about. Do you see? You can't give them any clues.' I'd looked it up. Having Nat and Thor about was turning out to be very educational for me, whatever Thor might or might not be learning.

He pulled a different face. 'Well, *duuuh*.'

'I think what Thor means to say,' Nat interjected now, 'is that he's very careful not to give away any specific details about the farm which would enable thieves to precisely target your sheep, Dora.'

'Yeah,' said Thor. 'That.'

I looked at the freckle-faced figure who was as tall as I was now and starting to gain shape, as though someone were shading in a cartoon sketch. He was only a boy, but a man in the making; he just still had the scaffolding up. 'Well,' I said. 'You said you've got a lot of local followers now. They may be able to pinpoint the farm from any details you show, the village or the road or even the view. Be careful. I know you will,' I added quickly to forestall an argument, 'just be double careful.'

Thor sighed deeply as though bracing himself for a conversation with the most stupid person on earth. 'It's like...' he gazed away into the middle distance for a moment, searching for the right words '... like, my followers are like, kinda, my *friends*. They comment and we chat and talk about sheep and farming and music and stuff. Loads of them are farmers too. They won't do anything well dodgy.'

Nat and I exchanged a look. His eyebrows were nearly in his hairline; he was probably remembering the conversation with the milker in the pub about the shed full of weed. My eyebrows remained at forehead level, because many of the dodgiest people I knew were farmers. When there's not a lot of money in the day job, but the day job is pretty much twenty-four-hours, there are a fair few dodges and scams going on behind byres and barns.

'Remember that talk we had about Internet safety, Thor. People online aren't always who they pretend to be.' I didn't know how Nat kept his voice so level and reasonable.

'Well, yeah, but that's like, people wanting pictures of you naked and doing all like stuff.' Thor cuddled the iPad closer to him, as though it might be corrupted by this talk. 'Pervs and shit. We talk about farms and houses and what it's like living in London and how we've got, like, clubs and bars and cinemas that stay open all night. Loads of them have never even *been* to London!' He said this with the wide-eyed amazement that hinted that he didn't know how they managed to survive this cultural deprivation. 'They want to know what it's like,' he repeated.

'Well, okay. Just be careful. And if anyone asks anything that you think is a bit – dodgy...' Nat looked at me again and I could see that he was trying not to grin '... then bring it to me. Or your mother,' he added, but with a tone of slight wariness. 'Or Aunt Dora.'

Knife butted at the back of Thor's leg. The lambs had been out around the yard, shouting at their fellow sheep through the bars of the paddock gate and eating random blades of grass that they found growing around water troughs or between the rough cobbles of the yard. Flick was probably in the kitchen again, tormenting Cass with her presence or trying to bully the dogs, who were too well trained to give the lambs the savaging that they clearly thought they deserved.

'Thor, we're going to have to start putting Flick and Knife out with the other sheep during the day,' I said. I wanted to distract him from dwelling too much on the thought that all adults were clearly idiots who knew nothing about online life and how grown up and aware he was about the dangers. 'They need to get used to being in the flock and they're big enough now not to get pushed around.'

Adult ewes could be brutal towards lambs that weren't their own, particularly if the lambs tried to take milk from them. Flick and Knife still fussed and pushed for bottles, but weren't dependent on the milk any more and were unlikely to try suckling from a ewe. The weather was good and they were, quite frankly, embarrassingly large to still be wandering around the house.

'Oh, but...' Thor began. Knife butted him harder in the leg. It clearly hurt, their little heads were remarkably bony, but he knew if he said 'ow' it would only give me more fuel.

'The sheep are Dora's livelihood, Thor,' Nat said gently.

'And they aren't pets,' I added. 'I know you're attached to them, and you've done a brilliant job of rearing them, but it's time they grew up and became sheep. You can still go down the field and visit them. They'll come running whenever they see you – that's what their mother used to do.' Another brief memory of

Willow's head hitting my knee when I tried to move hay bales. 'Honestly. They'll be trying for bottles when they've got lambs of their own.'

'Really?'

'Oh, yes.'

'Can't I take one back to London? We could keep it in the garden and I could take her for walks and stuff and down to the common and I could vlog that and all the cute girls would love her!'

I looked at him with the look I used on those people who came to see the flock with a view to 'keeping one as a pet'. 'Three words, Thor. Animal. Movement. Regulations. You can't just put a sheep in the garden – they escape. And need company. And need shearing and their feet done and all kinds of veterinary attention. They aren't like big woolly dogs, you know.' Plus Mum would have fifty thousand conniption fits at a sheep bursting through her bifolds and climbing on the sofa. Mum and Cass were very much alike on the animal front.

'Ooookaaaaaaayyyy,' Thor said on the falling note that indicated he was disappointed but wouldn't give up trying. 'Gotta go, Mum's got me another surprise present and she wants me in to open it. It's a pair of Nikes, those ones with the fancy trim – they're like two hundred quid a pair!'

Clutching the iPad and followed by Knife still bleating hopefully, Thor dashed out of the barn and back off towards the house.

'Not much of a surprise, then,' Nat observed.

I was more thinking about the two hundred quid. That was a lot of tractor diesel. 'She knows how to spend money, my sister.'

'To be fair, it's not difficult.' Nat came in closer. 'The back of your neck is really red.'

'That was from standing in the field while Thor went round and round. It was like watching the world's most boring F1 race.'

I felt him touch the nape of my neck, very gently. Just a finger stroke, but it made my spine feel as though it were going to burst through my skin. 'Nat.'

'I know.' He stepped closer still. 'No future in it, yadda yadda. And I understand. I really do. There's just something, Dora, something about you.' Another step until he was right in front of me, smelling of raw wool and heat. 'I felt it right from the first moment I saw you.'

I didn't like to admit that when I first set eyes on him my thought was of a shotgun. When I'd thought he was his brother, I'd wanted to kill him for what he'd put me through. 'That's a really cheesy line, Nat,' I said, very quietly, looking up into the shadow of his face.

'I know. I heard it in a film, and I've been wanting to try it out. But now I come to say it out loud, you're right. Far too cheesy. How about I really, really like being with you and I don't just want sex. I mean, I do want sex, but that's not the be all of it. I want *you*.'

'You can't have me. *I've* got me.' But my words were almost breaths.

'I don't have to be a tutor. I mean, I want to finish the school year for Thor, but he's moving on now. He needs proper structured education and exams and stuff. I could – I dunno, I could learn how to farm. Couldn't I?'

I looked into his eyes and they were so like Leo's eyes that half of me wanted to buckle, to just lean in and let him take control of the situation. But I'd done that with Leo and it had all gone badly. I had turned into someone I didn't want to be, even though I'd thought I had at the time. So, the half of me that kept control at all times leaned back out.

'It's not that simple, Nat.'

The hand fell away from the back of my neck. 'No. No, you're right.' He gave a big sigh. 'It really isn't. It's horribly complicated. I'm kidding myself here, thinking it will all be all right if we want it enough, aren't I?' The hand brushed my cheek now, gently pushing back my hair, which was escaping from its ponytail.

'Yeah,' I said, and the word nearly crumbled into letters under the weight of my regret.

'Okay. So, back to mild flirting, the occasional dirty joke and some dreams which I am definitely not going to go into.'

His sudden switch back to levity was encouraging. He wasn't holding my inability to get involved against me. Plus, he'd seen what my life was: how farming this tiny patch of upland Yorkshire was a constant battle that made *Game of Thrones* look like a rigorous Scrabble match. It wasn't a job, it was a life. I'd have said it was a life*style* but there was really not enough money for any style – you were lucky if you were wearing matching socks. Any man who wanted to be part of my life would have to think really, really carefully before he took it on.

I left Nat in the barn and went down to let the sheep out of the little paddock and down into the adjoining field. They'd been joyfully reunited with their lambs and there was a lot of impatient stomping about as they waited to be released.

Had I chosen this life? Certainly, I'd always loved coming up here and going round the farm with Grandad; the contrast between our squeezed life in London and the wide stretches of space up here was so huge, how could I *not* love it? But had I always wanted the farm?

The dogs joined me, and together we hustled the sheep out of the dusty, beaten earth of the paddock and into the field where they spread out from the gateway like a wide and woolly duvet being shaken over a bed. This was all second nature now. But *had* I always wanted it?

Back in that hallway, sitting with Leo, talking about life. Our futures. Him wanting to be creative, free, a wanderer. Me, wanting to – what had I wanted, back then? To be away from my family, chiefly, and away from Mum's stifling interest in Cass and her baby and their collective obsession with making sure that my sister was all right, healthy, undisturbed, solvent. The endless conversations about finding a flat for her to move into before the birth of her baby, Cass being there for six weeks and then having to come home because she wasn't coping. Mum walking the landing at night rocking a crying Thor so that Cass could get some sleep.

I'd wanted anything that took me away from that. And Leo had done that, for a while. It had all been – a whirl. A blur. A new world full of colour and excitement and my heart beating like mad and running through rainy streets, running, running, and laughing at anyone who tried to stop us. Hand in hand as we danced, the energy pounding through me, and thinking this, *this* was all I ever wanted and life couldn't be any better. But then the downside. When Leo wasn't around. The men, the parties that weren't fun any more. Throwing myself into things that left me feeling worse. Walking home at seven in the morning, through the crowds of people heading off to start their days in offices and shops and banks, all neatly dressed and clean, while I dripped and dragged my way down alleys with my shoes in my hand and my clothes soiled and split around the seams.

The farm had been an escape. I'd got dismal A level results, which my parents never even asked about. University was out; I'd blown that. I gave a grim smile. I'd blown a *lot* of things. So I'd come up to the peace and solitude of Folly Farm, to let the east wind that came straight from Russia blow through my life and rid me of all thoughts of Leo and that life.

Eighteen months of wrangling stroppy ewes, helping with difficult lambings, cooking meals that were edible because Grandpa hadn't really had a hot meal since Grandma had died and seemed to have existed on jam and tinned sponge pudding. Eighteen months spent learning how to manage grassland, where to sell the ram lambs that we couldn't keep, learning about bloodlines and breeding. Grandad might have decided that he was going to leave the farm to me when I was twelve, but I could have sold up, couldn't I? Split the money with Cass, watched the flock disperse to other people who cared about endangered breeds and gone my own way.

I looked out across the gently sloping field. Two lambs were leaping onto a bale, taking such joy in simply living that it made me smile. The ewes were all grazing, heads down and feet firmly splayed, their newly shorn bodies looking clean and neat. Above, the sky bent around us all in a blue haze, the odd cloud serving to show how relatively unblemished and pure it all was.

How could I ever think I would have done something else? I felt almost disloyal to have even let my mind wander on to other possibilities. This was my life and my home. And, to be honest, what else could I do? I made a mean bread and butter pudding, but that was hardly going to earn me a living wage, was it? I laughed hollowly to myself. *Farming* didn't earn me a living wage. But it did give me a roof over my head and the numbers of Upper Ryedales were coming up slowly. The breed was being recognised as important. We even had show classes now for our breed, even if the numbers were so small that, barring Mr Weird travelling over from New Zealand, the title was always split between me, two bachelor brothers from Kent and a couple who had a smallholding in Dumfries.

And at least I wasn't Cass. There was much to be thankful for.

A ewe limped out from behind me, following her lambs. It was the ewe I always thought of as Number Three, as she'd been the third ewe I'd ever lambed and, clearly, spraying a three in blue marker on a fleece was something that stuck with you. She was old now and probably these would be her last lambs, although I tended to get a bit soft-hearted about my 'retired' ewes and instead of sending them off to market to end up as pet food, I sold them on to people who wanted a couple of sheep for the wool.

She was very lame. All the sheep had been fine when I brought them up for shearing. Bugger, this was bad news.

I did a quick mental audit. Now that Cass had paid up for the decorating, there was money back in the account. Even if there hadn't been, I'd still have had to find it; I couldn't let an animal suffer. I said another few 'oh bugger's and a couple of 'bloody hell's, like a kind of anti-rosary, and pulled out my mobile to call the vet. Then I corralled the ewe back into the paddock with the help of the dogs, and went back into the house to grab something to eat while I waited.

Thor had put on his new trainers and gone off to vlog. A box lay on the table, tissue paper packing spilled over the rim and the lid on the floor. Cass was sitting with a tiny sliver of cake on a plate in front of her and her face in her hands.

'Are you all right?' It wasn't a question that came easily in regard to Cass.

'There's a sheep on my foot,' she said, muffled through her fingers.

I squinted down. Under the table, Flick was quietly chewing the hem of Cass's jeans. I didn't attempt to push her off.

'Did Thor like his trainers?' I cut myself a large slice of the cake. Cass could nibble tiny little Instagram-worthy pieces, but I was hungry, and the cake looked good.

Cass sighed. 'It was meant to be a surprise.' She lifted her face, by running her hands back through her hair. I noticed that her roots needed doing. 'I've no idea how he found out.'

'He's a child. That's what they do. Remember when you and I went hunting through the cupboard in the kitchen, looking for our Christmas presents?'

We'd have been about eight and ten. Left to our own devices while Mum had been upstairs on a telephone call, we'd decided to go on a treasure hunt. We'd seen parcels secreted away in the spidery depths of the huge cupboard and we'd snuck in to see what we could see.

'Oh, yes.' Cass damped a finger and sampled a few crumbs from the edge of her plate. 'That was the year we both got inline skates, wasn't it? And we found them under the cake tins. Mum was pretty rubbish at hiding stuff.'

Encouraged by the fact that my sister was actually talking, without complaining or mentioning money, I asked her something that had been bubbling away in the back of my mind for a while. 'Cass, why don't you move out from Mum and Dad's place? Get yourself a flat somewhere?'

She looked as though I'd asked her why she didn't strip naked and run through Leicester Square shouting 'I am a bumble bee, buzz buzz buzz' and stopped licking at the crumbs. 'Well, Thor, of course,' she said, as though I were stupid. 'He'd miss them too much and I can't manage him on my own.'

'You could send him to school. And he's old enough to get on a bus and go round and visit them, isn't he?'

Cass narrowed her eyes and gave me a ferocious look. 'Have you been talking to Nat? Are you both plotting something? Do you know something I don't?'

I opened my mouth to deny her allegations, then realised that, actually, it had been Nat's raising of the idea that Thor needed more intensive education than a home tutor could really provide that had made me think of it. 'No,' I said, unconvincingly.

'I've warned you before about trying to seduce him. Please stop having conversations with an employee about my private life and intentions for my son. If you carry this on, then I shall tell Mum that he needs to be replaced and send him back to London.'

'Then Thor won't have a tutor.'

She gave a sideways shrug.

'You'd have to teach him yourself.'

Cass did a 'tight mouth' face that reminded me of Mum, and got up to put her plate into the sink. 'There are tutors up here,' she said. 'Even in this wasteland of educational opportunity. Apparently there's an agency in York. So Nat isn't irreplaceable.' She whirled to face me so that her hair did a photogenic 'flick' around her head.

There was almost a note of panic in her voice. I heard it, and wondered what was getting to her. I wasn't worried about her sending Nat away, he was an adult and could make his own decisions about where he went or whether he stayed, but I couldn't help wonder about the way she'd reacted. It was as though the idea of moving out of Mum and Dad's really did scare her.

'Cass, you can manage Thor by yourself,' I said softly. 'He's thirteen. He's not going to try to get the lid off the Calpol when your back is turned any more.'

Her lips worked as though words were building up in her mouth and trying to get out, but what she did say was, 'There's a car in the yard,' and then she marched out of the kitchen with the hem of her jeans leg all soggy and half down. I didn't know if she'd noticed and didn't feel like attracting attention to it.

The car was Chris's. He was wearing his overalls already so he must have come straight up from the village. 'Hi, Dora! Got a ewe lame?'

There was something very grounding about Chris. Well, there had to be – he hadn't a spark of imagination in his entire, rugby-playing, body. He was big and sandy-haired, with the kind of square face that people always call 'open' and he looked as though, given twenty years or so, he'd be one of those big bluff men who play golf a lot and call their wives 'her indoors' or 'the little woman'.

I compared him quickly to the lean, honed darkness of Nat. It was like comparing Tom Hiddleston with Mr Tumble.

'She's in the paddock.' I took him in and showed him the ewe and he upended her and began feeling her leg. Whatever else Chris might be, and I was compiling a list, he was an excellent and dedicated vet.

'You know Elvie and I are getting married?' he said, probing the ewe's clearly swollen foreleg.

'That's wonderful,' I said, and meant it, to my surprise.

'Yeah, she thought she'd better make an honest man of me!' He did a laugh that was definitely a guffaw; he was further down the road to nine irons and patronising than I'd realised. 'What do you think of that?'

'I think it's a great idea.' I held his bag whilst he rummaged.

'Just going to give her an anti-inflammatory. She'll be fine.' He pulled out a bottle. 'So, you don't mind that Elvie's going to march me up the aisle, then? Not jealous?'

I remembered his selfishness in bed, his less than savoury habit of wiping his willy on the duvet and his snoring. 'Not at all,' I said. 'Good luck to you both.'

He injected the ewe. 'You and I could still... err... you know.' He gave me a nudge and a wink. 'Bunk up? For old times' sake? Elvie would never find out.'

'Well, that's a very kind offer, but it's not going to happen, Chris.' I stroked the ewe's irritated ears. 'Ever. Honestly.' I *wanted* to say that the sun could die a thousand fiery deaths and he could be the only man left on earth and I *still* wouldn't sleep with him again and if it was sleep with him or die I'd start choosing my coffin now. But his good-natured grin stopped me.

'Ah, it'd only be sex, though, Dora.' He patted the ewe and let her go. 'You take it all too seriously. You can just have a bit of rumpy pumpy now and again, doesn't have to mean anything! Doesn't have to be a big game-changer, just a bit of fun, bit of exercise and some bouncing tits. Lighten up!'

'Chris, my tits will never again bounce in your general direction,' I said, solemnly.

'Ah, never mind, then. Worth a shot, eh?' and he patted my bottom in the same way as he'd patted the ewe. 'She should be better by morning. Give me a shout if she's not, just some inflammation on the joint. She's an old girl, getting a bit past it now. Bit like you, eh?' And with another pat, which would have cost him his fingers if he'd hung around, he was off to his car, jauntily.

'Did he escape from the nineteen sixties or something?' Nat was leaning against the barn wall and had clearly watched the whole pantomime. 'He was practically *quoting* from a porn film there. Er, not that I'd know, of course,' he added quickly. 'Just – from what people have told me.'

'It's how Chris is.' I watched the ewe limp back on down the field to be reunited with her twins. 'He's so unreconstructed that he's practically ruins. But he's a good vet. He just likes to try it on with anything female. The ewe got away lightly.'

Nat was watching Chris's car bump its way back along the track, shaking his head slowly. 'I didn't know there were still men like that under sixty.'

'You've never been a woman.' I looked him up and down. 'Obviously.'

And as I looked at him, I was thinking about what Chris had said. It could just be sex. It didn't have to lead to anything, it could just be exercise and a bit of fun between two consenting adults. I was self-editing the bit about the bouncing tits though.

'Have you seen Thor?' Nat pushed himself away from the barn wall. 'Birthday or not, he needs to get stuck into some schoolwork, and he's already had an hour off for tractor-driving lessons with additional Nike time.'

'I think he's in the house,' I said vaguely, because my mind was full of swirling possibilities. 'Just beware of his mother.'

'You should get that printed on a sign, you know,' he said over his shoulder as he headed off in search of his charge.

I nodded and carried on standing in the sunlit paddock, watching his back view disappear into the kitchen and trying to stop those wretched tingles from climbing out of my body via my scalp.

9

'They've done it again!' Thor tore into the yard waving the iPad.

Two days had passed since Chris's visit and I was checking over Number Three. The swelling had gone down and she wasn't limping as much, but I'd made the decision that it was time for her to go. I had five yearling gimmers that were ready to go into lamb this year, the numbers wouldn't be down, and Number Three could go to a lady in Pocklington who kept some older ewes for the fleece.

'Who has done what again?' I let the ewe go and she strode off with dignity like a dowager duchess who's had her bottom pinched in a crowd.

'The sheep stealers!' Thor shook the iPad. 'It's all over everywhere! They hit my friend's place – took nearly a hundred sheep! He's just been telling us all. I'm gonna vlog it.'

Thor looked as though he was a mixture of very excited and quite upset, which seemed to be a semi-permanent state in young teenage boys. As though he was teetering on the edge of hysteria and looking for an excuse to launch it at someone.

'That's awful.' I straightened up. 'Where's your friend's place?'

Thor gave me a twisted look. 'It's out near Pickering. But I don't know exactly because you've told me not to tell anyone where *we* are, and I can't really ask for people's addresses when I have to be all, like, ingognito and stuff.'

'InCOGnito,' I corrected him without thinking. 'Yes, of course. That's actually very sensible of you, Thor.'

He beamed, switching from irritated teenager to praised child in less than a blink. 'Yeah. So, like, my friend put the call out for anyone who's seen a big lorry. Which was bloody – I mean, which was a bit stupid because *everyone* has seen a big lorry, but it has to be one that you could put a hundred sheep in, which is, like, not an ordinary lorry.'

'No.' I thought back to the night on the moor, the lorry that had passed us with the ramp half down. 'They're using a proper animal transporter.'

Thor was looking at me expectantly. 'So how can we catch them, Dora? Can we set, like, a trap? Put it out that we're going away and leave the sheep all in the field and have the police standing by and stuff?'

'No.'

'Why not?'

I looked at him sternly. 'Because that sort of thing only works in *Scooby Doo*. If you put it about that you're going away and leaving your sheep, the only people you will find coming round will be the RSPCA, and the police have better things to do than camp out for days waiting for a group of rustlers who may never turn up, if they've got bigger fish to fry somewhere else.'

'Oh.' Thor looked crestfallen for a moment. 'Why would they be frying fish?'

'It's just an expression. I really must have a word with Nat about your general education.' I looked around in the yard behind us. 'Is he around?'

'He's gone into York.'

I wanted to ask why, but didn't want to see that knowing look on Thor's freckly face, or have him start singing 'Dora fancies Na-a-at!', which I knew he was capable of. I couldn't help but wonder why Nat hadn't asked me to go along as well; it had been a long time since I'd had a day out off the farm.

What had been a beautiful sunny day, filled with wildflowers twitching in a half-breeze and the smell of honeysuckle almost drowning out the smell of a barn that needed mucking out, suddenly no longer seemed so beautiful and the smell of wet straw was definitely overpowering everything else.

'Oh.' It didn't really sum everything up, but it was the best I could do. I didn't want to swear in front of Thor because Cass would accuse me of teaching him bad language. I didn't know why, since Nat had spent the last few weeks trying to drum a little bit of French and Spanish into him, and he hadn't picked up a word.

'I'm going down to the field to see Flick and Knife.' Thor waved the iPad again. 'They still need to be inside at night, right, Dora? I'm gonna bring them back and film them coming up the track cos I've got, like, literally *millions* of viewers who want to see them doing that running-up-the-hill thing.'

With another joyful twitch of the iPad Thor was off, boots slapping against his thin calves like a round of applause. At least he'd had the sense to change out of the Nikes before he went down to the field.

I watched him go, running an odd run, mostly caused by the ill-fitting wellingtons, but partly by the fact that he didn't seem to have got used to his legs yet. Thor was heading for six feet tall already – further strengthening my idea that Kenny Oliver, known as 'Stringy Ken' throughout his teenage years, had been his father – and gave me the impression that he was a five-foot boy who'd been stretched to fit a six-foot suit, when it came to controlling his extremities.

This would probably be the lambs' last night in the house. The weather forecast wasn't indicating anything more than some wet weather and the girls were quite big and woolly enough to withstand a bit of rain. They didn't skip now, they galumphed, and spent more time grazing than they did playing. Thor would be fine, I was sure. I'd been proved right. They came barrelling up to him whenever he went down the field, knocking against his legs with piteous bleats about how hungry they were and could he, maybe, bring them a few pints of lamb milk, just for old times' sake?

I suspected he still smuggled them down the odd bottle when he thought I wasn't looking.

The sheep were all in the long field today. I'd opened it up after I'd cut it for hay, and closed a couple of the other fields up to let them grow for silage. Later in the season I would open all the gates and the sheep and lambs would have access to all forty acres, and once the grass stopped growing I'd have a word with Elvie about running some down with the horses in the final ten acres, for the extra grazing.

Thinking about Elvie made me think of Chris. I wondered if I'd be invited to the wedding; it might be nice to have an excuse to put on a dress and shave my legs. Then I wondered why I needed an excuse. Of course, sheep farming didn't really lend itself to prancing around in Balenciaga, but there was nothing to stop me putting on a skirt in the evenings, when most of the work was done. I could still do my nightly walk round; there was nothing magic about jeans that kept the sheep safe. And maybe Cass – awful thought – was right, in that I ought to make more of an effort with my appearance. Maybe not have my hair scrunched back into its practical elastic band all the time, make the effort to put on a bit of make-up now and again and buy some clothes that fitted rather than were just quick and easy to put on. Otherwise, given a few years, I was going to find that I never wore anything but elasticated waists and bobbly jumpers.

Then I stopped kidding myself. In the background to all these thoughts and ideas had run a film of Nat seeing me in a dress. Stopping dead with his mouth open. Gasping a bit, maybe. I didn't go so far as to imagine him saying 'Why, Miss March, you're *beautiful*,' because I couldn't stretch quite that far, but I did let myself think about his reaction to seeing my legs.

But, as I stared out across the acres and a tortoiseshell butterfly flickered its way down to some thistles flowering under the hedge, I pulled myself together. Nat liked me. I knew that. I was fairly sure, after that kiss we'd had walking back from the village, that he fancied me. But we'd agreed, hadn't we, that there was no future in it and neither of us were in it for a short-haul relationship that had a guaranteed end date? However much I wanted to slide myself over his lean, well-muscled body and whisper filthy things in his ear, it wouldn't work. Besides, I was still half hung up on his brother and couldn't admit it. If I told him the truth about Leo, about my life back then – well. Even *I* couldn't face up to that part of my past. If I had to come out and tell Nat...

I shuddered. This wasn't *fair*!

But then Chris's words came back to me. About how sometimes sex was enough. Just some good aerobic exercise with someone you liked. It didn't have to mean forever, it could simply be a pleasant way to spend some time. Plus, Nat made my mind turn to hot, dark places whenever I saw him slouching his way around the house in the evenings. Surely it couldn't be so bad just to have a hook-up? Two consenting adults? It didn't have to be a 'where is this relationship going' type of thing, did it?

That kiss. The feel of his mouth, the way his stubble had caught at my hair. His hands, firm against my back, holding me in...

'Dora! Your mobile is here and it's been ringing!' Cass appeared at the kitchen door, shaking the phone in question. 'Why are you just standing there? I thought sheep farming was all shovelling and walking up and down?'

I took some deep, steadying breaths. 'Just – thinking.'

Cass looked artfully disarranged, one strap of her painting overalls unbuttoned and a blob of blue on one cheek. If I'd been interrupted halfway through painting, I would have had plaster dust in my hair and a red face, but she managed to look as though *Vogue* were about to do a DIY-inspired fashion shoot. I remembered what she'd said, those half-whispered words. '*I'm the pretty one. It's all I've got.*' And I wished, for a second, that Cass and I had the kind of relationship where I could ask her what she meant.

'Here. It's annoying.' Cass handed me the phone and went back inside. 'I've got to put a second coat on that wall now,' she said peevishly, as though it were the phone's fault.

It was Henry's number. I returned the call, to find that he wanted to warn me about the rustlers striking again and remind me to be extra vigilant and ask if I'd seen any unusual large animal lorries about on the local roads. It was nice of him to call, nice of him to care enough to tell me, and I didn't like to say that I'd already found out through the medium of a thirteen-year-old boy and his 'followers'. It also didn't seem fair to tell him that his warning to watch out for my sheep made me feel that he was implying that I normally left them wandering about and only checked them over once a week, if I could be bothered. As though I were some kind of hobby farmer.

To refute the unspoken allegation, I walked down to the end of the field and looked back up over my flock. They ambled and grazed and the younger of the lambs jumped and skipped in the sun. All present and correct; healthy and doing well.

Then I looked further up, to where the roof of the farm was visible, like another crop growing out of the hillside, grey-slated. The date on the stone set above the door was sixteen ninety-three, although there were some doubts about how original the stone was and whether or not a previous generation of farmers had stolen it from a demolished barn and put it up because it was a shame to waste good stone. But taking it in good faith meant that the house had stood here for over three hundred years, and my family had been living in it and farming here for two hundred and fifty of those. My blood was partly diluted with the black water from the beck and the bell flowers of the purple heather that grew up on the moors behind.

I may have my doubts about whether I'd *really* wanted to take on Folly Farm, but the farm seemed to have no such doubts about me.

From this distance I saw my car, which really needed replacing with something bigger, and a lot more robust if Cass was going to keep driving it, approaching from the village road. It stopped at the junction where it met the smaller road that ran up and down the dale, indicated, although there was no other traffic besides a girl on a pony, and turned uphill towards the farm. Nat was evidently on his way back from York. The care with which he took the track made me smile. I'd never seen anyone take ten minutes to drive half a mile before. It meant I was in the yard before he was.

'Hello.' He got out and came over. I tried to pretend that I'd been busy doing things and hadn't really been waiting for him. 'Anything exciting happen while I was away in the big city?'

'More sheep rustling, but I have no doubt that Thor wants to give you a blow-by-blow account of that.'

Nat made a face. 'You don't think he's secretly behind it, do you? Like a criminal mastermind?'

'He's got freckles. I don't think they let you have freckles if you're a criminal mastermind. Boys with freckles have to be the plucky hero. Criminals have crew cuts and ferocious dogs, not footballer haircuts and a pair of lambs, although I'm wondering if my idea of crime was formed from reading Famous Five books and things may have moved on a bit.'

Nat laughed. 'Yes. He's become a lot more wholesome since we came up here, I have to say.'

I thought back to the sulky boy who'd stomped around the house and got his foot stuck between my floorboards. 'Yes, he has.'

'Compulsory removal from social influences. It's one of the reasons I don't mind him vlogging; he has to have some social contact with his peers and it's less of a risk via iPad than some of the things that were going on back in London. I think he had plans to be a gang leader down there, you know.' I must have looked shocked, because Nat hurried on. 'Oh, he wasn't actually going to join a gang or anything, so I'm not quite sure how he thought that was going to work, but... well. It's a different life down there now. London is changing fast – it's not like it was when we were young.'

'Nothing is.' I sighed. 'But this is such a quiet and untouched place, you sort of forget that there are places that are different.'

'The sheep rustling is a point of contact, I think.' Nat sounded serious. 'It's something that shows that nowhere is perfect. Even in this place that looks as though there hasn't been a crime since the Domesday Book writers nicked a pencil, there's the sheep stealing. It helps Thor realise that it's all one big world, we're not isolated somehow in an Arthur Ransome novel.'

'Nat!' Thor was yelling at us from the doorway. 'There's more sheep stolen! My friend says they got nearly a hundred!'

'Insurance scam, bet you,' said Nat with a half-smile. 'Probably turn out to be three.' He headed off towards the kitchen and I realised that I hadn't asked him what he'd been doing in York, or tried to mug him for relief parcels from the outside world.

* * *

I had a long shower that evening and washed my hair. The amount of straw and hayseeds that fell down the drain made me realise that I might have left it too long between washes, and it was odd feeling my hair brushing my shoulders rather than in a tight wedge at the back of my head. I pulled a dress out from the back of my wardrobe, realised that it had gone a bit mouldy stuck in there, and had to hang it out of the window for half an hour to get rid of the strange smell. It was the only dress I owned, so it was either do that or get back into jeans, and jeans wouldn't work for what I had half planned.

I even forced myself into some sexy underwear. Well, it had been Chris's idea of sexy, which meant it was scratchy nylon lace, with a low waistband and a high 'hoick' level which made my boobs look like they were sitting on a doily and my bum felt as though I'd wrapped it in chicken wire. Then I put the dress over the top, hoping that most of the smell had gone, put my feet into sandals, and went downstairs.

Fortunately Cass and Thor were in their rooms. The soundtrack to a game was thumping out of Thor's, and Cass was watching *Midsomer Murders*, judging from the music. Probably picking up tips.

The kitchen was empty. Well, emptyish. The dogs looked up as I came in, noted the costume change and put their heads down on their paws. I'd never notably given them much work to do whilst dressed as though I were off to the theatre and smelling like a drawer at the back of the pantry. The lambs were in there too, but the smell put them off from approaching me and they stayed under the table, exchanging suspicious glances and trying to get comfortable even though they were both now the size of small bunkers.

Nat usually came in to make himself a drink around ten. I sat at the table and tried to look 'casual', but it was a pose that I was so unused to that I could only seem to get as far as 'uncomfortable', which, given the chicken wire knickers, wasn't too far from the truth. In the end I gave up and cut myself a slice of Thor's chocolate cake, which was still doing the rounds from a tin with Christmas trees on.

The lamp glowed. The dogs snored. I drank several cups of tea, and still Nat didn't appear. I crossed my newly smooth legs and it felt weird not having several layers of fabric between them and the open air. There were chocolate cake crumbs in my cleavage too.

Oh, what was I doing? This was ridiculous! Wanting to seduce Nat, just because he was nice and I hadn't had good sex for a while and I knew he fancied me – how pathetic was I? I stood up and noticed how the heels of my sandals made the same tittuppy noise that Cass's shoes did. Was I turning into my sister? Was I going to start wafting around the farm in little dresses, because if I was, then I was going to pick ones that didn't smell musty and have weird little black spots all over them where the mildew hadn't properly brushed out.

There was no sign of Nat, and I was feeling stupid. I got up and kicked off the sandals. I might as well give the sheep a last check over before I got out of this ridiculous outfit and went to bed, so I put on my wellingtons and stomped out into the yard.

The dogs stayed in their bed, clearly assuming that I was off out for an evening of agriculturally themed wining and dining, but I left the door open in case they or the lambs needed a last wander round the yard.

All the sheep were grazing blamelessly in the moonlight. Bugger. What I really wanted was a good emergency to take my mind off things. Although, I thought as I adjusted my chest, which kept trying to escape from the bra, I was only dressed for the sort of emergency that you saw on saucy seaside postcards and if anything bad really happened, I was going inside to get my jeans on before I sorted it out.

Cloud had extinguished the moon when I came back up to the yard, so when I walked into Nat in the gateway I gave a high-pitched squeak and ruined what was left of my sophisticated act.

'Hell, you scared me!'

'Sorry, who were you expecting, the Easter Bunny? The kitchen door was open so I thought I'd check if you were out here.'

'I was just doing the evening rounds.'

The cloud moved and the moon came out rather shiftily. 'You look – interesting,' Nat said as my outfit was illuminated by the pale light. 'I like the boots.'

Wellingtons with a dress are never a good look. Thigh-high leather boots, yes. Even sassy little black biker boots with straps that hint at bondage, yes. Big green wellingtons that flap around your calves with a noise like a bucket filling, no.

'I...' I couldn't think of a single excuse for the way I'd dressed. 'I just wanted... er...'

'No, no, you're rocking it.' His voice was soft.

We stood there for a few moments, while the moonlight rapidly guttered over us and made the whole thing look like one of those flicker-book cartoons. Nat was still very close. At last he said, 'Did you get dressed like that for me?'

I *wanted* to say, 'Of course not! I'm an emancipated woman who fancied a change so I thought I'd do my hair up, put on a tight frock and underwear that, quite frankly, feels like being tied up with baler twine, and expose myself to some moonlight just in case I turned out to be a werewolf and I was the last to find out.' But I didn't. Instead, I whispered a quiet, 'Yes.'

'Wow.' He took a step back and looked me up and down. 'That's flattering.'

'I thought – something Chris said. About how we could just – enjoy ourselves.' I was still whispering.

'Ah.'

'And now I feel stupid.'

He stepped in close again. Put his hand against my cheek. 'Don't feel stupid, Dora.' He was practically whispering now too. 'Please. Don't ever feel stupid.' And then his mouth was on mine and he was pressed in so tightly that I could feel every zip and button from his shirt and jeans embossing themselves into my skin.

The moonlight flickered again, as though illustrating years passing.

We stepped apart, gasping. One shoulder of the dress was pushed down and I'd got my hands under the waist of his shirt.

'There's something – it's complicated,' Nat said, his eyes not moving from my half-exposed cleavage. 'I don't want this to go any further until I've had chance to…'

I moved my hand. 'Are you married?'

'God, no!'

'Well, I'm fairly certain you aren't gay.' I moved my hand again and he closed his eyes and let out a small moan. 'So, can't we just…?'

'Dora—' This was definitely a groan. He kissed me again, harder this time, and now I had my back up against the rough stone of the barn wall. There was something pleasing about the rough hardness of the texture of the stone and the smooth hardness of him in my hand.

He rucked my skirt and I felt his fingers slide inside the lace of the awful knickers. I could barely breathe as the pressure increased, his mouth slid down from my mouth to where my breasts had now completely escaped both bra and dress.

'There's a condom in my pocket.'

'What?' He raised his head.

'We can't do this without...' I saw stars, the wall behind me took my weight for a second as my knees buckled and I lost the power to say anything else for a moment. My whole body liquefied and then reformed. 'Oh, God.'

'In here.' He half carried me in through the doorway to the barn. I was still shaking and my legs were not receiving any messages from my brain, which was entirely concentrated on what he was doing to me and how best to reciprocate. We were suddenly lying down, deep in straw, and I was pushing at his clothes, sliding his jeans lower over his hips and unbuttoning his shirt.

'I need to talk to you...' He tried to stop me, but I clamped one hand over his erection and he shut up. I slipped the condom on and suddenly he was above me and there were no words left, just friction and him kissing me and my legs tight around his back. His shirt was unbuttoned, his chest firm and lightly haired against my uncontained breasts as we rocked and I felt every inch of him tighten briefly and then relax on an out-breath of my name.

'Dora...'

We lay like that, entwined, for a while, half dressed and decorated with straw, like entrants for a corn-dolly competition. I was still trying to catch my breath; he had his head down alongside my neck, keeping his face averted for so long that I wondered if he'd fallen asleep.

'Nat?'

'You have no idea how long I've wanted to do that.' His voice was muffled. 'No idea.'

I stroked his shoulder and went to push down the front of his shirt, which still had the cuffs buttoned, so I could touch flesh, but he stopped me. 'What's wrong?' I struggled to one side so I could see him better.

'I shouldn't – I'm sorry. This was all the wrong way round.' He sat up now and he looked shell-shocked but also devastated, as though he'd just broken a huge rule.

'It's fine. We both consented, we're both free agents, it was great – what's the matter?'

He cupped his face in his hands. 'I have no idea where to start.'

'You're scaring me now, Nat.'

He took a deep, deep breath, and began to unbutton his cuffs. 'I'm so, so sorry,' he said, and took off his shirt.

I stared for a second. 'You utter bastard,' I said.

10

I didn't know what to say. I wanted to walk out, to walk away to try to make sense of this, but I *also* wanted to kill him again, which wasn't compatible with the walking out, so I stayed. I contented myself with walking the length of the barn, up and down, tugging at the dress, trying to force it to cover more of me. He sat on the straw bale. He'd done his jeans up and slipped his shirt back up. Pulled the sleeves down over his arms.

'So, what?' I gestured. 'How long did it go on for? I'm assuming you're not still using?'

Nat rubbed at his arms now, as though he could rub away those marks. Healed, yes, but still evident. The track marks, scars from old needle sites. 'Dora...'

I took another deep breath. 'Did Leo get you involved too? Or was it the other way round, older brother getting his kicks, getting other people tied up in it all? Was it your fault he died?'

Nat opened his mouth again, but I was *angry*. 'So, what's all this "being a tutor"? Are you trying to atone for something? Does Cass know about your past? Because I can't see her willingly hiring an ex-junkie to look after her precious son. Hell, she wouldn't even give him Calpol for two years – she's not going to be overly happy to find out that his tutor used to jack himself up on anything going!'

Nat had stopped trying to speak now. He just sat, head down, so that his hair hid his expression. Moonlight occasionally peered in through the barn door and then crept away again as though embarrassed, leaving us with only a crepuscular kind of glow.

I paced a bit more. 'We had sex under false pretences!'

'You have no idea,' he said at last.

'What?' I whirled around. I could *feel* the fury on my face, as though it was trying to burst out of me and splatter him against the wall. '*What* have I no idea about? You haven't got a clue what I know or don't know!'

A breath. 'Dora, I'm Leo.'

He dropped the words into the darkness, which bent around them, wrapping them in black.

I was momentarily speechless. I took two very deep breaths, and the words came back. 'But you're dead.'

He raised his head now and there was no expression on his face. As though he was keeping everything deep down inside. 'I lied. Leo didn't die in a squat of an overdose. At least – part of me did. I watched a friend die, Dora, a good friend. It was drugs and I couldn't help him, I couldn't help *myself*, but when he died I knew I had to get out. So I did. The story is not as short as that, of course, or as simple as I make it sound, but I got out. Reinvented myself.' His voice went suddenly quieter. 'I left all that behind.'

'Shit.' It was the only word that contained enough venom and could be spat. 'Shit shit shit shit.'

All the implications. All the memories. That Leo, who'd sat with me on the bare wood floor of that hallway, that Leo who'd danced with me all night. That Leo, who'd never quite left the back of my mind – was here. Was *Nat*. Shit.

'And I know who you are. You were calling yourself Faith. You wore red lipstick and dyed your hair black and you were about six stone of angry, confused young woman; full of snark and sass but underneath you were so *scared*.'

I felt my outer self crumble. The past twelve years of building up, of farming and fresh air and outdoor life, fell away and left the core me standing there as though naked. Still that scared, confused eighteen-year-old, trying to wear a mask of certainty and sexuality.

'You *recognised* me?' I'd started to shiver so I wrapped my arms around myself. The dress offered no protection against the cold.

'Not at first. I thought I did, when we very first met, but you've changed so much – I thought I was wrong. And then you said something about making a living out of what you enjoyed and the world being a scary place. It was something Faith and I used to talk about, and it all just clicked. That was the moment when I knew who you were. And when you asked me to unlock your phone and the number was my birthday, I knew you'd remembered me. So I went with it. I knew you had your own reasons for never wanting to go there again and wanting to forget it, so I never brought it up. And anyway—' he was rubbing his arms now '—how could I? What could I say?'

'You could have told me the truth!'

He looked at me directly now. There was a cool steadiness in those hazel eyes. 'But you lied to me too,' he said. 'If I'd told you the truth, then I would have had to admit that I knew who you were. Which would have blown this whole thing open, wouldn't it? And you weren't ready for that, I could tell.' The steadiness in his voice didn't waver. 'And, by the look of things, you aren't ready for it now, either.'

'You had sex with me under false pretences!' I nearly wailed the words this time.

He grinned. Only a small grin, not lightening anything up, just an acknowledgement of the oddness of the situation. 'To be fair, Dora, I tried to stop. I wanted us to have had all this out first, but once you had your hand on my cock it was pretty much game over for me, so it was go with it or leave you standing.' He hitched a leg up onto the bale and sat with his chin on his knee; that pose that was so 'Leo' I couldn't believe I hadn't seen through the whole 'Nat' thing right away. 'And I wasn't really thinking clearly at that point, but even so I could reason that walking away and leaving you all dressed up and nowhere to go – that wasn't good either.'

'But...'

'If you remember, you were the one saying it could just be sex, just a bit of fun, so I sort of rationalised that you wouldn't mind who I was.' He stood up now and tucked his shirt back into his jeans. 'I think we might both need a bit of space right now.'

I didn't know what I wanted. To get away, to try to pretend that none of this had ever happened? To talk, to try to explain? To tell him what had happened, all those years ago, why I'd walked away and never come back? To kill him and bury his remains in the barn and pretend that he'd run away in the night?

'I don't know,' I said. They were the only words that meant anything. 'I don't know.'

He reached out as though to touch me, then apparently thought better of it and dropped his hand. 'I know it's not very gentlemanly of me to do this, but I really think it's better if we just sleep on this.' He ran his hands through his hair, and I looked again at those cheekbones, that mouth, and wondered how I'd ever not recognised him. 'Maybe we can talk about it tomorrow.'

The fury was back, flooding through me like an evil sugar rush. 'You bastard.'

'Or never,' he added hastily. 'Never works for me too.'

He started to walk out of the barn. Slowly, as though he was reluctant, but with a terrible inevitability. I felt the anger leave as suddenly as it had come.

'It was Buffy,' I said softly to his retreating back.

'What was?'

'Faith. I watched a lot of *Buffy the Vampire Slayer*. I wanted to *be* her. Hence the hair and the lipstick and – all of it.'

He paused for a moment. 'I know,' he said, quietly over his shoulder, and then walked out.

I didn't go to bed that night. Instead I walked the fifty acres until my feet were sore. I sat in the field in the darkness amid the reassuring presence of the sheep, who grazed around me unconcerned. I only went indoors as the first light started to tinge the grass with grey, then green and then gold as the sun came up over the moor, and then I didn't go to bed, I got in the shower.

I scrubbed and scrubbed as though I could remove all traces of him from me with the power of hot water and some grapefruit gel, as I alternated up and down the temperature scale as though I had a fever. One minute scalding with shame and embarrassment as I remembered who I'd been, *how* I'd been thirteen years ago. And then I'd be freezing, cold with shock when the implications hit me. Leo. Here. Nat was Leo. So he knew about it all.

I picked up the body-puff thing that had come with the grapefruit gel. It had probably been a Christmas present from Cass; this sort of Body Shop neutrality was her idea of a suitable gift. But then, I usually got her a magazine subscription or something equally personality-free, and it struck me again, as I scrubbed another layer of skin down the drain, how little Cass and I really knew about one another. We'd grown up together, close in age, similar interests – and then, what had happened? Well, she'd got pregnant whilst still on school dinners and I'd taken to sleeping on floors in unknown flats and having to find my way home from parts of London not even on the Tube map. But I *knew* what had happened to her. She – and I offered up a little prayer to any god that might be listening – would never know how I'd lived back then.

My brain skittered, as though it couldn't deal with facing all the implications and memories head-on; it got as far as the outlying facts and then shied away like a nervous horse. My mind went back to more comfortable thoughts, things I could control. Things that were blamelessly cause and effect: the sheep, the farm. Whether I needed to order more feed or whether I could get by on grass alone for the rest of the season. Did the tractor need new tyres and someone to sort out that timing issue? What colour was Cass intending to paint the hallway and could she be talked out of painting Farrow & Ball through the entire house?

It calmed me. Putting on my usual outfit of jeans and jumper and then my scruffy old farm coat calmed me even more. By the time I was back out in the fields, dragging feed sacks off the link box with the dogs at my heels and hungry, inquisitive lambs around my ankles, I could almost persuade myself that last night hadn't happened. It had all been a bad dream.

'You look shitty,' Cass observed, when I went into the kitchen for a cup of tea, having peered in through the window first to make sure that Nat – that *Leo* wasn't in there already. 'I hope you're not coming down with something. I'm not looking after those animals if you get poorly, you know.'

'I think I realised that,' I said, pouring boiling water. 'Your total lack of any empathy to date was a bit of a clue.'

'Well, they smell.' Cass gave a little shiver of distaste.

'And I'm not ill, I'm just tired. I didn't sleep well last night.' I dragged the chair out and winced at the noise it made on the flagstone floor, almost as though I were hungover.

'You should try some of my valerian and chamomile.' She

clopped her way to the sink; the sound of her heels was almost as bad as the chair-drag.

'Is that the colour of the bathroom?'

'It's tea.' She shook a packet at me. 'One cup a night, helps me sleep and it helps my anxiety too.'

I stared at her. 'What the hell have you got to be anxious about?'

Cass sighed, a sigh I considered to be overdramatic. 'Dora, when you are a mother, you don't know a moment's peace.'

'You have one thirteen-year-old boy, not two-year-old triplets. And you hardly spend any time with him because you've got – Nat minding him most of the day!' I stumbled over the name. In my head he was 'Nat', but overlaid with the whole past of 'Leo', like two people in one body. 'And when you're at home, Mum looks after him.'

There was a moment of silence. I could almost hear the dust motes swirling. 'Yes,' Cass said eventually and quietly. 'Yes, she does.'

It was another one of those instances. It felt as though there was something pivoting, as though with the right word I could turn Cass from what she appeared to be into something else. Something about her tone around those innocuous words hinted at so much unspoken. But I was tired and fraught and Cass barely left enough space to insert a knife tip let alone a sentence, before she spoke again. 'But you seem to think that lambs and dogs are your children, Dora, and it's really not at all the same. You can't put children into kennels if you want to go out, for a start.'

It crossed my mind to point out that my dogs could quite easily be left if I went out and were well behaved enough not to need kennels, but she wouldn't have listened. 'No, because other-wise Mum and Dad could just have sent you and Thor into some place with wire-mesh runs and underfloor heating while they did the extension.'

Cass looked pointedly around the room. 'It would,' she said slowly, 'have been an improvement.'

I sipped at my tea whilst she wiped around some surfaces with a damp cloth, like a scorned housewife in a nineteen seventies TV drama. 'How's the decorating going?' I asked eventually.

'I've nearly finished that bathroom. Honestly, Dora, why don't you put in some en suites? The rooms are big enough – my room has a bed and a chest of drawers and enough space to fit most of the Bakerloo line. You either need to do something with that space or buy more furniture. It's like sleeping in an empty dormitory.'

'But there's only me living here. Why would I need to have an en suite when I can just walk up the landing to the bathroom? I can skip to it naked if I want to – there's nobody to see.'

'But you could have *guests*!'

I stared at her. 'I've *got* guests. I've got you lot. And it hasn't made me incontinent; I can still make it to the bathroom in the night.'

Cass sighed. 'I meant, you could have bed and breakfast guests. People who pay money to stay on a farm. And then you can use that money to buy things, like heating. And carpets.'

'I'll think about it.' It had never really occurred to me before that I could open Folly Farm to guests. Now that Cass had suggested it, it was obvious. Six bedrooms, half the house practically unconnected to the other half, which would make perfect, self-contained accommodation for visitors. Bugger. My sister had actually had a good idea that I now had to think of a way of making into *my* idea or have her crowing about it for the rest of time. I might have to rule out the 'breakfast' part though, because

I was out on the farm too much to provide food, but I could certainly offer the other part of the deal.

Then I thought about the draughty cavernous rooms. Cass had another point there – the rooms were so large and under-furnished that you sometimes had to send out search parties for the bed. So in their current state, they weren't really lettable. The farm was more like a holiday camp for masochists.

But an additional income stream would help. It would buffer me against unexpected farm bills, and in the summer this place wasn't so bad as long as it didn't rain.

'I'll think about it,' I said again.

Cass just sniffed and tapped her way out of the room. I could hear her heels receding down the hallway to the front room, and then voices. Thor was in there. Was Nat with him? Or was he lurking somewhere around the farm, ready to burst out on me like the Ghost of Christmas Past?

I decided to go and find some more jobs to do a long way from the house. I'd pushed the whole of last night down, under all the practicalities of fencing and hay. Every now and then a moment, a word, would bubble back up and engulf me in a wave of horror, but I'd had years of suppressing my past. Twelve years of practice for this eventuality.

I would just pretend last night hadn't happened. And as far as I was concerned, if we never spoke about it again, it had never happened. Okay, he was still Leo, he still knew about it all, but if we just went back to being Nat and Dora, then the whole Leo and Faith thing was something that had happened to other people.

Yes. I could do that.

I replaced some fence posts and restrung some electric wiring where the lambs had been getting out onto the track. Fortunately they hadn't wanted to go far from their mothers, who'd been too big to squeeze themselves under the fence without getting a shock from the battery, but an extra wire lower down would stop the whole thing. I couldn't risk one of them getting out onto the road and being hit by one of the cars that sped up or down the hill too fast for comfort. The locals tended to know where sheep were liable to be, but we were getting into tourist season, and visitors saw only a long stretch of open road.

The lambs stared at me balefully for stopping their fun. Flick and Knife had been the chief culprits; with no thought other than that humans might have bottles of lovely milk for them, they'd be a danger out in the village or on the road. I could see myself getting irritated phone calls from people whose gardens had been trampled by a pair of rogue lambs trying to break into their houses, baaing pathetically and eating their bedding plants.

So, I made sure the fences were escape proof, and then went back up to the barn. It looked different in daylight. Small gaps in the tiling let sunshine through in controlled doses, where it shone onto straw bales and feed sacks and the remnants of the lambing pens I'd built with metal gating and baler twine. I sighed and started cutting the string. I might as well get the pens disassembled and mucked out now the sheep were all out. And it would give me something to do to keep me out of the way of Nat.

But it couldn't stop him coming to find me.

'We need to talk,' he said, standing in the doorway with the sun behind him, like a gunman entering a saloon. 'About last night. About all of it.'

'I don't want to.' I ferried my last armful of metal gate to where I was stacking them against the wall. 'You're Nat and I'm Dora and you're Thor's tutor. That's it.'

'But it isn't, is it?' He came further into the barn. 'Last night made it more than that.'

'We just had sex. That was all. Just two horny people, hooking up for a bit of light fun. There doesn't have to be anything other than that. That's what we decided.' I thought if I said it with enough force, I could make him believe that he'd agreed too.

He wasn't fooled. 'No, we didn't. And we can't leave this hanging. It's not good for either of us. I want to explain. Or try to.'

I sighed deeply, as though his explanation were nothing I had any interest in, even though I was itching inside to hear what he would say. What more was there to explain? That he'd pretended to be his own brother to cover up his past? We'd pretty much covered that last night.

But then, wasn't it better to get this out of the way? One quick conversation and we need never *ever* go back here again. I sat down on one of the bales of straw at the back of the barn. A beam of sunlight twinkled down onto my knee and I focused on it to stop myself from looking at him. 'Go on, then,' I said. 'I am dying to hear what you come up with.'

He sat next to me. 'We used to talk,' he said. 'We talked all the time, that year.'

'Of course, we did. We were out of our heads on drugs. Everyone talked bollocks for hours, danced all night and then fell over. It's what ecstasy and cocaine are *for*.'

'I never got to say sorry. For introducing you to all that. I was young and I was confused and I just wanted to have a good time and forget that my family had broken up, and I should never have got you involved in the whole "drugs and party" scene.'

He wasn't looking at me. He was talking to the toes of his boots.

'You didn't coerce me. I was there of my own free will.' Yes, I'd played the part of Faith to the hilt, careless and carefree; promiscuous and party-girl to the max. I'd wanted Leo but he hadn't been interested in me like that. After that – well. It was anyone who'd have me.

'But you were so – fragile. I could see it, even then. Right through the whole "Faith" act, like she was this shell you had on. I mean, we never talked about *us*, did we? We talked about how shit the world was, how nobody understood young people, how we just wanted to have a good time – God, we thought we knew it all back then, didn't we?' A half-smile flashed my way. 'But we never got to know each other as people. I wanted to. But you – talking to you was like handling a bar of soap; I'd just get close to getting a grip on you and, whoops, you'd be off on some tangent, like you didn't want me to know who you were underneath it all.'

He dug his fingers into his hair as though those memories of the past were threatening to push their way out of his temples.

'I really liked you.' My voice was so quiet that it almost didn't come out at all. It was just a little whisper amid the rustling of the breeze in the straw and the cawing of some rooks on the roof. 'I liked you and you were my friend. That year was – then things happened. I wanted to talk to you, to tell you, but – I had to get away.' My voice gained a bit of volume. 'And then, of course, I just wanted to kill you.'

He nodded solemnly. 'That was only fair.' He put an arm out behind us. Not embracing me, in fact he was hardly touching me, but it felt as though he was steadying both of us. 'Can you tell me now what happened? Because you just stopped coming. I mean, you were there, every party, every gig, every rave; it was you and me and a wrap of coke or a couple of Xs, and then you just dropped off the face of the earth.'

Faith. I'd been Faith. It had all happened to Faith, not to Dora. Dora just told Faith's story.

'You remember the end of the nights? When it would get light and we'd all be high and still have too much energy to burn? We'd dance and dance and then talk and dance some more. But you never, ever made a move on me. I waited and I waited but you never so much as touched me, and I wanted – I *couldn't* go home.

And I couldn't tell you. So I'd go home with whoever I'd been dancing with when the club shut or the party kicked out, and I could see you there, watching me.'

'You always looked happy enough to me.' He was watching my face.

'I was out of control, Leo. My parents had no time for me, it was all about my sister and the baby. I had no one, only you, and you wouldn't kiss me or take my hand; all you seemed to be interested in was the talking and the dancing and I didn't know how to make you want me.' I took a deep breath. 'So, I'd try to make you jealous. I'd dance with all the other men and then you'd vanish and I'd find myself on my own with some random bloke and off my face and wanting – something. Someone. To feel that someone cared.' I looked at him directly now. Right in the face. I wanted to see his reaction. 'I wanted you. Why did you never just take me home?'

He met my eyes for a moment, then tipped his head to stare up at the roof. I watched his gaze trace the little beams of light. 'I don't know,' he said. 'I wanted to. I wanted *you*. But you were busy playing Marianne Faithfull out there. I wasn't grown-up enough to see how unhappy you were; I thought you were this free spirit who didn't want the boring guy who bought your drugs and talked to you. Plus, of course, I was also completely off my tits and barely knew which way the door was. I'd see you draped around some bloke who was trying to look like Usher, I wasn't about to barge in and drag you away, was I?'

I had to look away now and my eyes found a small pile of damp straw that instantly became the most fascinating thing in the world to look at. 'The worst thing happened. Well, no, the *second* worst thing, after getting pregnant. I got a sexually transmitted infection. All that sex with no condoms, who'd have thought?' I sounded bitter now, and I didn't know why. I'd been having unprotected sex with men for months, what had I expected? What had I *wanted*? To get pregnant? To go home and force my parents to have to pay attention to me and not just my sister? I hadn't known then and I didn't know now. 'A bad one.'

I flashed a look up at him and saw him pull a face. 'That sounds rough.'

'You could say that. I didn't know what it was for ages. I thought I had cancer.' I gave an odd little laugh although it wasn't funny in the least. 'I was terrified. I was eighteen and scared, I couldn't tell anyone, I didn't know what to do. I wanted to come looking for you, you were the only person I could think of who'd understand, but – suddenly it all seemed so meaningless. The drugs and the partying; I thought I was going to *die* and I thought you'd be better off not knowing what happened. After all, we weren't – we hadn't – you were just this guy I saw around. I was ashamed of myself, somehow. I thought I'd brought it on myself by having all that sex with all those men; just shagging about with people I didn't care about and didn't even know.' That odd laugh came again. 'I thought it was some kind of divine retribution. Turns out all that Sunday School stuff that Mum made us do must have sunk in deeper than I knew.'

'Oh, Dora,' Nat said, half under his breath.

'And I had nothing. It was like I was facing death with no life behind me. I came up to the farm to help Grandad and to get away from home and Mum's Mary Poppins complex. While I was here I read up a bit on my symptoms and got to a local doctor who gave me antibiotics and it all went away after a number of very embarrassing consultations and some quite painful swabs. Grandad needed me on the farm, and it was so different out here, so I made up my mind. Get away from the music and the drugs and the all-night dancing scene.'

'And away from me.'

'Yes.' I took a deep, deep breath and cast Faith off. 'All right. Your turn.'

'Sorry?'

'What was your excuse?' I waved a hand to indicate his arm. 'I'm assuming you moved on up from the amateur weekend using? You didn't get all that from an EpiPen or giving blood.'

He went very still. 'No.'

There was an element to his stillness that made me think he was remembering things he didn't want to remember. The hair on the back of my neck prickled as I thought about the things he'd forced *me* to remember. I'd been *eighteen*, legally an adult, mentally a child and psychologically very, very lonely. So I'd assumed a personality I had no right to, and acted a part. What the hell had he done?

Leo stood up and began pacing the barn, much as I'd done last night, as though movement could somehow take away some of the power of the awfulness. 'It started out just fun. Just something to take the edge off, to give me enough – I dunno, something. Confidence? And I was having fun, *we* were having fun.' He gave me a quick look but I kept my face neutral. 'All those nights we sat and talked, I didn't think you'd like me if I wasn't a bit – extra, you know? Without the drugs I thought I was boring. Certainly not someone you'd be bothered with. You were Faith, you could have anyone you wanted.'

Maintaining my neutrality was a real struggle now. I wanted to interrupt, to ask him how the hell he could have thought that I only liked him out of his head. Had it not been obvious how I *really* felt about him? Did he think I'd spent so many evenings waiting for him to ask me to dance, ask me to go home with him, ask me to stay, just because of the drugs?

'I guess I got used to you being around. Being some kind of constant,' he went on, still pacing. 'Then one day you stopped coming and I waited. Thought maybe you'd just got caught up somewhere, that you'd be back, with all that dark hair whirling around and the eyelashes and that red smile that I could see halfway across a room.'

'So this is *my* fault?' I stood up too. 'You're going to find a way to blame me?'

'Oh God, no!' He stopped pacing, at the far end of the barn. Between us, a rain of sunbeams formed a curtain. 'Of course not. This is all down to me.' A deep breath. 'My parents were divorced, and then when I was nineteen Mum went to Canada, Dad had taken off somewhere. I lived with my sister, but then she moved up to Scotland, and I was on my own. Twenty-one, on my own. I was working, trying to save enough to go to university, but – well, the parties were more fun. Drugs were more fun. And I guess I just – spiralled, I suppose. Then, when Jamie died...' He tailed off.

'How come you could just change your name? I mean, they do checks on people who teach, don't they? Please tell me Mum and Dad did checks on you.'

'Yeah, Nathaniel is my middle name. I just tell everyone I go by that, rather than Leo. So all my paperwork is right, just back to front.' He seemed happier to be talking about practicalities, rather than his state of mind back then.

'Oh,' I said, somewhat mollified by the fact that my mother wasn't *actually* the most careless person to employ a teaching professional since the uncle in *The Turn of the Screw*. 'Sorry. Go on.'

'Do I have to? I mean, that's pretty much it.' He pushed his hands into his pockets and raised his shoulders. At that moment he looked so much like Thor sulking about being made to do schoolwork that I almost laughed.

'I want to know it all.' A tiny, warped little piece of me wanted him to suffer. Wanted him to feel as bad having to rake up the past as I had.

He took a deep, juddering breath. 'Okay. So, when Jamie died, I got clean, got myself through uni – reinvented myself. There was nobody left who remembered Leo, so I sort of killed myself off and became Nat.' He turned thoughtful for a moment, looking down at the straw-covered floor. 'So, I'm like the other end of the spectrum to you, really. You took an identity first up, then went back to being you. I did it the other way round. Where are you going?'

I headed for the door. I still didn't know how to feel about all this. I needed space; I needed to see the sun. 'I've got work to do out here, you know. This isn't a hobby farm, it's not just something to do to prop up my backstory, it's my livelihood. Those are animals out there that need looking after. I can't sit here all day navel-gazing and playing "do you remember?" just because you want a therapeutic experience.'

Outside the air felt clean against my face. All those memories had made me feel every inch the confused eighteen-year-old Faith again, walking in a skin that didn't fit and trying to be a person I could never be. But here, with the breeze coming off the moor bringing the promise of summer, the sheep calling in the meadow and the permanence of the old buildings, I could forget all that as though it really had happened to someone else.

Nat caught up with me as I started down the track. 'So, what do we do?' he asked.

'Well, there's another length of fencing that wants looking at down near the beck, and the gateway has got a bit poached up in the bottom field so I want to check that and maybe get an order for some hardcore in to sort it out.'

'I mean about us.'

'If you're going to say "you know too much about me to be

allowed to live", then I'm afraid I shall have to laugh and refer you to the *Midsomer Murders* scriptwriters' club,' I said, with a blitheness I definitely didn't feel.

He put a hand on my arm. 'Please, Dora. This is probably the biggest thing that's ever happened to me. Finding you again after all these years.'

'Great, now I feel about ninety. And it's not like you were looking, is it?'

'Well, not directly, no.'

I kept walking. 'I have to say, the "pretending to be your own older brother" thing, it's not really that attractive. I'd have had more respect for you if you'd been honest and said that you used to have a drug problem but you'd sorted yourself out.'

He strode alongside me. 'I don't think your family would have hired a tutor who had a past like that, do you?'

'So, what was all that about? I *know* you never knew my real name. So, it's what, pure coincidence that you're here tutoring Thor?'

We'd reached the gateway. Several sheep clustered up against the gate to see if I'd brought any food and their inscrutable faces pressed against the wood were so in contrast to the myriad expressions on Nat's face that it almost made me laugh.

'Coincidence? Maybe. But maybe it's also that when I applied to be Thor's tutor we did a Skype interview first, your mother and your sister. They wanted to check me out before I met Thor, I guess. And there was just something about Cass...'

'An air of brimstone and horns, I should think.'

He half smiled. 'Something that reminded me of you. Of Faith.'

We were talking. It suddenly hit me that we were talking. With each new snippet of information the words came more easily; that stilted self-conscious conversation we'd had in the barn was being swept away. I wasn't sure how I felt about that. I wanted to hold the hardness I felt towards Leo against me as a shield against Nat, but the resentment and anger were breaking up in the face of his openness.

'Please don't tell me that there is anything about my sister that is like me, except possibly hair colour and, as nobody has seen her real hair colour for a decade, that is unlikely.'

'There are similarities. You have the same shaped face, similar eyes. Patterns of speech. That sort of thing. Plus, she's got something of that wary "putting on a front" thing that I remembered from you, from Faith.'

'My sister doesn't have a front.' I unclipped the gate and waded through the curious sheep, Nat still striding beside me. 'She's purely one-dimensional. In fact, I think my mother didn't give birth to her, she cut her out of a magazine.'

'*Hellfire Weekly*?' As though he was also relieved that the tone of the conversation was becoming more normal, Nat grinned at me. 'I hear they do subscriptions. Anyway. Maybe that was part of me taking the job. The fact that your sister reminded me of someone I'd known and lost.'

We crossed the field to the offending piece of fencing between some willow trees, now waving their spear-shaped leaves greenly, with sheep trailing a tail behind us. There were still some hopeful baas, and Flick and Knife gallivanted over to check out bottle-likelihood.

'I want to forget any of it ever happened,' I said, averting my face to pretend to examine a fence post. 'I want to forget who I was when I was being Faith, the things I did – it all makes me feel —' I shook my head '—dirty, somehow. I mean, it shouldn't, I was more than up for it all, but it's like that wasn't *me*. Almost like I was possessed by Faith, doing stuff that the real Dora wouldn't have dreamed of. Why the hell I couldn't have been possessed by

Buffy and gone out and kicked some ass, I don't know.' I rocked the fence post. It needed knocking deeper into the earth; the sandy bank of the beck had worked loose around it.

'You were possessed by the spirit of drugs, that's all.' Nat sat down on the bank. An old ewe stuck her head in his pocket, convinced that we must have food about us *somewhere*. 'Lowered inhibitions, altered mental state. Great if you're stable, not so wonderful if you're a bit rocky. As I found out to my cost.' He rubbed at his forearm through his jacket. 'But maybe we had to go through it to become the people we are now.'

'I liked Leo,' I said, leaning on the fence. 'I liked who you were then. You were gentle and funny and you never tried it on. You must have known I would have gone for it. I'd have done pretty much anything anyone asked back then. But you never did.'

He moved his jacket away from the ewe's enquiring nose so she started on his trouser pocket. 'I liked you too. When we talked and you were the real you, full of ideas and plans and so witty and sharp and smart. And then we'd go out and dance and it was like the world was there just for us. But then the guys would move in and you'd be dancing with them and I knew I'd lost you.' He sighed. 'I didn't want to take advantage of you. When you were being Faith, you got all hard and brittle, like you were trying to keep from getting hurt. I didn't want to sleep with Faith, I wanted *you*. But I knew if I made a move, I'd get Faith, because you were using her to protect yourself.'

'You make it all sound like I had a split personality.' I leaned on the post to see if I could bodily push it deeper into the soil, but it didn't budge. It was going to need the lump hammer or even the front loader on the tractor brought down on it. Bugger.

'Maybe.' He frowned at the sheep. 'Why do they do this? When normally they're all about the running away?'

'I'm not sure. I think it's because we're sitting down.' I gave up on the post. 'Cass thinks I should start doing bed and breakfast.'

It was all I could think of to say. He'd got it so right and I felt a bit stupid now. If he *had* kissed me back then, in that hallway, when I'd thought he was going to, when he'd moved across in front of me and I'd been waiting, he would have got Faith. Because Dora wasn't good enough, wasn't sassy enough. Oh, she was fine for conversation, clever and funny and all that, but when it came to sex, to opening myself up physically to someone? That was where I slipped into Faith's feisty, protective skin.

I knew I'd done it again last night. The sexy underwear, the heels – I looked down at myself in my farm coat, jeans and wellingtons. Yep. This was Dora. I hadn't really been aware of it, but last night I'd been Faith.

'That's not a bad idea.' Nat rubbed sandy hands down his leg. 'Don't tell her I said that though, will you?'

'Oh, no, I'm busy trying to work out how it was my idea all along. But could it work?'

He looked around at the green acres with the little dark beck swirling over unseen rocks into coffee-froth. 'Maybe. This is a great location, handy for York and Leeds, not too far from the coast, and you're right on the moors.'

'But it's just more work though, isn't it?'

His expression was direct, as though there were things I wasn't seeing. 'You aren't afraid of work though, are you? I mean, I have the feeling that you've been using farm work to avoid mixing with us back at the house – it's not usually quite as intense as you've been making it look, is it?'

Well, he'd got me worked out, hadn't he? 'Sometimes it is,' I admitted. 'Lambing is a bit full on. But, no. I mean, yes, there's a lot to do, but it's only fifty acres and a hundred or so ewes.'

'You could get help. If you did decide to do B&B – girls from the village or something, to help in the house?'

'But then I'd have to pay them and that would take away the whole point of using B&B to earn more money,' I said reasonably. 'And yes, okay, so maybe the farm isn't quite as time consuming as I've been making it look these last few weeks, but it's still busy. And running a B&B as a business would be busy too, if you do it properly. I'm not sure I can do both without having to take on someone else, which might end up costing what little extra I might make.'

We both looked back up the field towards the house. The windows twinkled in the sunlight, not showing the dirt or the unwashed curtains, and it all certainly looked very picturesque and brochure-worthy.

'Plus, it's hell in the winter,' I added.

'Right.'

I sighed and sat down on the grass next to him. The ewe wandered off, now it was apparent that we weren't going to turn out to be carrying sacks of feed about our persons. 'I think I've made a mess of everything,' I said.

'Don't be bloody daft.' Nat waved an arm. 'You've got all this.'

'It's sheep. All I do is feed them and get them to make more sheep. It's all a bit pointless really. They aren't a commercial breed, there's no meat on them, and the wool is all very "special interest" and arty-crafty stuff. I've got a horrible feeling that I'm only here because of hipsters and people who like quinoa.'

He laughed. 'It's fifty acres of upland Yorkshire. What else could you do with it?'

'I don't know. Rent it all to Elvie for grazing? The riding school makes tons more money than I do – loads of parents from York bring their children out here for lessons every week.'

'Quinoa-lovers to a man, I bet you.'

Now it was my turn to laugh. 'Yes, it's all very middle class up here. You've got to go a bit further onto the moor to get the gnarled old men who carry feed sacks on their backs through snow.'

Nat put a hand on mine and I felt every atom of it. 'But this farm is in your family,' he said quietly. 'You're carrying on what your grandfather did. You're helping an endangered breed back from the brink. There's value in that, even if you can't see it.'

Underneath his hand I turned mine, so we were palm to palm. His fingers gradually folded until he was holding my hand, very gently. 'I know,' I said, and it was in answer to more than the statement about the farm.

His whole body relaxed. I hadn't realised how tense he'd been until then. Above us a skylark started singing, a little warbling dot rising through the blue.

'I'm still Leo,' he said. 'You know that, right?'

'I know. It's just – twelve years? It's a long time.'

'Thor's entire life, practically.' He leaned against me, the weight of his shoulder reassuring. 'I think we sort of embody the whole "it's complicated" thing, don't we? But, maybe, if we want it enough, we can work something out?'

I looked down at our hands, clasped together on the soft grass. 'I think I'd like to try,' I said very quietly.

'And I'd like you to be Dora when we next – I mean, if we ever get to do that again. Faith is great, and, wow, yes, actually, now I come to think of it, you can keep some of her but – can I have the real you?'

'I think I'd like to try,' I repeated.

We sat there in silence, surrounded by the sounds of nature. We didn't speak. There were still things to be said, obviously, still feelings to work out from all those years ago, but maybe, if we wanted it enough, we could do it.

* * *

A couple of weeks dragged their weary way past. When Cass wasn't looking, I prowled my way around the farmhouse, trying to see the rooms with visitors' eyes. If I played up the whole 'seventeenth century' angle they didn't look so bad; small windows were *de rigeur* back then, but so were four-poster beds, which I wasn't sure I could afford, and some degree of floor covering, ditto. I'd also have to do something about the unreliable nature of the floorboards, which had a distinct moth-eaten touch, and the electrical wiring, which tended to mean all the lights went out when someone leaned against the airing cupboard door.

Plus, most of the unused rooms contained spiders, which seemed to have raised generations of offspring and probably regarded the place as more theirs than mine. I wasn't sure I could take an arachnid uprising.

The weather improved. Nat and Thor took a lot of the lessons outside now, sometimes down in the field where Flick and Knife participated in their rotund, woolly fashion, with such subjects as the history of field measurement, art and maths, which Thor persisted in calling 'algebaa'.

Nat and I circled one another warily. There were smiles and the odd hand touch – things that reaffirmed our desire to try to reconnect – but we didn't get to spend much time together since Cass had started decorating the kitchen, so everyone had migrated elsewhere in the house. It had all definitely become something more akin to *Jane Eyre* now, with careful manners and no sex. With the longer days setting in, Thor was also largely omnipresent, and we could barely manage a whispered conversation in the hallway before there was the sound of running feet and a teenage appearance. It was a bit like being haunted by Reebok.

'We should go to the beach,' Nat announced one morning as we ate varying forms of breakfast at the table, which was now in the middle room. In the house's heyday this had probably been the parlour, but Grandad hadn't been overly bothered with the niceties of eighteenth-century living so it was mostly used to store furniture left over from other parts of the house and, occasionally, hay.

We sat and ate toast or, in Cass's case, two dry Ryvita and a tomato, and ignored the fact that it looked as though we were eating in Steptoe's yard.

'Beach!' Thor exclaimed. 'Can I swim?'

'I don't know, can you?' Nat asked.

Cass raised an eyebrow over the crispbread slice. 'Of course. Thor had professional lessons from the age of three. You could have been an Olympian, darling,' she said to her son, 'if they'd let you keep the armbands.'

'Granny used to take me.' Thor ignored his mother. 'Every week.'

Cass put the Ryvita down and got up from the table. 'I hate beaches,' she said.

'You hate everything, Cass.' I slathered more butter onto my toast and watched her watch me do it, her eyes following every stroke. 'It's your defining characteristic.' I avoided catching Nat's eye as I spoke because I didn't want to giggle.

'So, you can all go if you want. I need to second-coat the walls and do something about that window. I've got a Pinterest page.'

I had no real idea what Pinterest was. I'd heard of it but never visited. It didn't sound like a site you'd order feed or equipment from.

Thor cheered. 'Can we go now?' He jumped up. 'Is it far?'

'It's about half an hour away,' I said. 'We'll take towels and head to Robin Hood's Bay. There are lots of educational rock pools there when the tide's out, and less toddlers.'

'Half an *hour*?' Thor looked stunned. 'That's, like, next door. Why haven't we been before?'

'Because it's freezing,' I said. 'You'll find out.'

So we packed up the car with an astonishing amount of stuff. Thor wanted a football and all his swimming things. I didn't want to ruin his fun by pointing out that the North Sea in May felt not unlike the Baltic in February, but reasoned that a thirteen-year-old boy wasn't going to be put off by that. Cass and I had always gone into the sea whenever we'd been taken on rare trips to the coast, ignoring our mother's advice to just walk along the beach and pick up shells and interesting stones. It struck me again that our mother had had a very odd view of children. But then I wondered, for the first time now I had so much new information, what her upbringing had been like as the only survivor of six. Had Grandma been overprotective, not wanting to lose her only remaining child? Or accepting that death happened? She must have grieved those little lost lives so badly...

So much made sense now if I viewed our childhood through the lens of my mother's life. Then her worry over Cass's pregnancy – had she been cast back into remembering her own losses and those of her mother? No *wonder* she'd been manic about hospital appointments and cleaning and making sure everything was done by the book.

'Are you all right there?' Nat quietly laid a hand in the small of my back as I stood by the car, smelling the sun-baked upholstery. 'You look deep in thought.'

I pulled myself away from the wonderings. 'Just mentally preparing to leave the farm,' I said. 'I haven't been off the premises since we went down to the village for that drink, and I'm a bit worried that the place might cease to exist once I'm out of sight. But then, Cass will be here, so ceasing to exist might be a good thing.'

'We're going to the beach, not interstellar space,' Nat observed. 'I think the place will survive without you for a day. And Cass can get on with the kitchen without us all bursting in every two minutes. I'm selling this to her as an educational trip for Thor though, so we'd better come back with Educational Things.'

'We always bought pencils on school trips. Mum didn't like us spending money on anything else really, but it was fine because we played sword-fighting with them all the way back on the bus.'

'Okay. No pencils.'

Thor sat in the back and made observations all the way, while I drove and Nat pointed out places of interest from the map on his phone. Since I already knew them, and Thor wasn't bothered, the overall effect was of three people travelling separately.

The tide was out when we arrived, and Thor immediately ripped off his clothes and dashed into the sea, leaving Nat and I sitting on a towel on the little ridge of sand that formed the beach, whilst being surrounded by dog walkers, school trips and families on holiday with pre-school children. We were the only people sitting down.

'We haven't really had a chance to talk for a while, have we?' Nat squinted out across the rocks to the ribbon of sea. 'I miss that.'

'I still don't know if – I mean, how would we play it? You'll go back to London with Cass and Thor – you can't just leave him in the middle of the school year – and if you did move up here, what would you do?'

Nat sighed. 'I told you, Thor needs to move on.'

'But he likes you! And he seems to be learning stuff.'

'Well, he'll have to learn to manage without me. Maybe go to school. And surely the house is big enough for both of us to exist in separately if we find the whole relationship thing doesn't work? Obviously, I wouldn't hang around for long, but you need never see me if you didn't want to. Oh, and you never asked why I went to York the other day.'

'You've clearly thought it all out,' I said, slightly tersely.

'Yeah, I certainly have.' Nat stretched his legs out. Now I knew he was Leo it was all so *obvious* that I felt stupid. The long legs, the way he sat. The curve of his face. Okay, so twelve years had added some flesh to his face, a higher stubble-level and a degree of poise that he'd lacked at twenty-one, but I still should have realised it was him. I *had* realised it was him. When I first saw him get out of the taxi, I'd *known* it was him, I'd just let myself get talked out of it.

Could we make it? Caution and the passing of those twelve years told me it might be difficult. Then I looked at his profile, the half-smile on his mouth, the way those hazel eyes were travelling the horizon, and I let my inner Faith have one last go.

'Good. We'll just have to watch ourselves while Thor and Cass are here, because my bed squeaks something dreadful.'

He knew what I'd done. I knew that from the sudden glance and then the big grin. 'There's always the floor.'

'That squeaks too. It's even worse, in fact.'

'Or the barn. Or does that squeak as well?' He was grinning even more widely now.

'No. But I'm hoping I will.' Channelling Faith gave me that little burst of confidence. Just enough to get me over the worries, the shyness, the doubts. When I let Dora back in, I felt I had to qualify the statement. 'I mean, I know you're pretty good already. Grandad always said you should test out equipment before you took it out on the farm; you don't want to walk two miles with a chainsaw only to find that it doesn't work when you get to the tree.'

'Your grandad was very sensible.' Nat coiled himself back up again. 'He must be freezing out there.'

'No, we buried him – oh. You mean Thor. Well, of course he is, but he's not going to admit it to us by coming back in, is he? He'll stay out there until he's blue, pretending that he's having a great time.'

'When I went to York, I went to the agency that provides tutors,' Nat went on as though this news were part of an ongoing conversation. 'They'd be happy to put me on their books. So I could still work up here. There'd be a lot more travel, but I reckon I could work it around the farm, give you another pair of hands when you needed it. What do you think?'

I couldn't speak. My mouth flapped open a couple of times.

'I'm going to take that as a positive sign.'

I was stunned. He'd actually thought about it. Thought about how he was going to earn a living if he moved in with me, how he could make it fit around the farm. *That* impressed me almost more than anything. He hadn't blithely decided on how his life would be, he'd considered the fact that the farm would need him sometimes, and started to sort out work accordingly.

'You've really got this sorted, haven't you?' I said, when words returned. I remembered him before, Leo, the *old* Leo, the one I'd known. With his plans for his future, travelling around the world with all his belongings in a rucksack, teaching English to pay his way, doing it for a couple of years and then deciding where he'd like to settle down. 'You were always so organised,' I added, softly.

'I was. Then I let other things get in the way.' Almost without thinking, he rubbed at his arm again. 'I let myself get distracted by immediate fun. I should have held the line, saved up, gone to uni and gone out and found you. I tried, you know.'

'What?'

'Like I said, I went round the clubs asking about you. I even tried round some of the local shops, putting little cards in the windows, I put an ad in the paper too. "Looking for Faith." Blimey, I got some weird answers to that one, but it was my own fault. I never knew there were so many religious nutters in Streatham.'

I stared at him. 'You really tried to find me?'

'You'd disappeared. I wanted to know if it was because of me, or something – I dunno. I just wanted to see you, one last time. Hear you tell me to bugger off, if that's what you wanted. But, of course, Faith wasn't who you really were, so nobody knew anything.'

'And I didn't know because I'd come up to Yorkshire. Otherwise I might have seen something.' I took a deep breath. 'You really cared that much?'

'I did. You must have cared a little bit too. Otherwise you wouldn't have wanted to kill me.' He gazed back over the sea again. 'And I should never have got you started on the pills and stuff. Sorry about all that.'

'I did it of my own free will, Nat,' I said softly. 'You hardly held me down and forced me.'

A sideways nod acknowledged the truth of this. 'I think Thor may have had enough. He's gone navy.'

Thor dashed back up the beach towards us, scattering spaniels and small children. 'This is *amazing!*' he said, through teeth that chattered so hard I feared for his jawbone.

He let us persuade him to put some clothes on, and then he and Nat went off searching the rock pools for sea urchins and starfish. I watched them walk off, Thor clutching Nat's big coat around him as he tried to warm back up. Leo had tried to find me. He hadn't just shrugged and moved on to the next girl. Not that

I'd really thought he would, he'd been too – too nice for that, but I had wondered. Wondered how big a hole my leaving had made in his life, whether he'd miss me at all.

And he had.

There was a nice warm glow starting deep inside me. My inner Faith raised her eyebrows. And then she fanned that glow into flames.

11

I couldn't stop giggling.

We'd moved the bed away from the wall, put a variety of things under the legs, tightened up the brass knobs until they were rigid, and the bed *still* squeaked. We stood up in the end, me half hitched onto the window ledge, which brought me to just the right height, and I hid my face in his shoulder to muffle my voice as I gasped and cried out.

'Now *that* was Dora,' he said, breathlessly. 'Much better than Faith.'

'You think?' I dug my fingers into his bare back. 'I learned a thing or two from Faith, you know.'

I showed him. He was *most* appreciative.

Afterwards, we lay in the bed together, not caring about the squeaks. 'I'm sure they won't hear anyway,' I said. 'They're over the far side of the house.'

'Then why did we go through that whole performance of moving the bed?' Nat had his arm behind me, and was lying facing me. It was all very relaxed and comfortable. He didn't even care about being naked and letting his scarred arm show.

'I just like seeing you work naked.' I giggled again, and then hastily corrected myself. 'I mean physical work, not, like, teaching. That would be wrong.'

'Your sister would certainly have something to say about it.' He smiled and pushed my hair away from my face.

'Probably in a police station at full volume. Which would be fair enough, now I think of it.' I wriggled my body against him. He had none of Chris's wideness, formed by years of rugby-playing and subsequent beer drinking. Nat was slender but muscled in all the right places. *All* the right places. I wriggled again with delight.

'What time is it?'

He reached his phone around. 'Just after two.'

'Wow. Three hours. I'm impressed.' I sighed. 'But we ought to get some sleep. I've got someone coming to look at a couple of the gimmers tomorrow.'

'Would you like me to go?' Nat half sat up. 'I don't mind.'

'No. Stay here.' I wriggled again, and felt him react.

'Oh, well, if you put it like that...'

We did, eventually, fall asleep. I didn't know how long for, but it was still dark when I woke up.

It took me a moment to work out why I was awake. Nat was still curled around me, eyes closed and his breath gently puffing against my hair. I smiled, but then realised that it was my phone buzzing that had woken me, the screen green and flashing with urgency.

I moved Nat gently off my arm and picked up the phone. I answered the call.

'Yes?' I whispered.

'Your bloody gate is open!' Elvie's strident voice split the dark more completely than the buzz or the fluorescent green glow. 'I've got horses all over the village!'

I struggled to sit up, Nat waking up gradually beside me. 'What?'

'I had a phone call from her who lives opposite that field of yours. Django is currently eating her philadelphus and she's got two Welsh ponies in the greenhouse. Did you leave the gate open today?' Elvie's voice held a tone of panic.

I frowned at the phone and tried to remember when I'd last been down and checked the gate onto the road. 'No. I've not been near the bottom field today. All the sheep are in the middle field apart from some youngstock up in the paddock, I've had no need.'

'Oh.' Elvie sounded slightly mollified, but it wasn't like her to be in the wrong for long. 'Well, you could come out and give me a hand to get the buggers back in. There must be a hole in the hedge somewhere for them to all get out like that. Django is a lazy bastard at the best of times, no way he'd squeeze himself through a hawthorn just to eat someone's perennials.'

I sighed. 'We'll be down in a bit, Elvie.' I hung up the call. No way was I going to rush just to round up a bunch of sullen horses at – I checked – quarter to four in the morning.

'What's up?' Nat was sitting up now.

'Horses out.' I got out of bed. 'I'd better lend a hand.'

'But they aren't your horses?' He looked at me blearily. 'And you're naked, and it seems a shame to waste it.' He winked. 'Even if I will probably fall asleep halfway through.'

I gave him a stern look as I pulled my trousers on. 'Nat, this is farm stuff. We help each other out if we get the call, and, besides, it's my field they got out of.'

He sighed and swung out of the bed. 'Suppose I'd better start getting used to this lark, then.'

'You don't have to.' I was a bit surprised by his reaction. 'You can stay in bed.'

He was already struggling into his clothes. 'Dora, this is your life. If I want to be a part of it, then I have to be there for the middle-of-the-night escaped horses as much as I am for shagging you senseless, don't I? Come on.'

We emerged onto the landing, to be met by Thor, who was clutching his iPad and wearing a bizarre assortment of clothing. 'I was coming to get you!' he said to me, and then stared at Nat. 'Why were you in there?'

'Checking the plumbing,' Nat said without missing a beat. 'What's wrong?'

'They're here!' Thor shook the iPad. 'I just got an alert from Moorsman250. He lives in the village. The rustlers are here! They're down in the field now!'

'Shit. They must have either taken the gate off its hinges or driven straight through it. That's why the horses are out.'

'Stay here, Thor, and call the police. We'll go down to the field and try to stop them.' We were all running down the stairs together now.

'No chance. Moorsman says he's called the police, but the lorry is loaded up and they're leaving. I'm vlogging this.' He held the iPad up and said, 'They've got my fucking lambs on that lorry. We're gonna get them.' I wasn't sure if he was talking to us or to his followers.

I ran now, through the kitchen with the dogs attaching themselves to me as I went, out across the darkness of the yard with the first green streaks of dawn just tinting the far horizon over the sea to the east. 'Stay here!'

'No chance!' Thor and I tussled for a moment. 'Moorsman is watching the lorry. They're just going out of the village.'

'You're really vlogging all this?'

'Oh, yeah, everyone's online.' He gave me a small smile. 'It's better than GTA cos it's real.' He spoke into the iPad as I hesitated for a moment then flung open the doors to my car.

'Everyone in. Nat, you let the police know what's going on, Henry's number is in my phone. We'll try to find them.'

All three of us got into the car and I didn't even wait for seat belts before I whirled around in the yard, leaving the dogs standing behind us looking confused. We took the track at such speed that I was sure we were airborne for most of the time.

'What's happening?' I spun the wheel.

'Moorsman lost them out of the village. But American Dad has seen a big lorry go past Pickering, and Pip-Boy is waiting on the Scarborough road to see if they go through his place.'

We belted down to the village turn. Sure enough, there was a big bay horse standing dreamily eating in a garden opposite the field, while a lady in a dressing gown tried to shoo him out with a yard brush. The field gate was lying flat, smashed, as though something very heavy had gone over it.

I slowed down long enough to shout to Elvie, who was just coming out of her yard with an armful of head collars. 'We're following the lorry!'

She gave me *A Look* that indicated that I should just let my sheep be rustled, claim on the insurance, and come back and help her round up her errant equines, but I wasn't going to.

'Police say to update them as we go.' Nat passed the phone into the back of the car. 'Thor, you tell them where we're going – you've got the inside information.'

So, guided by a thirteen-year-old boy with an iPad, who was being talked to simultaneously by what seemed to be his entire group of followers, we hurtled down the dark lanes towards Pickering.

'They just went through Thornton!' Thor shouted. For some reason he seemed to think that the police had substandard telephone equipment and needed to be informed directly. 'They've got Flick and Knife!' he said then, on a note of rising desperation that made his voice end in a squeak. 'We've got to stop them before they...'

Nat and I glanced at one another.

'If they get off the main road, we'll lose them. I mean, your people will lose them.' I pushed my foot down hard and the little car made 'brrrrrmmmmmm' noises without much actual gain in speed, as though we were in a cartoon. 'Where are the police?'

'Coming out of Scarborough.' Thor held up the iPad again. I assumed he was still live-vlogging this entire event and wanted a view of the outside of the car, as we picked up the lights on the outskirts of Pickering, where nothing much was happening. There was no other traffic and I broke several speed limits as we hurtled past the town and out up the hill towards Thornton.

'Henry and James are behind us somewhere,' Nat added.

'What happens if they get away, Dora?'

I glanced round. Thor had the iPad facing me. He was broadcasting me, with my sex-tousled hair and middle-of-the-night face, but this was no time to suddenly acquire vanity. 'They get them all to some rural location and slaughter them there. Then they load the carcasses up and take them somewhere to sell that isn't too fussy about provenance,' I said shortly. This was no time to mince words. Although the rural followers would already know this, I suspected that most of Thor's fan club would be city people, for whom sheep were just fluffy things that gave a good roast dinner.

'So they die,' Thor said, flatly.

'Yeah. They're too traceable alive. They all have ear tags. Once they're just meat, nobody really asks questions.'

'Can we go faster?'

'I'm trying...' We flew into the countryside, passing the occasional car on its way to milking or an early shift somewhere.

'Big lorry going like shit down a drain, just gone through Brompton,' Thor reported to both us and the police. And then, somewhat proudly, 'Mutant got his whole family up to watch the road. He says his sister just spotted them when he'd gone for a piss.'

'Thor, remind me to have a word about your use of language when this is all over,' Nat said mildly.

'Yeah, yeah.' Thor had gone back to broadcasting, holding up the iPad to the car window again. Still nothing to see, except a glimmer of dawn just topping the moors to our left. He was monologuing quietly into the device as we went.

'I never thought this vlogging thing would come in useful,' I said. 'But I'm bloody glad of it right now.'

'Dora, remind me to have a word about your use of language when this is all over,' Nat said, and grinned.

I smiled back. Our smiles were rather tight and tense, but it was so good to have him here beside me. I'd been prepared to do all this alone, but I was realising how much better it was to have company.

My hands were stiff on the steering wheel as we bucketed along the straight stretch of the A170, and my leg was shaking slightly as I tried to force the accelerator through the floor. I had absolutely no idea what we'd do if we caught up with the lorry, other than follow it, and if they stopped, then I rather feared for all of us. I suspected that the sort of people who earned their living from stealing other people's animals probably weren't going to pat us on the head and tell us to drive away and not tell anyone. And my nephew was in the car. God, never mind the rustlers, Cass was going to kill me for this.

Although, without Thor we might well have lost them.

Followers who weren't local were busy contacting anyone in the vague vicinity; Thor was getting people from Malton buzzing in to ask how it was going; there were even some who, with an obvious vague knowledge of Yorkshire and how big it is, had got in touch with people in Sheffield. But it was nice to know that the big city was alert in case a lorry full of stolen sheep should suddenly appear in its midst.

'They turned off!' Thor suddenly yelled. 'Pulled a left at Ayton!' There was an excitement in him that was clearly a mixture of fear for his lambs and what they were all treating as a live-action computer game.

'They're going up through the forest.' I gritted my teeth. There were too many turn-offs up there once we were off the main road. Too many places to hide.

'Marlborough has got people up there!' Thor's volume was increasing. 'They're coming down from – Silpho? That's not a real place, is it? Sounds like a disease.'

There were lights in my mirror now. I took my chances on being stopped for speeding and went faster. The car was rattling; it sounded like the space shuttle coming through the atmosphere. I was almost sure that the bonnet was starting to glow red.

'Okay.' I lifted my foot as we turned off the road and into the quiet of the narrow roads that led through Forge Valley. The trees, just starting to come into leaf, hung over the road. Undergrowth was matted and dripping, a shower must have passed up here although we'd stayed dry, and it gleamed in the headlights as we hurtled along, woods steeply banked to our right and a drop down to the river on our left that I didn't want to think about on slippery wet roads with sudden bends.

'There!' Thor suddenly shouted. 'Down there!'

We'd shot past a turning into a car park in what would be just the Nature Reserve in civilised hours. It was big and well surfaced, but the turning was hard to see from the road.

'Are you sure?'

'There's a lorry in there with its lights off, parked right back under the trees.'

I drove on more slowly, then turned the car in the road and bumped it down a small sidetrack, so we were hidden behind the trees.

'What do we do?'

'Wait for the police,' Nat said.

'We can't,' I said sharply. 'They'll drop the ramp and unload the sheep. They can disappear here, hide the sheep in the woods, head back to the main road and get picked up and just come back and get them later. All the police will find will be a lorry and a lot of trampling.' I cut the engine. 'Oh, hell. It all just got a bit Scooby Doo again.'

'We need to stop them.' Thor was opening his door. 'They can't kill Flick and Knife. They just *can't*.'

He was out of the car before I could stop him, dashing down the bank towards the lorry.

'Oh, hell,' I said. 'Cass is going to *kill* me,' and then I was out too, slithering down the drop that led to the small car park where there was, indeed, a lorry pulled way back in under the trees. I couldn't see the ramp; they'd backed right up to the river.

Then we could hear them. The baaing of distressed sheep, the clatter of small hooves on stones. They were unloading, driving the sheep across the narrow strip of river here, where, in nicer weather, children would paddle and adults would shoulder rucksacks for long walks through the woods. They'd be off up the far bank and away into the woods soon.

'Thor!' I tried to whisper a shout. 'Get back here! Wait for the police!'

'They've got my *lambs!*' He was gone, still holding the iPad, tearing towards the lorry. I hoped that he'd updated the police so they'd know where to look for us. These woods were a mass of small roads and tracks and car parks; we were all invisible tucked away off the road here. They could drive right past us and not see what was happening until it was too late, and 'too late' wasn't something I wanted to think about.

I ran across the open expanse of the car park. In the cab of the lorry a small dog was barking, staring at me through the window and scrabbling its paws against the glass and I wondered if it was the early warning system. Thor was already under the trees around the back of the lorry. I flattened myself against the body of the truck, hearing the terrier getting hysterical inside, and slid round. Behind me, Nat was keeping to the cover that surrounded the car park. He reached me in time for both of us to hear Thor scream.

'Where the fuck did this one come from?' a man asked.

Nat and I did a comedy head slide, where we both peered around the side of the lorry, one above the other. Thor was being firmly grasped by both arms by a man who looked as if he meant business.

The man shook Thor. 'What are you doing here?'

The iPad dropped into the river beneath them. Behind the far side of the lorry, the sound of sheep being moved was getting fainter.

'You've got my lambs,' Thor said, in a louder voice than I would have been able to manage. 'They're not yours.'

'Got a snooper!' the man called. 'What do we do?'

There was a lot of splashing as I assumed, but couldn't see, the sheep were being assembled on the other side of the river. Another voice shouted, 'Are there any more?'

Nat put his arm across me and pushed me back into the body

of the lorry, so we were flat against it. It meant we couldn't see Thor any more though.

'Must be. He didn't fucking run after us, did he?'

'Shit.' More splashing and the other voice, louder now, right beside Thor. 'Okay. Okay. Not a disaster. Just let's get these beasts away safe and then we'll deal with them.'

He presumably meant us, but Thor thought he meant that they'd kill the sheep and started to shout. He was also, probably, quite angry about the wrecking of the iPad, which would by now be under a foot or so of water.

'Oh, and shut the kid up.'

There was a slap and Thor went quiet. At this point I could feel the spirit of my sister rattle into my brain. Over my dead body was someone going to start slapping my nephew.

And then every Buffy episode I'd ever seen thundered into my head. I presumed it was the anger and fear for Thor that did it. I let my alter ego, fuelled by adrenaline, hurtle to the fore and I marched out from behind the lorry, to the evident consternation of the man holding Thor by the upper arms.

'Let that child go. We've got the police just behind us,' I said, in my best 'Faith getting sassy with vampires' voice. I might even have put my hands on my hips at this point. 'You may as well give up now.'

The man looked around for a second. 'I don't see no one,' he said, but he let Thor go. 'I reckon...' then he was hit in the knees by two hugely overgrown lambs, bleating happily in their attempts to get to Thor, who could only have been there, clearly, in order to give them illicit bottles of milk for which they were several weeks too old.

He collapsed and suddenly the car park was full of light. Nat was beside me, grabbing Thor to hold him up. The man who'd slapped him was being trampled over by Flick and Knife, who had no respect for persons who tried to get between them and milk, and there were people everywhere.

I counted four cars, all with their lights on. Every car seemed to hold a family; there were adults and teenagers, two dogs and one small girl in a nightdress.

'Sorry,' said one man, who was wearing a Barbour jacket over pyjamas. 'We lost you when you turned off the road.'

There was a lot of noise. People were running through the wood, there was baaing and splashing and voices and lights, the smell of newly emerging wild garlic being crushed, wet wool, hot engines, diesel. I just stood. Nat decanted Thor into my arms and we clutched at one another while activity whirled around us, as though we were a frozen shot in an action film.

Two dogs were fighting in a desultory way as the rest of the sheep joined Flick and Knife, and milled around in front of us. Sheep follow other sheep, and mine had clearly decided that the lambs were onto a good thing, so they'd all headed back over the river. I didn't kid myself that they'd heard my voice and come running to me, but at least they weren't straggling off through the woods, impossible to find.

Nat and Thor and I just hugged each other. Then Thor disentangled himself and there was a lot of cheering as he was recognised. Some of the cars were occupied by his followers, or, rather, the parents of his followers, who'd been persuaded to get up before dawn to join the rescue attempt. The others were friends, relatives and general associates of other followers, who, being geographically unable to join in, had dispensed anyone local to help.

So, by the time the police arrived from both directions, as the Scarborough crew had come down as Henry and James had come up behind us, in a far-too-late pincer movement, it was pretty much all over. The three men who'd stolen my sheep were being pinned to the side of their own lorry by some big, scary-looking blokes. My sheep were all present and correct and eating every blade of grass in the car park. Flick and Knife were following Thor around and hopefully chewing his leg and all the dogs were lying together in the first rays of the early sun. Except the terrier, who was still barking in the lorry cab.

Nat and I stared at each other. I wondered if my face was as pale as his.

'That,' he said stickily, as though his mouth was dry, 'was a night to remember. On so many levels.'

I looked over at Thor, who was happily chatting to a group of teenagers, while parents and siblings talked to the police. The small girl in the nightie was playing with the dogs. Everyone was wet, tired, filthy and slightly smug, except for the men being escorted into the police car, who looked as if they were only seconds from saying, 'We would have got away with it, if it hadn't been for those pesky kids.'

'I will never say another word against vlogging,' I said, through lips that felt as though they were shaking. 'They could have done anything if this lot hadn't turned up.' I waved an arm to indicate the car park, which was now nearly full, subsequent cars having joined us. 'We didn't really need the police at all. Apart from the whole arresting thing.'

Thor galumphed over, accompanied by the lambs. 'Did you see?' he yelled excitedly. 'They all came to help out! That's Moorsman250 over there...' he pointed at a family group; I presumed that Moorsman was the gangly young lad among them '... and that's Monster's uncle and his family, and Pip-Boy's sister and her husband and...' He pointed randomly. The place was jammed with people in varying degrees of nightwear, except for one man in a suit who had evidently just been off to work and two lads in overalls who might have either started or just finished a shift. 'Everyone came out to help! Can I have a new iPad?'

'Yes, probably. Very, very probably.'

Right now he could have asked me to buy him Manchester United and I probably would have gone with it.

12

By the time the police had interviewed us all and let the terrier out of the lorry cab, where its increasing levels of frustrated barking had infuriated everyone, and rounded up the sheep and we'd found a lorry to take us all back to the farm, it was nearly lunchtime. I sat in the lorry cab with the police-mandated driver, while Nat drove my car, Thor and Flick and Knife, from whom he refused to be parted, behind us.

We got most of the way down the drive to Folly Farm, to be confronted by my tractor. I'd left it parked in the small shed, yet here it was blocking access to the yard at an acute angle with two wheels wedged in the bank that lined the track. The driver stopped the lorry and looked at me.

'Can't get past that,' he said bleakly. 'We'll have to unload them here.'

So we arrived in the farmyard behind a flock of sheep and lambs who were all looking as though this was the best adventure they'd ever had, and who'd had to be ushered past the tractor whilst trying to eat every single bit of grass all the way down the track. The dogs, who would normally have helped, were nowhere in evidence. In fact the farm looked closed up. All the curtains were drawn, the doors were shut and the gimmers that I'd left in the paddock for looking over by the woman who wanted to buy one were baaing at me from the barn. Where the door was also shut.

'Where is everything?' Thor seemed baffled. 'Even the chickens...'

'I shut them in at night. They're still inside.' I could hear the muffled, and slightly annoyed, clucks and squawks from the henhouse near the barn.

'It's like the *Mary Celeste*,' Thor said, happily. 'We did that one last week. That and the lighthouse where all the men disappeared, didn't we, Nat? It's like that. Like, deserted.'

Not quite deserted. As we got into the yard, there was a lot of noise of furniture being moved from behind the kitchen door and Cass flew out to embrace her son, followed at a wary distance by two collies who looked as though being closely confined with my sister had driven them to PTSD.

'Where did you all go?' She wrapped her arms around Thor. He was about six inches taller than her and it looked ridiculous, as though she were trying a high tackle. 'I heard you shout about rustlers down the field, next thing I knew everyone vanished!'

'Did you move the tractor?' I asked, trying to disrupt her hold on her son because he was beginning to go blue.

'Yes! I was worried that they might try to drive up to the farm and burgle everything! And then take the sheep up here – so I put them in the shed out of the way.'

I stared at her. She was wearing her tight jeans again and one of my big waxed jackets, which made her look like a balloon on a stick. '*You* did that?' I was impressed. I'd not even thought about there being another vehicle, but she was right. The lorry could even have been a decoy – while we were all out chasing about replacing the gate and getting the horses back, anyone could have come up to the farm and helped themselves to the gimmers and two well-trained sheepdogs. They could, as Cass had said, have had a go through the house too, not that there was much worth taking, but there was a lot of feed stacked in the shed that would have been worth a bit. 'I didn't know you could drive a tractor.'

'Thor showed me his video.' Cass sounded defiantly proud. 'A lot of times. And he told me about it. In detail.'

She and I locked eyes for a second, in which we exchanged a degree of understanding. Thor could be a little bit relentless in his recounting of adventures. But she only had herself to blame for that.

'So you put the tractor over the drive to stop them getting in?' Nat was trying to beat off Flick and Knife, who were assaulting his knees.

'Yes. And I shut everything up inside. I had to barricade the kitchen door. You really need to get some proper locks for the house, Dora.'

I had a sudden image of my sister dragging the kitchen table against the door and didn't know whether to laugh or sympathise.

'I didn't want them to get into the yard.' Cass had let Thor go now.

'We chased them all the way to this car park, Mum!' Now he could draw breath he was determined to milk the situation, evidently. 'And we got the sheep and this bloke was trying to scare me but he didn't scare me really and the lambs came and hit him and he let me go and Dora's said she'll buy me a new iPad!'

'Ten out of ten for precis skills,' Nat muttered.

'A little bit worried about the dwelling on the iPad,' I muttered back. 'Are they expensive?'

'He *did* use it to best advantage though.'

'True. I suppose I can't begrudge him a replacement.' I gave

Nat a slightly wobbly smile. The adrenaline of the whole thing was beginning to leave me now and I felt a bit shaky and a little bit afraid I might burst into tears. Only the fact that my sister was there, behaving as though she'd single-handedly beaten off a gang of armed robbers, stopped me from throwing myself into his arms and weeping like a wuss.

'You let my son face a gang of desperate men?' Cass finally got to the point. 'And you didn't think to let me know what was going on?'

'If you followed me on YouTube, you would have known, Mum,' Thor pointed out. 'I was live-vlogging the whole way.'

'It was the *middle of the night!*'

'Yeah, computers work all the time, they don't have to go for a sleep, you know.' Thor was being very reasonable, I thought. But then he was probably still high on having saved the day. This was going to get wheeled out a *lot*, I suspected. Probably every time he wanted to do something normally not allowed.

'I think I'd better put the sheep out in the paddock,' I said, trying to edge past Cass, who I feared might have quite a lot of frustrations she wanted to take out on someone. 'They've had quite an ordeal.'

'What about *my* ordeal?' Cass wailed. 'You all just went off! *Anything* could have happened! And that tractor is, quite frankly, dangerous. Surely it can't be safe having to drive around in that?'

'It's all I've got. But thank you for thinking of it, Cass, honestly. You were right, they *could* have had accomplices who were just waiting for the farm to be empty. Good thinking.'

I whistled to the dogs and ran them around to collect the sheep and drive them down through the gateway, but the look on my sister's face etched itself into my brain. She looked astonished and flattered and a little bit taken aback, as though nobody ever praised her or thanked her and she wasn't sure how to react.

She carried on standing there, just at the entrance to the paddock, while I let the gimmers out and opened the far gate so all the sheep could head down into the middle field. None of them seemed to have taken any harm from their adventure, even Number Three's limp wasn't any worse, but they did seem to be very grateful to be out with the sun on their backs and the new grass under their hooves. Flick and Knife weren't among the flock, but I didn't begrudge Thor wanting to keep them close for the time being. They had had something of a close shave.

When I came back up onto the yard, Nat was waiting for me.

'Where's Cass?' I asked.

'She went back into the house. There's probably a little light disembowelling she wanted to get on with.'

We leaned on the gate, companionably. It felt rather nice.

'That was one hell of a night.' I took a deep breath. 'Thank you for being there.'

'It's just part of country life.' Nat flicked a quick look at me. 'Please tell me it isn't. I don't think my nerves can stand that sort of thing more than once in a lifetime.'

I laughed but didn't want to make any promises. 'Do you think we can make a go of it?'

'What, us?' He looked down at me. There were shadows under his eyes. 'Well, we have waited for twelve years to give it a shot, that's got to count for something.'

'We were different people back then. Literally, in your case.'

'All right, don't go on about it.' He looked rather shamefaced. 'I know I should have been honest with you from day one. But it took me some time to recognise you, and it would have been bloody strange if I'd met you straight out of the taxi going, "Hi, I'm Nat but my real name's Leo," wouldn't it? Plus, it would have been pointless.'

'I suppose so.' The wood of the gate was very warm under my

hand and his shoulder was bumping mine in a comfortable way. It made me hopeful. 'And could you really stay here? And learn to farm? Would you be happy? Or would you start to pine for London after a while? I should warn you that the nearest cinema is thirty miles away, and you've seen the local pub. I don't think Brig is really cut out for the hospitality industry.'

Nat gave me a slightly twisted smile. 'To be honest, I think I've outgrown all that London has to offer. I may be dangerously close to becoming a born-again rural dweller; you know, fifty uses for nettles and a winning way with rhubarb. Plus, you're here, so...'

'It wouldn't have worked back then, would it?' It was a question that had burned its way through my mind, often at three in the morning. Leo had been my ideal for all these years but now, looking back, he'd been scared and lonely too. Together we could have halved one another's loneliness and fear or we could have doubled it.

'No, I don't think it would.' He reached for my hand. 'You were looking for anything to hold on to, any kind of certainty in the world. I wasn't that. I was too busy looking for my own solidity. When we were together it was a bit rocket-fuelled, wasn't it? We talked a lot but we never tried to explore what the hell we were doing to each other. We were just companions in misery, really. Now...' He tailed off.

'We've grown up a bit. We've stopped looking for solace in chemicals,' I said. 'Apart from the stuff I have to paint on to stop fly strike in sheep.'

'What the hell is fly strike?'

'You don't want to know.' I linked my fingers through his. 'But you're right. We were too young, too unsettled. Too scared, back then. Now we're grown-ups.'

'Yes. But the good end of grown up – the end with plenty of

time to do stuff.' He pulled at my hand until I sort of swivelled into his arms. 'Shall we go back to bed?'

'The lady is coming to see the gimmers at two.' But I didn't move out of his embrace.

'Okay. Later, then. We've got to work on that squeak.'

'Mine or the bed's?'

He kissed me then, properly, and I didn't care if Cass or Thor saw at all.

13

The warmth of the summer nudged spring aside, and brazenly moved in.

The grass began to brown but the Ryedales were used to foraging and doing well on not very much, which was why they thrived on this thin, upland soil. They spent a lot of time nosing around under the hedges for fresh blades of anything green, then lying in the sun like contented cats, or bunched into the shade of the big tree in the long field.

The heat spread over the whole farm. Thor became tanned and even more freckly, despite Cass pursuing him with a bottle of factor fifty every morning, and he learned to drive the tractor well enough to be allowed to take feed down to the far field on his own. Cass watched him go and watched him come back, keeping her eyes on the track the whole time he was gone, as though she were a war wife waiting for her husband's Spitfire to return to base.

Thor was also enjoying his history lessons. Nat was encouraging him to study the history of the farm, where Thor clearly considered seventeenth century to be pre-Big Bang, and the inhabitants that long ago to have lived a troglodytic existence. I had tried to help with any of Grandad's reminiscences that I could remember, but I didn't like the 'one day, son, all this will be yours' expression that Cass always gained during those lessons, so I now tried to keep out of the way.

Nat and I discovered a lot about each other. We sat and talked outside most days as the dusk drew its skirts around us and the rooks sneered on their way home. We talked about everything: TV programmes, books, the state of the world, how life had been growing up. The past, the future. It was all easy and comfortable. He learned to handle a sheep, to grab a diagonal hind leg and roll it onto its bottom until it sat, disgruntled but accepting; then how to check feet, dose lambs for worms, and even look out for the dreaded fly strike, although he did balk a bit at dagging.

I started to relax and stopped using the farm as an excuse to stay out of the house. Thor was learning to handle the sheep alongside Nat, although he got bored a lot and went off to vlog his own stuff on the new iPad. We couldn't really begrudge that, and, if we did, he'd just shake the iPad at us and say, 'I saved all your sheep, Dora,' and that was that until the next time.

Cass continued the decorating. The newly renovated kitchen table was scattered with catalogues for furniture and paint, where it had once been scattered with farm debris. The walls were a sunny yellow colour that was intentional rather than the scars of fat fires, and the wobbly and mismatched work surfaces had been replaced with one continuous wooden block. It made me uneasy. It looked at me as though I should have been rolling pastry or doing something arcane with suet, as though I were failing in my domestic duties, but I shut it up by putting a marble slab from the old dairy on top of it.

There was also a seemingly endless stream of tradespeople. They came to talk to me about extending the plumbing to put en suite bathrooms into the bedrooms, or to show me samples of carpet. One came bearing a brochure for radiators and talked at some length about central heating, but when I found out roughly how much it would cost to 'sensitively install', I had to go and sit down.

'There's sensitive and there's sensitive!' I wailed to Cass, who was the only person around, making some herbal tea in the kitchen. 'For that price I could get therapy!'

'If you want guests, you have to have *some* form of heating.' Cass poured boiling water and the smell of disappointment rose from her mug. The herbal tea smelled like hot squash but tasted, to my chagrin, of lightly dampened hay. 'You can't expect people to pay to come and stay somewhere they have to keep their coats on indoors.'

We'd kind of skipped over the whole 'whose idea it was' stage, and dropped right down on 'this is going to happen'. Even the bank manager seemed to think it was a good idea and had made encouraging noises about business loans. I'd looked at the repayment rate and had to sit down again. Plus it was going to mean the whole of future summers would be basically spent rushing from housework to farm work and back again. Nat would probably be able to pick up students who needed extra tuition for exams, so he'd be occupied and the majority of the farm work would, inevitably, be down to me.

'And you'll need a proper washing machine.' Cass pointed an accusatory finger at my twenty-year-old Zanussi, which did laundry like a sulky maid and left strange blobs on clothes, if it was particularly displeased. 'For the bedding.'

'Oh, God, the bedding!' I put my head down on my arms. At least the re-stripped pine surface of the table no longer gathered crumbs semi-professionally. 'Sheets and duvets and stuff!'

'And towels.' Cass perched her tiny bottom on the edge of the table and sipped at her flavour-free tea.

'I think I may go and live in the barn,' I said weakly. 'And why are you dressed up?'

She was wearing a floaty little skater dress, which demonstrated that she'd got the legs in the family, and heels.

'I,' she announced, 'am going Out. You remember Out, Dora, although probably only vaguely. It's anywhere that isn't this place.'

I stared at her. 'Where? And why? And, most importantly, have they been warned?'

Cass gave me a strange look. It was that half-pride half-daring look again, the one she'd had when I'd congratulated her on her foresight at blocking the drive with the tractor. As though she'd almost frightened herself by having an original idea. 'James is taking me to Scarborough.'

This sentence fell into my brain like a brick through slurry. '*James* James? Policeman James?'

'Yes. It's his day off.'

'But – how did he ever manage to find enough words to ask you out?' I had a tiny frisson of jealousy but only for one second. Nat was worth a hundred Jameses, and also knew how to construct a sentence.

'We got talking when they came to interview you all about the sheep theft.' Cass put her mug down. 'And he comes over, when he's not busy.'

'I *wondered* why the police car was in the yard so often when I was down the field! I thought they were just doing lots of security checks!' I smacked my forehead. Things made a bit more sense now.

'Well, they were. Sometimes. Quite often James came on his

own, just to check up on us, you know. Make sure the farm was secure.'

'*After* all the sheep rustlers were put away,' I pointed out.

'Well, yes. But he wanted to make sure that...' Cass was groping for excuses. I didn't help her out, I just watched. 'That there weren't any more rustlers,' she finished at last, putting her mug down in the sink. 'And that's him just driving into the yard now, so I'll see you later.'

'Scarborough,' I muttered as she swept out of the kitchen, in her flicky little skirt and with her long brown legs. 'Hasn't that poor place suffered enough?'

Cass and James. Well, she'd be going back to London soon, wouldn't she? And he was probably good for a fling. Cass didn't really want deep conversation from her men, so James's lack of chat wouldn't be a barrier.

'Mum!' Thor crashed into the room, making the marble slab bounce with his energy. 'Grandma's on the phone! Oh. Where is she?'

'Gone to Scarborough to help the police with their not very in-depth enquiries,' I said. 'Do you want me to talk to Grandma?'

Thor spoke into the phone, which he had clutched to his chest in the position usually occupied by the iPad. 'She says no, she'll talk to Mum when she's back,' he said. 'She says she'll ring you another day, but she's got to hurry because Grandpa is stuck in the deckchair again.' Then he whirled out of the back door, which was propped open with a wire basket to let the sun in. It gleamed on the flagstones, which Cass had treated with something that made them shine and look as though they were made of concrete.

I only really spoke to my mother on special occasions like birthdays and Christmas. She came to stay, once a year, and roamed the farm like a rehomed cat, muttering about how it had been in her day, as though 'her day' had been the Victorian era, rather than the sixties.

But in the spirit of starting again, maybe she and I could find a new relationship in the same way as I had with Nat. I just had to ask the question that was looming over all of this – in the back of my mind along with the hay bill and the worries about the barn roof. 'Thor!' I yelled and waited for the footsteps to patter back across the yard.

'What?'

'Can I just have a quick word with Grandma, please?'

He held out the phone. However quickly my mother wanted to get off the phone, I knew she'd hang around to chat to Thor. She was probably trying to get him to give a blow-by-blow account of what went on up here, where she had no influence. Well, good luck with that. Thor was becoming as untalkative as most teenage boys and had developed all the communication skills of Flick and Knife, which consisted mainly of shouting loudly for food and ignoring everyone the rest of the time.

'Mum,' I said. 'It's Dora.'

'Yes, I know it is,' she said testily. 'What do you want, dear?'

At the sound of her voice I started to waver. How did I ask? There was no way I could frame the question 'did Grandpa give me the farm under duress?' without making it sound, well, like some kind of accusation. And we definitely didn't have the kind of relationship where I could ask her how she felt about her past. All those lost boys, all those lost chances for him to pass the farm down to his own sons, or even a grandson. Why did I get the farm? Did they all give up waiting for a boy to inherit? But that sounded terrible.

'Do hurry up, dear. I only rang to check that Cassie was all right; there's your father to extricate yet and the dinner is on.'

Hearing her impatience, I chickened out. The conversation

was too complicated, too emotional to fit in between now and getting my father out of the deckchair. And it was almost certainly a conversation that should be had in person, if I could ever bring the subject matter up at all. But I needed to say *something* as my mother already thought that all the outdoor work was turning me into an extra from *Last of the Summer Wine*.

'Do you know where the old farm diaries are?' It was a flicker of inspiration. 'Thor is studying history and he's been looking up the history of Folly Farm. It might be nice if he could have a look back through Grandad's old farm diaries.'

'Oh.' Her voice became thoughtful and she said something away from the mouthpiece to my father, who was, presumably, still trapped in the deckchair. 'I think they are up in the loft somewhere. He used to file them away, year by year, so they could be in one of the old trunks, in the far attic, you know the one. Where you two weren't allowed to play because of bats.'

It hadn't been that we weren't *allowed* to play up there, I remembered, as I climbed the precipitous stairs that led up out of a cupboard in one of the smaller bedrooms. We'd gone up there once and startled a colony of roosting pipistrelles and Cass had screamed so loudly and had such a bout of hysterics that we'd just simply never done it again. She'd been too terrified and there hadn't been anything of interest up there for me. Apart from the bats, of course.

But now I thought about it, I did vaguely remember Grandad talking about the old diaries when we still came up to visit several times a year. Grandma had still been alive. The farmhouse had still been full of the smells of steamed puddings on the Aga top, fresh baked bread, and the dusting and ironing had been done daily. When I'd been doing family history at school and I'd asked about the farm, Grandad had dug me out a couple of the diaries that had been kept, journalling the price of fat stock, the weight of wool from that year's shearing, the number of ewes that had lambed and those that had failed. They were a kind of business diary, a way of comparing one year to another, annotated with comments about the weather, observations on the house and garden, sometimes the odd pithy remark about a neighbour, and I'd clutched these tangible proofs of my family's existence before my birth all the way back to the start of the new term.

When I'd come back to take over the farm after college, I'd read the recent diaries that had been kept in the study. I didn't know where the older ones were, but I remembered that he'd kept all of them. They went back to when Grandad's dad had farmed these acres. I didn't know what previous generations had done about record keeping, but they might well have been illiterate.

And I hadn't had time to worry about the older ones. Long evenings over books were a luxury I'd lost ages ago.

The attic stairs were dusty. Not the hair-clogged dust that you got under the beds, or the bits of old cooking that the hens hadn't found that cluttered the kitchen floor, but the sort of dust you usually see as a special effect in horror films or *Doctor Who*.

'Dora!' Nat was calling through the house. 'Are you around?'

I hesitated. I wanted to pull out the books, brandish them to Nat and Thor as treasures of history, but I had to find them first, and I wanted to do that in secret.

But the dust made the decision for me. I sneezed, extravagantly and hard enough to make me lose my footing and stumble down a step. There was a moment of distant thundering, broken by a leap and a curse as Nat cleared the still-broken floorboard on the landing, and then he was standing at the foot of the attic staircase.

'Why are you in a cupboard?'

'Well, I heard someone mention a lion and a witch and I—'

'Does this go up to the attics?' He was behind me. 'Blimey. Mrs Hinch didn't get to you, did she?' He poked a toe at the dust. 'I'm guessing the attics aren't much used? Can I see? I've been wondering what was up here. You can see the little windows from outside so I knew there must be—'

'Yes, yes, these are the stairs to the attics. Shall we go up or shall we stand here debating on how many bodies my sister has hidden up there to date?'

I'd spoken rather sharply. Nat bounded up a couple more stairs and turned to look down into my face. 'All right. What's going on? You haven't developed a sudden need to look at the farm from really high up. Why are you creeping about and being all furtive?'

'I'm not! Am I?' I sneezed again.

'You are a bit. You've never even mentioned the attics before, except, as previously stated, as somewhere for your sister to put the mangled corpses.'

'She's gone out with James,' I said suddenly.

'What, Police James?' Nat looked at his hand. It was dusty from the rail. Everything was dusty. 'Do we expect an emergency call to find nothing but a desiccated corpse, a still-crackling radio and a mysteriously empty parked car?'

'Probably.' I smiled now. His normality cheered me up. I'd always liked Leo for his ability to be grounded; even when he was flying high, he'd been sensible. Sensible enough, I now realised, not to get involved with me when I was a mess. 'I want to look for something. Give me a hand?'

'Always, Dora, my love,' he said, and headed off up the stairs, to precede me into the attic.

I stood for a moment before I followed. *My love?* The words felt as though they'd been punched into me, like a ewe's ear tag. Love? That was a word I hadn't heard for a while.

'Are you coming, or what?' Nat appeared again in the attic doorway. 'Because I have no idea what you want up here, or where to start looking. It looks like the *Cash in the Attic* summer special.'

He was right. The attics were full of stuff. Mostly old furniture that had come up here to die, some piles of old newspapers, broken toys—

'Ooh, Mousetrap! We used to love that one!'

'Leave it alone and keep moving.'

—crockery and cutlery in cardboard boxes, framed pictures obviously designated too ugly to remain downstairs, old stationery and some balls of wool. We picked our way across the floor to another small door.

'This is the one we didn't go in. There were bats.'

'Are there still bats?' Nat looked a bit nervous. 'I'm not sure about bats. They're small and silent and come out of nowhere, and don't they bite?' He used his fingers to make a 'fang' face.

'You're thinking of my sister again. And no, no bats. The roof was redone and they decamped to the old barn by the river.'

'Oh,' said Nat in a tone that clearly meant 'good'.

I pushed the door open slowly because, despite my sounding confident, I wasn't 100 per cent certain that all the bats had moved on. The door opened onto a tiny room tucked right under the eaves of the old house. Maybe once it had been the room given to the maid who'd run the dairy, whose job it had been to care for the calves and turn the cheeses. It had one tiny, high window that showed only the bleached sky and the top of a tree as its view. The floor was covered in old chests of varying types, some tilted at angles, some stacked on other chests.

'It looks like the hold of the *Titanic*,' Nat observed. 'Pre-iceberg, obviously.'

There were wooden chests, and other chests with domed lids

covered in leather, small boxes with their lids half off, a few tea chests and one or two small wicker boxes.

'I'm surprised that Cass hasn't raided this place for feature objects,' I said, gingerly opening a trunk with a fingertip. 'She says "feature objects" a lot, have you noticed?'

'As long as she's talking about things, not people.' Nat rubbed at a pane of the little window. 'There's a really good view from up here. You can see practically the whole farm.'

Dust pillowed around us as we flipped open trunk after trunk. Most were full of junk, like the big attic, just in boxes.

'What are we looking for again?' Nat asked from the far side of the room.

'Farm diaries. They could be any kind of book. Big journal-type things or even exercise books. The ones downstairs, the ones from just before Grandad died, are in these big black things, like account books.'

'Like this?' He produced a big book, its cover wrapped around with brown tape and pages escaping.

'Exactly like that, in fact.' I went over. The trunk was full of books, all standing on end, jammed in. I rummaged further through the trunk. The books were arranged library style, squeezed in so tightly that none could fall, but the space Nat had made had allowed some to flop loose and I could see cardboard slices interleaved between some of them. I pulled one out.

'Photographs?'

I laid them down on the lid of a nearby trunk. They were tiny black-and-white photographs, with scalloped edges of the old-fashioned type, showing small children, some babes in arms.

'That's Grandma,' I said. Grandma as she must have been in her heyday, still plump, still aproned, but with dark hair swept up in curls. Sitting on a bench outside the kitchen door, with hens at her feet, holding a baby in her arms. Looking proud.

I turned the card over. *Betty and Jimmy* was written in faded blue ink on the back – *1957*.

One of the brothers that my mother had never known.

I picked up another one. Two girls, one a baby just starting to learn to walk, the other a toddler, of maybe two, wearing matching dresses with the kind of embroidery smocking at the front that were obviously home-made. *Deborah and Janice summer 1955*.

I couldn't look any more. My mother's sisters, her family. A family she'd never known. My grandma, who should have been mum to six bouncing children, bringing up her one surviving daughter as an only child, rattling around in this cold barn of a place.

So much loss. And all I had to worry about was the fact I'd fancied a boy when I was eighteen, who'd disappeared and then come back. I whirled around and hugged Nat tightly for a moment.

'What the hell was that for?' He was grinning though.

'I'm just so happy that you found me again.'

'Oh. Okay. And you can get that from two photographs?' He blew at my hair, from which dust whirled. 'I'm going to stick around to see what happens when you find an album.' He wiggled his eyebrows and I laughed. 'I thought you were looking for books?'

'Yes...' I pulled another one out to an accompanying puff of dust. This one had a mock crocodile-skin covering, cracked now, but the pages were legible when I flicked. 'I thought you may like them to help Thor with his history. They're the old farm diaries.'

'Wow. Shall we take this downstairs to read? It's a bit...' He fanned his face. 'We can come back and get the others later. I might get you to go through them before I let Thor have a look, just in case there's anything – well, sensitive.'

His eyes were huge in the filtered light that came through the dusty windows.

'Thank you,' I said. It encompassed so much. Him just being here, his thoughtfulness, everything. Just him.

'It's okay.' His voice was very quiet. Everything was very quiet up here at the top of the house. Even the birdsong came filtered through tightly closed windows and dust, as though we were somehow outside time in this room. As though all these memories of years gone had created a time trap; it could have been any of the four centuries the house had been standing.

We stood facing each other over the trunk full of books.

'I meant it, you know,' he said, very quietly.

'About the photo album?' Between my fingers the cover of the farm diary crackled. The textured cardboard had dried and peeled up into little curls that I couldn't stop picking at.

'When I called you "love".' He was looking down, almost as though he didn't want to see the expression on my face, looking at our footprints and the way they disturbed the dust around the trunk into swirls. 'I wanted to wait until I was sure it was real.'

'And now you are?' I pulled a strip of cardboard away from the cover. My hands wanted something to do and they were on autopilot because my brain was concentrating too hard on his words to have any control.

Now he looked up. Looked right in my eyes. 'Yes,' he said softly. 'I'm sure. How about you?'

If it hadn't been for the trunk between us, I would have closed the gap. 'I've been sure for twelve years,' I said, equally quietly. 'It was always you, Leo.'

Leaning in awkwardly, he put his arms around me and hugged me. I tried to reciprocate, but hit him on the head with the farm diary as I did so.

'I fear that may be some kind of metaphor.' He rubbed his

head. 'But we'll manage.' Then he kissed me, a proper, deep kiss that somehow echoed down through the years. It was all those kisses we should have had twelve years ago if only we'd not been so messed up, twelve years' worth of pent-up affection. And then back further, and it became all those kisses that should have been, between all those children who never got to grow up and their lovers. We were kissing for an entire family.

We broke apart eventually. It was too hot and too dusty to stay there for long.

'Is this bat guano?' Nat poked at something on the floor with his toe, arms still holding me, the trunk still preventing us from a proper embrace.

'It might be.' I straightened away. 'There may be some hangers-on still getting in somewhere.'

'Then I think we should leave. Before their master comes back and drains our blood.' He let me go and we moved out of the room.

'Have you ever *seen* a pipistrelle? They're tiny.' My heart felt light, in fact my whole body felt light. I could have floated down the stairs and out of that cupboard.

'Have you ever seen Dracula? He's bloody huge and I don't think I could take him in a fair fight.' There was a note of levity in Nat's voice that made me think he'd got similar feelings of some kind of load having been lifted. It hadn't been a real load, of course, no huge problem had been overcome, but the words were said. We loved each other. This whole thing was real. 'And I'm fairly sure your sister controls him. She looks the sort to have minions.'

'She doesn't need minions, she's got me.' We reached the cupboard in the small bedroom and stepped out into fresher air and a thankful lack of dust. Well, not quite so much dust, anyway. I wasn't wasting housework on a room nobody went in.

'Yes.' There was a weight to the word that made me stop and look at him.

'What?'

'Well, you being so capable and your sister having this sort of learned helplessness – does it not make you wonder?'

We went down into the kitchen. Outside in the yard Thor was trying to vlog teaching Dax to shake paws. Dax, a dog who was professionally trained to move sheep to whistled commands, was pretending not to understand, and kept jumping up and licking Thor's ears.

'I have to be capable. When you run a farm you can't flap about and be all "save me, save me" because everything is your responsibility, from a spider in the bath to knowing when to call the vet. Everything depends on you; if you drop the ball, animals can die.'

He made a kind of 'I suppose so' shrug and sat at the table. I made tea – as a trained minion I couldn't let a tea opportunity be wasted – and we spread open the farm diary, which left little trails of dust on the pine surface as we moved it between us, sometimes reading passages aloud, sometimes having to jointly decipher something that had been written in pencil and was now just indentations on a page.

Dax slunk in and hid under the table. Thor went and sat in the paddock and carried on vlogging. We read on. More tea was drunk.

We got to June and had to stop.

Nat blinked hard. 'Sorry, Dora,' he said. 'But I never thought I'd read a book that made James Joyce look like a coherent narrator. This is tough going.'

'It's not so bad if you know what he's talking about.' I stood up too and stretched my back. Six months of vague notations: feed prices, sheep weights and the odd remark about stone or grass. Nat was right, it was tough reading.

'Definitely needs more emotional impact.' Nat looked out of the window. 'Talking of which, your sister is back.'

Thor had dashed across from the paddock to greet his mother, who'd clearly been planning a lengthy and affectionate farewell to James, and looked somewhat peeved to be practically forced out of the car by an eager teenager who wanted to show her what looked like the products of his entire afternoon's vlogging. A couple of words were exchanged, which, for James, *was* a lengthy farewell, and the car left the yard, scattering bantams who tore away with their 'old lady with failed knicker elastic' run before resuming pecking at the dirt.

Cass and Thor came into the kitchen. She smelled of the seaside, candyfloss and salt air, and there was a plaster on her foot where her heels had rubbed, so there had clearly been more than sitting in a parked car and talking, about Scarborough. Her hair was a bit rumpled but she looked happy. Or as happy as Cass ever looked. Thor talked relentlessly at her and punctuated his speech with frequent recourse to the iPad until Nat said, 'Right, Thor. It doesn't look as though this farm diary is going to give us vivid first-hand insights into the history of the farm. Shall we go and do some research into building methods instead?'

'Can we do an archaeological excavation? Can we, Dora? There's this programme, right, where they dig up things in people's gardens – can we get them to come and dig here? There must be, like, *thousands* of years of stuff in the garden!'

Nat grinned at me. 'We can put in a couple of test pits if you like,' and then he and Thor were gone again, back out into the bleaching sunlight.

Cass sat down wearily. 'Why does he want to keep *doing* things?' she asked, rhetorically, I hoped.

'He's clever and he likes his mind to be occupied. Did you have a good time in Scarborough?'

Scarborough, the land of chips, twopenny shove machines and crowds of men with their shirts off. I wouldn't have thought it would have been Cass's sort of place.

'Mmmm. Very nice, thank you. James is good fun.' She crossed her legs and leaned back in her chair as though she was exhausted.

'How can you tell? No, sorry, I'm sure he's lovely, he's just not very – talkative, is he?'

Cass threw me a look. 'Not everyone needs to jabber on all the time. You and Nat are well suited.'

'Oh. Ah.' I didn't know what to say to that.

'Didn't you think I'd notice the pair of you creeping in and out of each other's rooms at all hours?'

That was it. I was going to get an en suite bathroom as soon as possible. 'Mum rang to speak to you,' I said, to try to distract her. 'Did Thor tell you?'

'No? I'll go and ring her back.'

'Yes, do. She may have got Dad out of the deckchair by now.'

Cass sighed. 'That deckchair!' as though I was supposed to know what went on with it when I hadn't lived at home since I was nearly nineteen, and those had been resolutely garden-chair-free years. She pulled her phone out of her ridiculously tiny handbag and went off into the front room, where the signal was strongest, apart from out in the yard.

I breathed up a silent prayer to any passing deity that Mum had been ringing to say the extension was finished, Cass and Thor could go home and Nat could stay with me. We'd be able to scuttle to the bathroom any time of the night we liked without the fear of Cass or Thor appearing in front of us like avenging angels, asking us what we were up to. We could kiss in the kitchen. We could spend evenings curled up together on the sofa in the front room, watching television, once all the farm work was done, and he'd finished marking. We could, in short, be a proper couple.

But Thor would miss him, I thought, looking out through the kitchen window at the pair of them stalking around the yard and looking at the lower courses of stonework on the barn. There was an element of hero worship in the way Thor looked at Nat. It was the way he'd used to look at our father. When Thor had been small and Dad had played football in the garden for hours with him or spent ages poring over sticker collections and animal encyclopaedias, Thor had regarded him as only one step down from God. And he was giving Nat something of the same look now.

Bugger.

Well, as Nat had said, Thor was ready for school. He could go to the school his mother and I had attended, which wasn't bad academically and only had the usual number of teenage pregnancies and fights.

I looked again at the gangly figure of my nephew, who'd grown again and whose ankles were visible as the hem of his trendy joggers was now heading towards his shins. There was an unworldliness about Thor that was going to get the crap beaten out of it going into Year Nine at a school with over a thousand pupils. And if I was honest, I'd miss him too.

Bugger.

I went back to the farm diary. I was practically at the date it was now, eighteen years ago. Nothing in Grandad's notes jogged my memory about that time; it was still sheep prices at the markets, repairs to the old trailer, a brief paragraph on a possible diversion of the beck lower down the valley and whether it would mean our acres would be more or less liable to spring flooding.

I remembered Grandad as a man of few words, but the words

he had had were more interesting than this. I closed the book again. Thor could have a read through later in the interests of research. It would probably bore him into an early night.

Cass came back into the kitchen and she had been crying. As I looked at her face I felt my heart drop through my chest with fear. 'Cass? What's wrong? Has something happened?' Had Mum or Dad had bad news? Dad had a persistent cough, but had always been told it was due to his asthma – please don't let it be anything sinister. Or Mum's varicose veins – could they turn nasty?

Cass nodded slowly and began filling the kettle.

'What? What is it?' I went over to her. If anything was wrong with either parent, we'd need to face it together. Or sort of together. Several hundred miles apart.

'The extension is finished,' Cass said faintly. 'We can go back to London.'

I waited for the 'and…' but it never came. 'Yes?' I prompted. 'So, what's happened?'

She whirled around, kettle in hand, and water slopped over my feet. 'Isn't that enough?' she practically shouted, then went and slammed the kettle down on the Aga plate so hard that Dax crept from under the table and took himself back out into the yard. 'Mum wants us back before August. She wants us all to go to France.'

Fresh tears started to fall and, obviously not wanting me to see her crying, she went to the sink and bent her head as though she were assessing the level of washing up, which was a ruse so transparent it was practically invisible.

'I'm still not getting it,' I said helplessly. 'What's wrong with that? Going home and then a lovely holiday to France? Sounds brilliant.'

'You don't understand.'

'I know. I just said that. What's so awful? Cass?' I put my arm around her as she let out a sob. It was the first time I'd actually touched my sister with affection for years. I'd given her a congratulatory hug when I'd first met Thor in the hospital, him lying in his little plastic crib and her looking terrified and rigid with shock, but since then she'd almost used him as a shield against any tactile imposition.

'Oh, Dora…' The words were quiet, but sounded as though they came from the heart. 'It's *awful*.'

The kettle squeaked to a boil and I released my arm. In deference to Cass's obviously unhappy state, I made two cups of fruit tea and set them down on the table.

'Right.' I steered her to a chair, gave a quick glance out of the window to reassure myself that Thor and Nat were a good distance away and unlikely to burst in, and sat opposite her. 'Tell me.'

She hesitated, eyes on her mug. She was still crying, but silent, heavy tears now, as though she'd been holding on to them for a long time. 'I don't know – you'll think it's stupid.'

'Cass.' I spoke gently and she looked up. 'You are obviously unhappy. Why would I think anything that makes you this unhappy is stupid?'

She took a deep breath. 'It's Mum,' she said. 'She does everything for me and Thor. Everything.' More tears fell and there was a pause.

I caught myself before I said, 'And that's what's making you cry? Don't be stupid.' Instead I took a deep draught of the vaguely fruity hot water in my mug and carried on looking at her.

'From the moment I told them I was pregnant – it's like she went into overdrive, Dora. You remember the flat that they got me? When I was about six months pregnant? And then said I couldn't manage on my own so they moved me back home?'

I nodded. I hadn't really been involved that much, and had never even visited the flat. I'd been busy. Partying.

'I was happy there. I'd made friends with a girl opposite with her baby, I was getting it all decorated and lovely, and it was my *home*. Then Mum turned up unannounced one day, I'd got some dishes in the sink and some laundry piled up ready to do, and she told me I obviously wasn't coping and I had to come home. She packed up my stuff while I sat there, next thing I'm back in my old bedroom and she's telling everyone that I can't manage and I need to live at home so she can keep an eye on me and the baby.'

Oh. I suddenly remembered my mother back then. Micromanaging Cass's hospital appointments and doctors' visits. Taking her shopping for baby things and always seeming to come back with her own first choice of pram and cot and clothing. I remembered how quiet Cass had got. How she hadn't seemed to look forward to the birth of her baby at all.

'She meant well, Cass,' I said. It was the only thing I could think of. Those days seemed so far away now, and I'd barely ever been home. Too busy sitting in hallways with Leo, having the luxury of time to talk over potential futures. And then, when I thought he didn't care, dancing away my unhappiness and trying to hide it all under lots of sex with random men.

'She was the first to hold him, you know,' Cass went on, almost conversationally. 'When Thor was born and they lifted him up, she practically wrenched him out of the midwife's hand before the cord was cut. And from then on, she's taken over our lives.'

Learned helplessness, wasn't that what Nat had called it? I was beginning to see where it had come from now.

'I couldn't *possibly* manage to feed him myself.' Cass sounded as though she was quoting. 'And Mum used to take him whenever he cried, give him a bottle, rock him, walk him at night. She said she was doing it so I could sleep. But I didn't *want* to sleep, Dora! I wanted my baby! But every time I did anything I was doing it wrong and she was just helping me out.' Cass took a gulp of her tea and I saw her hand was shaking as she lifted the mug. 'In the end – it was just easier to let her.' There were tracks in her make-up where the tears had washed it off her face. She suddenly looked very, very young and slightly afraid. 'I wanted to do it by myself,' she said very quietly. 'I wanted my baby. And a place of my own, and a job. But Mum keeps telling me I can't manage.'

I reached across the table and took her hand. 'I never knew,' I said. 'I'm sorry, Cass.'

Another bunch of words came in a rush, as though they'd been building up behind the dam of years. 'When Thor was tiny Mum told me that I shouldn't waste my looks being awake all night. I needed to find myself a man, and now I'd got Thor I only had my looks to fall back on. And then you got the farm and everything and I'm stuck there, and she won't let me send Thor to school or do anything that goes against her ideas of how to bring up a son!' Cass took another deep breath. 'Dora, I want to ask you something.'

She sounded so serious, so depressed, I wondered if she was going to ask me what I'd been doing all those times I hadn't been around. Where I'd been. Who with. And I was trying to construct a cover story so that I didn't have to admit to having been a drug-using promiscuous party girl, because, while it had suited Faith in *Buffy the Vampire Slayer*, it now sounded a very thin excuse for a girl from Streatham whose parents had worried more about her sister than her. I'd decided on heavily edited highlights, when Cass went on.

'Would you consider letting Thor and me stay here at the farm? No, before you say anything, I've been thinking about it. We could convert one of the barns into a little house. And we could live there and help out with running the B&B or whatever. And Thor can help on the farm because he loves it, and he can go to the local school if he wants, and he's been asking about it because it turns out a lot of his local followers go there. He's got a bit of a reputation now,' she added proudly. 'Because of saving your sheep from the rustlers. He's a local hero, apparently. So he could join the Young Farmers and have friends and things and it's all stuff Mum never wanted; he had to grow up and be an architect like Dad, and only have friends that were *her* friends' grandchildren so she knew them from birth. No "unpleasant influences", you see.' Cass stopped. The words had fallen out of her, swift and unconsidered but with a caution behind them that sounded as though she was expecting to be slapped down.

'Oh,' I said again.

If I said 'no' could I really send Cass back to London and condemn her to permanent life under our mother's influence? Now she knew there was an alternative – that she and Thor could be a family unit? That she could be a perfectly good mother on her own? Well, maybe not perfect or good, but Thor was rapidly passing the stage of needing a fully involved maternal presence and starting to need to make his own way in the world.

Then I thought of our mother and her way of either guilting us into behaving or making her disapproval known so volubly that we would comply just to stop her talking. How even I hadn't wanted to ask why Grandad left me the farm, for fear of bringing on one of her 'moments' and having her refuse to speak to me for six months. I knew that Cass wouldn't have the resilience to break away if she went back. She might intend to make her own life, but she'd cave. And spend the rest of her days being controlled. I felt momentarily guilty. All those years when I'd felt so jealous of Cass being cosseted and cared for, never a moment's worry about money or where to live or how to care for her son. All that resentment I'd felt against her for taking and taking and not doing anything for herself. It all made sense now.

But could I really put up with living with my sister?

'Could it be a barn on the other side of the farm?' I asked. 'Maybe we could get permission to convert that one down in the horse field. It's nearer the village,' I added hastily, so as not to look too ungenerous. 'Closer to the school bus stop.'

Cass leaned over the table and kissed my cheek. 'Thank you,' she whispered.

We drank the rest of the horrible herbal tea in silence. She was presumably thinking of how to break the news to Mum. I was wondering what I'd let myself in for.

14

'No, I think it's a really good idea,' Nat said later, after I'd put Cass's proposition to him. I'd waited until after we'd had very good sex though, just in case he had the same reaction as I had at first.

'Honestly? You think we can co-exist with a semi-vampiric horrible person who just happens to be my sibling?'

'If she's far enough away, yes.' He slipped his arm round my shoulders. 'She's not really that bad. And it will be extra help on the farm and in the house. You do have to admit that she's done a brilliant job with the decorating. The place looks almost habitable now.'

'If we take photos of it now, in summer, with the sun shining and the hens in the yard and all that, we might manage to get some visitors,' I said. 'By next year we'll have the plumbing sorted and maybe some heating in.'

'You can fool some of the people all of the time,' Nat said solemnly. 'Just let's not have them during the winter.'

'And we can get planning permission on that barn that's far, far away more easily than the ones in the yard, because they are in the National Park. The boundary goes through my land. But don't tell Cass that. I'm saving that one in case she decides she wants to be closer to the house.'

Nat hugged me. 'This could all really work, you know.'

'I know.'

I'd stopped feeling the dread at the thought of seeing my sister every day. Once I'd seemed to accept her proposition of moving to Yorkshire, she'd got very practical about it, with talk of using her fifty per cent of the farm profit to reinvest into the B&B business and her savings to turn the barn into a little house for her and Thor. She seemed to have got over the whole ISA and savings for Thor thing now that there was something concrete to put the money into. Plus I had hopes of her helping to bail out the farm accounts if things got sticky. And Thor was already useful around the place; having two extra blokes to help with heavy work would be wonderful and would mean I didn't need to beg for help from neighbours whenever I needed something really hefty lifted. Thor had already started looking through tractor catalogues, which was worrying.

It could work. It really could.

Mum could video call Thor and he could go down and visit for holidays, when London would seem more of an attraction. And, as Cass had said, up here Thor had gained an almost deific level of noteworthiness because of his standing up to the sheep rustlers to save his lambs. It wouldn't hold much water in Streatham, but up here he was regarded with the same level of awe as Captain Cook or Dame Judy Dench. We didn't get many heroes coming out of North Yorkshire.

Most important of all, Mum couldn't mould him any more. She couldn't try to turn him into the Perfect Son and he could be a proper boy, running across fields and going to school and making friends like a normal child. I understood Mum's reasons, or, at least, I thought I did. All those lost babies. The loss of her chance to have her own son. So she'd taken Cass's.

So, Thor was happy to stay. Cass was happy. Nat was looking forward to farming and taking on more tutoring work. It seemed almost churlish to say that I was the only one who wasn't totally over the moon with the whole thing. I was still dwelling on what Cass had told me about Mum and Grandma wanting the farm to be left to a son, and on Grandad's thinking behind leaving the farm to me. Whether it had been grudging or glad. Whether that loss of sons and grandsons had hung over him in his last years. Whether, in short, I'd been the best of a bad bunch, just a compromise.

The uncertainty meant that the farm and I were at odds. Before I'd always felt that I was part of the land here, that the farm accepted me. As though I'd seamlessly stepped into Grandad's shoes and everything was all right. Now it was almost as though the fields juddered under my feet, trying to shrug me off.

I told Nat this and he laughed. 'It's your farm,' he said. 'By rights. And you always felt all right about it before – why should thinking that your Grandfather wanted it to go to a boy make it feel different? After all, if he'd *really* wanted it to go to a boy, why didn't he leave it to Thor? He was, what, five, when your grandfather died? So he could have done.'

'But who would leave a farm to a five-year-old, who may want to grow up to be a fashion guru or to star in cooking programmes on TV? Wouldn't it mean that you were deciding the fate of a child? Like a Norse god or something?'

Nat gave me a level look. 'Did your grandfather ever give you Norse god vibes?'

'No! That's exactly my point! And he knew if he left the farm to Mum she'd probably just sell it.'

'Well, then. He did the sensible thing leaving it to you, with an interest to your sister. Why would you even question that?'

But I couldn't explain it. Couldn't explain how I felt dislocated now, like a caretaker rather than a landowner.

In the end, it was Thor who solved the problem.

He was going through all the farm diaries, with a little deciphering from me and some mathematical help from Nat, working out the price of hay per ton in 1963 versus the price now and whether it was more or less valuable these days than back then. He was noting down the increasing price of sheep and anything pertinent about the development of the farm. He'd already found the details of the building of the old stone barn that we wanted to convert, back in those pencilled-in days post-war, when Grandad had just been taking over the running of the farm from his own father; when there were still details of the horses they'd used to plough up the big field and the yields of the dairy cows that they'd milked when the feed shed had been a shippon.

He was poring over the books at the kitchen table one late summer afternoon. Nat was fielding a hay delivery, Cass was doing something with fabric swatches in one of the bedrooms and I was cooking something for our evening meal. A vat of stuff bubbled on the Aga and I stirred it now and again, hoping it would turn out to be edible.

'Aunt Dora,' Thor said, 'I've just found you.'

He'd marked his place with a ruler, which was wise. Grandad's handwriting tended to wander, and, although it was neat, it was often interleaved with later notes in different colours and could give you a migraine if you tried to concentrate on it for too long.

'What do you mean you've found me?' I stirred the pot again. It was supposed to be a bolognese sauce, but there was a disturbingly large mushroom element about it. 'I'm right here. I don't take much discovering.'

'In the book.' Thor pointed. 'Here.' He flipped the book shut over the ruler to show me the cover. 'This one.'

'It's the year I was born.' I bent over. 'Where am I?'

He tipped the book open again. It was the day of my birth. It had been a Wednesday, and Grandad had seen fit to write in green ink that day, which, even though it had faded over the years, still held an element of 'strobe' to it.

Sold barren heifer: £3
Fenced lower paddock, need more timber. George has
promised a load before Christmas.
Betty made puddings.
Brought the flock up to the shed, frost forecast.
John phoned. Karen had a baby girl this morning.
Ordered more poultry food, had to come from Marishes as
Pickering short.

Above the note about the baby, Grandad had added, obviously later and in pencil:

Baby named Pandora. 7lb 3oz. Thriving.

And then later again, in the ruled margin of the page, sideways on to the rest of the writing so it stretched up the side of the book, almost hidden in the fold of the spine, another note, this time in blue ink.

She's to get the farm, being the firstborn. Betty and I decided a
long time ago. Any more children can have a share, Betty

hopes for a boy to help with the heavy work, but eldest gets the land.

'Eldest gets the land,' I said aloud.

'Oh, is that what it says?' Thor wasn't particularly interested. 'I thought it said "elevens gosland" but that's not even real words, is it?'

So, I'd always been meant to have the farm. Even if I'd subsequently had brothers, the land was mine.

'Just thought you might want to see what they wrote when you were born,' Thor carried on. 'Seven lub? Why did he write seven lub, three ozz?'

'It's old weights,' I said vaguely. 'Ask Nat about it.'

Just then Nat walked in through the door, smelling of hard work and hay, with the dogs behind him looking smug because they'd been mousing in the bales. Thor immediately launched into questions, and Nat grinned at me over his head, washing his hands at the sink and shedding hayseed all over the newly swept floor.

I felt the acres wrap themselves around me again, as though there had never been any question of ownership, and everything seemed so right I could have cried.

Cass had been wrong about everyone wanting boys to inherit. Grandad and Grandma had agreed even before I was born, 'eldest gets the land', and Grandma had only wanted a boy as an addition, not instead. It didn't matter that I'd been a girl.

The lost babies would always be mourned and I'd get those photos out of the attic and put into frames – those children would never be forgotten. But Folly Farm was mine.

I gave a quiet smile and an inward nod to Grandad, then went over to hug Nat and stir the bolognese.

MORE FROM JANE LOVERING

We hope you enjoyed reading *Home On Folly Farm*. If you did, please leave a review.

If you'd like to gift a copy, this book is also available as an ebook, digital audio download and audiobook CD.

Sign up to Jane Lovering's mailing list for news, competitions and updates on future books.

https://bit.ly/JaneLoveringNewsletter

The Country Escape, another funny and warm-hearted read, from Jane Lovering, is available now.

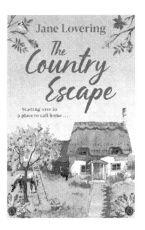

ABOUT THE AUTHOR

Jane Lovering is the bestselling and award-winning romantic comedy writer who won the RNA Novel of the Year Award in 2012 with *Please Don't Stop the Music*. She lives in Yorkshire and has a cat and a bonkers terrier, as well as five children who have now left home.

Visit Jane's website: www.janelovering.co.uk

Follow Jane on social media:

- facebook.com/Jane-Lovering-Author-106404969412833
- twitter.com/janelovering
- bookbub.com/authors/jane-lovering

ABOUT BOLDWOOD BOOKS

Boldwood Books is a fiction publishing company seeking out the best stories from around the world.

Find out more at www.boldwoodbooks.com

Sign up to the Book and Tonic newsletter for news, offers and competitions from Boldwood Books!

http://www.bit.ly/bookandtonic

We'd love to hear from you, follow us on social media:

facebook.com/BookandTonic

twitter.com/BoldwoodBooks

instagram.com/BookandTonic